Alice at 80

BOOKS BY DAVID SLAVITT

Fiction

ALICE AT 80
RINGER
COLD COMFORT
JO STERN
KING OF HEARTS
THE KILLING OF THE KING
THE OUTER MONGOLIAN
ABCD
ANAGRAMS
FEEL FREE
ROCHELLE, OR VIRTUE REWARDED

Poetry

BIG NOSE
DOZENS
ROUNDING THE HORN
VITAL SIGNS: NEW AND SELECTED
    POEMS
THE ECLOGUES AND THE
    GEORGICS OF VIRGIL
CHILD'S PLAY
THE ECLOGUES OF VIRGIL
DAY SAILING
THE CARNIVORE
SUITS FOR THE DEAD

Alice at 80

A NOVEL
BY DAVID R. SLAVITT

SEVERN HOUSE PUBLISHERS

This title first published in Great Britain 1985 by
SEVERN HOUSE PUBLISHERS LTD, of
4 Brook Street, London W1Y 1AA

Copyright © 1984 by David Slavitt

British Library Cataloguing in Publication Data

Slavitt, David R.
  Alice at eighty.
  I. Title
  813'.54[F]   PS3569.L3

  ISBN 0-7278-1147-9

Printed and bound in Great Britain by
Butler & Tanner Ltd, Frome and London

For Anne Sue, who prompted it;
for Marion, who believed in it;
and in memory of my mother, who liked it.

1 9 3 2

AS SHE IS PERFECTLY WELL AWARE, they look at her as
they would look at a relic, with the same rude wonder they
might feel for the knucklebone of St. So-and-so in its gor-
geous gem-encrusted receptacle of tarnished silver. She is
St. Alice, the patroness of childhood, the playmate each of
them would have loved to have.

She knows how to play her role well enough, understands how to be gracious but not too regal—particularly
here in America, where an English accent can be intimidating. But if she is sweet enough, she can put her Englishness
to use as a reminder that she comes from across the divide
of the centuries as well as from across the sea. Americans
admire distance, perhaps because they have so much of it.

Still, to play any role is demanding. She is no relic, cannot radiate holiness or goodness, cannot cure illnesses by
her mere touch. Mortal and alas too human, she has to work
at the more modest and immediate tasks of living. She must
demonstrate to her sister Rhoda the appreciation Rhoda is
sure she deserves. Even more difficult is the task of dealing
with Caryl, her son. Rhoda and Caryl have come with her to
New York in order to look after her, but Alice spends considerable time and energy looking after them and worrying
about them, about Caryl particularly.

For one thing, he drinks even more than in England, as if
prohibition made him thirstier. And even when sober, he

dwindles away to a respectfulness that more and more approximates that of her public admirers—which is distasteful to her. Caryl, her youngest, dimmest, and only remaining son, depends upon her financially, which may be a pity but is not a shame. She has tried to let him know that the world has not yet come to that sorry pass where a man's worth is to be judged solely by his capacity to make money.

The trip to New York is, nevertheless, an indirect result of Caryl's financial predicament, to try to establish him in some security which he clearly requires and is not able to contrive for himself. True, his wife's family has money, but what they do with it and how they may decide to tie it up are questions beyond Alice's control or interest. She can determine only what will happen to her own money, and can reckon perhaps on the likelihood that Rhoda will leave to Caryl, her only nephew, the house at Hoseyrigge. To whom else would she leave it, anyway?

But beyond the money and beyond her concern for Caryl's prospects, there is a part of Alice that enjoys these academic ceremonies, their rituals so formal and familiar. At the proper distance, even the gawking of the crowd is not intolerable. It is like a coronation, or like a wedding, and she can still close her somewhat faded blue eyes and imagine herself a young woman again, a bride, or even a girl. It is irksome that Caryl cannot even admit to himself the possibility that she might, in some measure, be enjoying herself. He is too wrapped up in his own misery, delighting in his obligation and his guilt. That is his style, these days. He feels guilt for not having been killed in the war like his two brothers. And any other guilt is congenial and even welcome, mixing in like another ingredient in one of those loathsome cocktails he enjoys. That he gives her too much credit and attributes to her an altruism she doesn't feel might be flattering, but she has no patience for it. She dislikes being misunderstood, even if she has conspired in the misunderstanding. Or all the more, because she has conspired.

She has not disabused him of the idea that she has merely consented to be made into an object here at Columbia University in the City of New York, for its centenary display of Lewis Carroll first editions, translations, and memorabilia. They even have the table from the rooms in Christ Church where Carroll wrote *Alice*. And Alice is here to receive from Dr. Nicholas Murray Butler, *honoris causa*, Columbia's doctorate of letters. Hers is only a convenient neck upon which to hang the hood. She is, like that table on display, what they call an "association item."

A delicate, wispy-haired, frail-boned old lady, she has, nevertheless, a toughness and shrewdness that will not suffer nonsense and cant. She has spent an observant lifetime, much of it in a university older than this one, so she understands that deals have been made. She is well aware that this display, the celebration, and her honorary degree are not quite spontaneous. Columbia will get something out of it, one way or another, either from the Rosenbach brothers, who are the rare book and manuscript dealers, or from their client, Eldridge Johnson, of the Victor Talking Machine Company. Columbia is certifying the book as a classic, but someone will have made it worth the university's while to have put on this carnival.

On the other hand, it is not something they'd do for just any book. There is a respect and affection for this particular work, and for her too, however clumsy and bumbling. In acknowledgment of that real affection as well as its contrived display, she must endure this attention, must sit here on the platform not far from Caryl and Rhoda, and be made much of for three quarters of an hour.

Her back is militarily straight. The afternoon sunshine is of almost tropical brilliance. She is a bit dazzled by it. The robes, hoods, medallions, and staves of office are also dazzling—but are meant to be. She does not take them seriously except as playthings. There is a quality of playacting about them, all the more endearing for their studious solemnity. " 'Curiouser and curiouser,' said Alice," Alice thinks. So much of life can be summed up by that line, the line given to her so long ago and from which she is still reaping benefits.

And, no doubt, still paying the costs, too. She is a woman quite different from what she might have been had her path and Carroll's never crossed. People expect her to be like the little girl in the book, full of fun and games, spontaneous and gay. They cannot imagine her bitterness at the loss of that light, her awful feeling of exclusion from Wonderland. She is straight-backed because that is the only comfortable way to bear the burden she has carried so long, the feeling of exclusion. Those whose hopes have been raised and dashed are worse off than those who were hopeless all along.

If it is a wedding, then she and Carroll are the bride and groom, even if posthumously and by proxy. Regi—her late husband—would have hated it. He always hated Carroll, or Dodgson. He'd have been pained to see her going through this ceremony, even though it is in part for Caryl's benefit. And poor Regi was right, after all. His whole life long, he resented Dodgson, and Alice thought he was being ridiculous. Now she sees that it was as if Regi could peer into the future and predict, gypsy fashion, this unimaginable event.

Her father, Dean Liddell, would have been antagonistic too, even more than Regi, having known Dodgson better and having hated him longer and at closer range. And yet, as much as her father had detested Dodgson, he had been unwilling to make a scandal. For the sake of Christ Church, and Oxford, and for the sake of his own family's reputation, he had kept silent and suffered Dodgson to remain in the college. The Dean had been a practical man. He might,

therefore, have condoned her participation in this ceremony, might even have found something wonderful in it—
in the strictest sense of that word. (He was often strict, and
always so about words.) Worthy of wonder. Not necessarily
a good thing but a remarkable thing. A wonder, for instance, that he had been the one to suggest the title to
Dodgson. *Alice's Adventures Under Ground* became, at Dean
Liddell's prompting, *Alice's Adventures in Wonderland*. To that
extent, the Dean was a collaborator.

They were all collaborators—her father, her husband,
Carroll, and Alice herself. And the adventure they contrived together has only the most tenuous relation to the
one the public has read. Their understanding of what happened is not the same as Alice's. If it were, she could not
bear it, could not face them at all, would not be here to
receive their tribute. She looks out at the sea of faces, all of
them healthy, earnest, open, and honest. And she looks
across the group on the platform with her, to her sister and
to her son, Caryl.

What shall she tell him?

She cannot face the question, or not now. She looks at
the lectern, listens, and then reaches into her purse for a
handkerchief with which to dry her hands.

THE MAN INTRODUCING HER is Professor J. Enrique Zanetti,
from the chemistry department. Alice wonders how many
there were from the English department who contrived to
let this cup pass from them. Or, no, that is unfair. Even if
chemistry professors do not ordinarily concern themselves
with literary birthdays, Carroll's is a special case. His enthu-
siasts are not limited by department. The worst that can be
charged against Zanetti—an altogether amiable and cheerful man, so far as she has had a chance to observe him—is
that he seems ambitious. Assuming her expectations are
correct that Columbia will somehow find its reward for

these exertions, and in the not too distant future, then
Professor Zanetti's efforts may also find some recompense.
He is doing well enough, for whatever motive, talking
about "the little girl whose magic charm elicited . . . seventy years ago the story that has brought such delight to
humanity, young and old," and so forth and so on. He
speaks slowly, and his voice booms out over the loudspeakers of the public address system. "Carroll did not realize at
the time," he says, "to what heights his creative imagination had climbed. But little Alice Liddell instinctively knew.
She pleaded that it be written out for her and Carroll
agreed, fulfilling his promise the following Christmas when
he presented to her the famous manuscript of *Alice's Adventures.*"

It was so long ago. She can hardly remember it. What she
does remember seems to be from a story about somebody
else.

But if the presentation has become unreal, the cash is no
less hard for that. She catches at the phrase. It was harder
cash than she could have imagined.

"Well might he write years afterward to his little friend
grown to womanhood," Zanetti concludes, quoting from
one of Carroll's few surviving letters to Alice, " 'Of its
existence you were the chief if not the only cause.' "

He turns, smiles, and says, "Mr. President, permit me to
present to you Alice Liddell Hargreaves."

They doff their mortarboards to her and to each other.

It is her cue to rise and walk to the rostrum.

She takes the few steps, a bit nervous, feeling her breath
come in difficult gasps. What on earth do they want of her?
What can they expect of her? That she try again to be that
young muse, inspiring each of them to write a masterpiece
as she once inspired Mr. Dodgson? Impossible and beastly!
They have no idea! And she is reluctant even to take credit
for having inspired Carroll. She knows it is not altogether

the truth that she simply asked him to write it down. There was also the war between her and her sister Edith.

The truth hardly matters now—certainly not to Edith, who has been dead for years. The truth only embarrasses decent people—as Regi insisted and she herself always knew, having learned from her parents how unpleasant it could be.

Dr. Butler does not strike her as being the kind of man who would allow any but the best-behaved truths anywhere near him. He addresses her formally, speaking slowly and clearly, for her or for the microphones and loudspeakers: "Alice Pleasance Liddell Hargreaves—descendant of John of Gaunt, time-honored Lancaster, daughter of that distinguished Oxford scholar whose fame will last until English-speaking men cease to study the Greek language and its immortal literature; awakening with her girlhood's charm the ingenious fancy of a mathematician familiar with imaginary quantities, stirring him to reveal his complete understanding of the heart of a child as well as of the mind of a man, to create imaginary figures and happenings in a language all his own, making odd phrases and facts to live on pages which will adorn the literature of the English tongue time without end, and which are as charming, as quizzical, as amusing as they are fascinating; thereby building a lasting bridge from the childhood of yesterday to the children of countless tomorrows—you, as the moving cause, Aristotle's 'final cause' of this truly noteworthy contribution to English literature, I gladly admit to the degree of Doctor of Letters in this university."

Applause. They put the hood over her head. She moves the tassel from one side of the mortarboard to the other as they instructed her earlier on, just after the luncheon. She turns and waits for the applause—sustained and very generous—to subside. She looks down. Most of the people in the audience are standing. Caryl, behind her on the platform, is applauding with more vigor than is becoming. What is she to do with him?

When it is quiet, she speaks into the microphone to make her reply. "I thank you, Mr. President, for this signal honor bestowed upon me. I shall remember it and prize it for the rest of my days, which may not be very long. I love to think, however unworthy I am, that Mr. Dodgson—Lewis Carroll —knows and rejoices with me."

There is another wave of applause, even louder, and continuing from instant to instant so that her impression is of enormous duration. She is moved by it, or more accurately she is shaken. She cannot help but allow the feelings she has tried to dam up for all these years to trickle through, to run for just this once, gushing free. It is her marriage to Carroll, the marriage she wanted back when she was a little girl. For Regi was right in that way, too. She did love Carroll, adored him, has never recovered from that first irreparable loss. They are still clapping; and although she knows that it cannot possibly be the case, she entertains the absurd idea that they can somehow see into her soul, that they can all together divine the truth that she has kept hidden for so long, that they understand and forgive, even approve. She dabs at her eyes with the handkerchief she has wadded in one hand. They are beating their stinging palms together in a frenzy, like sea lions in an aquarium, like wind-up toys, like zombies.

How long ago it was! And they are all dead, all of them but herself. This is what Edith understood and craved, and what Alice's younger sister was shrewd enough to be envious about back at the very beginning. Alice was ten then and Edith was eight, but Edith had understood that their whole lives were at risk, that the long dull years that were to follow would hold nothing so fine, ever. Oh, Edith! Poor, dear Edith.

Poor Alice, too. It is a lifetime ago, and the woman on the

podium feels a thundering in her blood, in her ears, in her inmost heart that is as close to pity as she has ever allowed herself to come: pity not only for herself and for the little girl she once was, but for Edith and for Regi, and for her two dead sons, and for Caryl, too. And for Carroll himself, that terrified, adorable, fussy, wonderful man, the man whom she has loved longest and best.

What harm is there? Her father is dead. And Regi is dead. The dead are beyond our hurt. In her gloomiest and most doubting moments, she has believed that. Regi can have no idea that any of this is happening. Or, on the other hand, if by some amazing suspension of order and reason and sense there turned out to be some kind of afterlife, then Regi would understand, wouldn't he? The effort he made, before he died, was to understand her, to reach out, whether he understood or not.

How can she endure it? Her whole being is about to shatter like something brittle. They keep on clapping, in their foolishness or their wisdom, and she stares out at them, her eyes only a little blurred from her tears. They are posterity. They are immortality. What they suppose of her will become the truth, and what she knows of her own life will be buried. Many of them are carrying copies of *Alice in Wonderland* with them, which frightens her. How can they expect her to sign so many books? Or have they brought them just to be blessed, or to show them to her—or her to them?

She holds onto the lectern to steady herself. It would be dreadful to faint, she thinks. But it would be acceptable to die here, to be translated at this instant out of time, buoyed into timelessness by that indefatigable applause. To be restored to that Wonderland she has glimpsed but never known, or lived in so briefly she can barely remember anything of it! Carroll's eyes she recalls as being limpid and woeful, even when he was telling jokes, even when he was laughing. To be restored to that sad gaze or to be freed of it at last—either would be acceptable.

But the dizziness begins to pass. And the applause at last shows signs of subsiding. She will get through the ceremony, and no doubt she will contrive to get through the rest of the day. She still must collaborate with Caryl on the article they have promised the New York *Times*. And then, tomorrow, she must return here for the university's luncheon and the closing ceremonies for the Carroll exhibition. After that, they will be finished with her and she with them.

She nods, acknowledging the very generous, very affectionate ovation. She returns to her seat. There is one more musical selection from the chorus, during which she is very stern with herself for having let those tears well up that way, for having allowed herself to go all mushy. She will not let that happen again. Still, she is interested to discover that the river of old emotions is still running, no matter how deeply submerged. That works two ways, however. In loyalty to Regi and in consideration of Caryl's feelings, she must be very careful how she treads. Caryl is at her side now, the attentive son, ready to help her off the platform during the recessional that concludes the ceremony. He looks solicitous and concerned, as he often does when his salivary glands have begun to work in the expectation of a drink.

What will become of him? She leans upon his arm and allows herself to be escorted back toward President Butler's office, where she will be able to get out of the cumbersome cap, hood, and gown of the doctorate.

WHAT CARYL CANNOT UNDERSTAND is why his mother ever agreed to subject herself to this awful public display. She could have declined easily enough, either making some excuse or flatly refusing to participate. The only explanation that makes sense to him is that she finds some good in this, sees something enjoyable or satisfying to herself. But if that's true, then it calls into question all of Caryl's assumptions about his family and his own history, his very memories, which are all that remain to him of his father, his two elder brothers, and his Liddell grandparents. Have his understandings of a whole lifetime been wrong? The only other explanation is that they all knew the truth but conspired to withhold it, either agreeing together or each of them spontaneously deciding, for whatever reason, to keep little Caryl ignorant by lying to him or just by keeping silent when he asked them questions.

And he asked. It is difficult to be the child of a woman who is more or less famous throughout England and not have anything to tell one's friends, one's schoolmates and their parents, or even one's teachers about Lewis Carroll. Naturally, he asked, putting the question to his mother and discovering that she was not at all forthcoming. And then he asked his father, who was just as reticent and who in addition glowered. His brothers, Alan and Rex, told him only that their experience had been much the same. Rex even warned him never to mention that man's name—either name—to Grandfather Liddell.

Children learn patience, mostly because they have no choice. They endure mysteries that go on for decades. All Caryl knew was that something bad had happened and that his father and grandfather hated Lewis Carroll because of it. He lived with mystery for long enough to be able to make at least intelligent guesses. It was his impression, moreover, that his brothers had made the same guesses. How else could one explain the icy fury any reference to Carroll produced in their father or grandfather? Both these men clearly felt themselves to have been affronted, even dishonored, by "that man" whose fame was a joke and whose great book was an obscenity.

If all that is true, however, it is mystifying indeed to hear his mother speak of Carroll not just with pride and affection, as required by the occasion, but with a show of conviction that seems persuasive to Caryl, himself. It is, first of all, her willingness to undergo these ceremonies that is so inconsistent with what he has always believed. He feels like some amphibian that has just dragged itself out of the water to lie on the beach, gasping, trying to extract oxygen from the air, able to live, but whose every new breath is an adventure. He assumes it is his fault, of course. Had he not made certain unwise investments, trying to improve his shaky finances by accepting risks (how else, actually, can one improve one's finances?), then his mother would not have had to sell the damned manuscript. That's what it all leads back to, his incompetence and his need. The rest derives from that, even including his mother's strange sense of obligation to the Rosenbachs or to Mr. Johnson.

It is flimsy and some of the connections aren't quite convincing, but one can make a logical argument, draw a line. And yet there are still questions. Why, for instance, did she undertake to sell it, herself? She could have left him the manuscript and the job of disposing of it. Did she think him so incompetent as to be unable to perform that simple bit of business? She had never let him think she distrusted him so deeply. Has she been, then, so skillful a dissimulator? Had she, for all those years when his father was alive, merely feigned that compliant simplicity?

They are two different sets of questions, but they overlap, so that Caryl feels the chagrin of his fiscal needs and his mother's having in this way to take care of him and at the same time is aware of a serious error somewhere in his knowledge of his family and of himself. Either area of doubt would be uncomfortable; together, the doubts are particularly onerous. He looks about him for reassurance, but the fake Palladian buildings of Columbia only mock him. It is not, after all, the strangeness in those fun-house mirrors but the distortions of what is recognizable that one finds disturbing.

Several times he feels his hip and the comforting edge of the rounded aluminum flask, slender but solid, and promising solace and courage as soon as he can get to a place of some privacy. Like Fotheringay, who also was a secret snorter. Fotheringay, a fellow officer in the Scots Guards, once admitted ruefully that the man who drinks in private is the worst kind of drunk, but when Caryl asked him why he didn't then get hold of himself, Fotheringay replied, "Have a heart, Caryl. Those people who can get hold of themselves just don't understand the problem. They haven't any idea what life is. They live in a dream. For us, the only way to do is with help."

Caryl never quite knew whether that "us" was to include Guards officers, veterans of the trenches, victims of shell shock, or just drunks. But there was a kind of honor that carried over from one category to the next. Caryl wasn't exactly proud of himself—but didn't feel any shame, either —if a drink or two could help him through a morning, or give him that stolidity he needed in order to confront the problems of life, whether he understood them or not.

He feels the sun as if it were a weight overhead. It will not move. Time is caught, as it always seems to be caught in Carroll, in some surrealistic snag. Caryl lets the blather break in waves upon his head. Don't they understand anything? Don't they have any glimmer about their freaky idol who was mad for little girls? Have they no sense of shame?

He can imagine what his father would have thought of this, the rage, that lofty distance that would come into his father's face. When other boys told him how their fathers got angry, Caryl was surprised. The way children expressed annoyance or frustration or fury was to shout and carry on, but grown-ups, gentlemen, were quite different. His father always got quieter and quieter. His sentences became more and more inflected. His lips pursed a bit. And he became curiously Latinate in his vocabulary. It was as if he were withdrawing into some interior sanctum from which formal diplomatic messages could be sent only after calm consideration.

Caryl knew officers like that in the war. They'd gone mad. Or been killed, most of them. And one or two had emerged as generals.

It isn't Caryl's own way, but he admires it. And he can all but hear his father, chiding in elegant hypotaxis the smug president of this colonial college, or the Rosenbachs, or, most probably, Caryl himself. And he has no answer to make. He made a mess with the money, digging himself even deeper into the hole than he'd been before. No good arguing about the expense of running a place like Cuffnells. He made his investments, took his gamble, and suffered the consequences.

My God, but he never *asked* to be bailed out this way.

It was his mother's idea, her initiative, her responsibility.

Had she liked the old pervert? Had she liked whatever it was the monster did to her? Or is this her way of brazening it out, pretending that nothing happened in order to protect her own reputation?

It's possible. She has to save Carroll in order to save herself. And she has to save herself for all their sakes, Grandfather Liddell's first of all.

Caryl and Rex talked about that, once. Both of them Christ Church men and grandsons of the Dean, they arrived at the same conclusion—that their grandfather had kept still all those years, even though it must have galled him each day, every time he laid eyes on Dodgson, because there was no way of firing Dodgson without bringing disgrace on both the House and his own family.

His mother is doing the same thing, isn't she?

No, she isn't. Caryl knows perfectly well that neither his grandfather nor his father would have lied this way. Or would they? Wasn't their silence, grandfather's particularly, a kind of lie that went on for decades?

Silly, really, all these questions. Matters of honor. Like the honor of Montenegro or the honor of Serbia. Or a hill fifty yards to the north. Hardly worth all those dead bodies, stinking and gnawed by the rats. But what else is worth dying for? What else is life about?

He watches as President Butler drapes the hood over his mother's shoulders. For all Caryl knows, this is his mother's way of getting back at old Dodgson himself.

The celebration was originally scheduled for late January to mark Lewis Carroll's hundredth birthday, but his mother refused to consider a midwinter crossing. Has she contrived to expropriate the whole celebration, seizing it for her own birthday? She will be eighty in two days and there is another ceremony scheduled for the closing of the Carroll exhibit then, on the fourth of May. He has waited for her to explain herself, or at least to share her feeling of satisfaction. In her position, that's what he is sure he'd feel. Instead, she has kept her own counsel, letting him suppose whatever is comfortable. Or to suppose nothing at all, just sit quietly and endure his way through it. She has contrived, however, to make him an active participant. There is that piece for the *Times* in which he is to pretend to interview her. She has consented to that arrangement and it means that they will have to talk, he and his mother, about Carroll. Either she will continue to lie to him or she will tell him the truth and admit that she has been lying for forty-four years. Either way, there will be no benefit to either of them, and a great deal of embarrassment.

Caryl's duty is nevertheless clear. To soldier through and protect her, insofar as possible. That's the objective. And not to think too much, which only gets in the way. He learned in the army not to think too much—a hard lesson for intelligent people. But there it was. The flask would help. Real Scotch, the man has promised him, but after the first couple of swallows it doesn't seem to make much difference. Even the fake Scotch can get you drunk, which is what one needs to avoid excessive cerebration.

Thank God, it's time. The first notes of the recessional ring out from the band. The people on the platform are rising. Is it the national anthem? No, it is indeed the recessional. His mother is waiting for him. He goes to her side, takes her arm, and walks with her, helping her down the steps and leading her along in the procession that passes through the audience and toward the building in which Butler has his offices. There will be a lavatory there, and he'll be able to pop off for a moment. Aunt Rhoda is following? Yes, all in good order.

Their progress is slow, and while Caryl is pleased that his mother is not pressed to exert herself, he is also tantalized. The privacy of that paradisiac W.C. recedes at every pause. He contrives a wooden stoicism, not quite identifiable as military but surely related to his time in the Guards. Nicholas Murray Butler's office seems more like that of a captain of industry than of a scholar, but Americans have no idea of limits. For all Caryl knows, every instructor in the university has such impressive quarters, those green leather sofas with their brass nails, those polished tables with brass lamps of baronial proportions, and the marble pen-stands. Does Butler sit at that huge desk and sign treaties with other colleges?

His mother is seated in the chair of honor beside Butler's desk. Caryl excuses himself and goes off to find the loo. He sees Aunt Rhoda taking note, a recording angel. Well, too bad. He has no doubt that he has earned his reward, and he goes out to have a quick drink. When he returns, Aunt

Rhoda welcomes him back with another meaningful look.
Has the woman no mercy?

"It's almost over," she says quietly. "Just a few more
minutes."

"Yes," Caryl agrees.

"You've done very well so far."

"Have I?"

"Just hang on a bit longer."

He is mollified. He has misjudged her too, perhaps. She
did not say a word about his drinking. All she was trying to
do was help. And this morning? He remembers back to the
moment in the living room of their suite at the Waldorf
where she took advantage of a moment they had alone
together to say that he shouldn't push too hard. He assumed that she meant he was not to push too hard about
the details of what happened between Dodgson and his
mother, that he ought not take the *Times* piece too seriously
or use it as an instrument of torture. But quite possibly he
was wrong. It is not altogether implausible that she meant
no more than to tell him not to push himself too hard, not
to be too demanding or critical of himself.

Or both? That would be more than likely. It would be her
way to defer, delay, deny, in the hope that any unpleasantness would simply get up, excuse itself, and go away.

It is also possible that his improved outlook is not so
much the result of Aunt Rhoda's friendliness as of the genie
in the bottle, the friend in the flask. He feels soothed,
eased. The nurture of that condition is an exacting business, an art really, as the work at the distillery is an art too.
The trick is in the striking of the right balance, the finding
of the proper proportion, as any Greek philosopher could
have said, stoic or not. Too much, and he gets belligerent
or sleepy; too little, and he still feels the pain of things. But
there is a fine edge, or more accurately a fine dullness, and
with practice one learns how to reach it and stay there,

keeping to that delicate ledge beyond which lies the abyss of drunkenness. It is more like the intricate oriental refinements of lovemaking than anything else, the ability to climb to that plateau and hang there until the plateau almost disappears and one imagines oneself to be floating, soaring free.

He is able now to float through the flatteries and the nonsense of Dr. Butler's office and offices. He accepts the compliments of strangers as if he were really pleased, as though he had done something to deserve praise, as though any of this meant anything. What it means is that they begin the process of disengagement. He can feel the party breaking up, like a frozen river in the north of Canada. Rex had been in Canada, had brought home specimens of trees for their father's arboretum, and had described, with his knack for precise detail, the look and the spirit of the wilderness there. It's where he'd have gone back to, if he'd lived. The opening up of spring . . .

Caryl feels the opening up of doors. He escorts his mother outside and they allow themselves to be deposited in the back of someone's luxurious Packard. His mother and his aunt take the rear seats. There is room for Caryl between them, but he prefers the little jumpseat that unfolds from its receptacle and turns the large limousine into something that feels almost sporty. The car belongs to Butler? Or one of the trustees? Perhaps to Mr. Johnson? It hardly matters. Caryl looks out of the window and waits for his mother to say something so he'll know what tone to take with her. He does not wish to make fun of her. But if she is inclined to make light of the ceremonies, disengaging herself from them, then he will be happy to join in her humor.

"Are you all right?" Rhoda asks, again proving herself to be an ally. It seems a simple enough question, but Caryl doesn't want to risk the appearance of pushing.

"Yes, just a bit tired," his mother tells them.

"Perhaps you'll lie down at the hotel."

"I believe I shall," his mother says. "We can work together later on, can't we?"

This last is to Caryl. He'd be happy to put it off. The only difficulty is that he must remain undrunk for several more hours. But the nice balance of dullness is better than the ordeal out in the sunshine on the green lawns of Columbia. "Whatever you like," he tells her. "I think a rest would do you good."

She nods, agreeing, even perhaps thanking him. She closes her eyes, indifferent to the street scenes of Manhattan. She is fatigued. Or is she smiling?

It is not impossible that she is replaying the speeches and ceremonies of the past hour. Or that she has left them far behind, going way back to her recollections of another university, in another age. Or maybe she is simply taken by the humorous quality of their misunderstandings, Butler's, Caryl's, everyone's. She has a half-smile that anyone else would compare to that of the Cheshire Cat.

It's just fatigue, Caryl tells himself, and he looks out at the impressive sight of the Hudson on their right and the cliffs of apartment houses on their left. He decides to allow himself a drink or two while his mother sleeps. At the very worst the *Times* can survive without their piece about Alice. His mother will take the blame and bail him out, yet again.

Whether he wants her to or not.

1926

IT WAS IN THE OLD HOUSE, Cuffnells, Lyndhurst, Hampshire, a grand sprawl of a place down in the New Forest, on a gray April morning, the latest in a rather long series of gray mornings. They were at breakfast. Annie had brought in the mail, offering it to Reginald Hargreaves, Esq., J.P., who glanced through it as she poured him a little more tea.

He was tall, lean, wore a mustache, and combed his hair —silvery now—straight back from its pronounced widow's peak. He could hide his feelings as well as any Englishman; still, he had all he could do not to betray surprise at finding the note. It was not a guilty surprise. He was old enough to have accommodated himself to the customs and necessities of his own life and intelligent enough to be reasonably free of illusion. Had he been required to give an account of himself, he would almost certainly have likened his situation to that of a man married to an invalid, unwilling to abandon her, feeling for her a loyalty and affection in no way diminished by the impossibility of normal conjugal relations, but requiring for himself some occasional indulgence. There was no chagrin, then, as he opened the plain envelope and noted the signature of Glenda Fenwick. But he was startled by Mrs. Fenwick's disregard of the proprieties.

He put a Blackwell's catalogue over the letter from

Glenda and opened another letter, this one from a botanist with whom he had been corresponding about forcing roots from cuttings of certain kinds of trees.

"Anything interesting?" Alice asked, her tone betraying no particular curiosity.

"No, just a note from Soames about the rooting thing."

"Mmm."

"And a Blackwell's catalogue," he said. He put Soames' letter over Glenda's note and offered her the bookseller's catalogue. She accepted it.

His success in the little sleight of hand was irksome. He did not mind deceiving Alice when it was necessary to do so, but his proficiency distressed him. He was, he believed, an honorable man. If he kept some of the truth from Alice sometimes, it was only out of decency and kindness.

It was not a bad marriage, although Reginald Hargreaves never thought to appraise it in terms of good and bad. It was beyond such qualifications, for they had gone through forty-six years together and had endured the loss of first one and then another of their sons in the Great War. They were like two people who survive a shipwreck and are pulled out of the lifeboat in which they have been drifting for days. They do not ask ridiculous questions about whether they enjoyed the voyage or each other's company.

Alice offered, "Another slice of toast?"

"Yes, thanks," he said, not wanting any. He forced himself to keep her company a little longer, to chew and swallow the slice of toast, to put off until that courtesy had been done the inspection of Glenda's letter.

He watched while she thumbed through the catalogue. Nothing arrested her attention. She offered it back. He put the other mail, including Glenda's letter, into it and went out to the orangery where his seedlings burgeoned in the simulated rain-forest. Here he could be assured of privacy. He looked again at the simple laid paper and read the writing, large, clear, and rather schoolgirlish, that said: *My dear Reginald Hargreaves, I have a matter of some interest to disclose to you having to do with the subject of our recent conversation. Please let me know when you next plan to come to London. Sincerely, Glenda Fenwick.*

Nothing in the letter was even suggestive. There might have been some questions, but nothing for which an inventive man could not have fabricated answers. Still, it was annoying to be forced to fabricate.

On the other hand, he had to suppose that Mrs. Fenwick was risking as much as he, if not more. She was jeopardizing his patronage and friendship. It wasn't an action she was likely to take frivolously.

The subject of our recent conversation.

Alice.

Even in the orangery, where the temperature and humidity were subtropical and there was no stir of air, Hargreaves felt a chill, thinking of that occasion and feeling a pang of mortification. To talk about one's wife with one's mistress or one's whore? Unforgivable. And banal!

There had been extenuating circumstances. But still . . .

He burned the letter.

TWO MONTHS EARLIER. It had been one of Hargreaves' periodic visits to London, ostensibly for a new hacking jacket and a conference with his banker, but also for reasons of health. A gin drinker, he needed to have his prostate occasionally flushed. It was a kind of duty, like brushing one's teeth or eating one's roughage. He visited Mrs. Fenwick's, as was his custom. Quite late in the evening, they were sitting in the parlor, sipping champagne that was sweeter than he liked, making the desultory remarks and pointless jokes that are a part of the end of an evening. It is merely good manners for people to try to persuade one another that they have all had a good time. One of the young ladies remarked that it—the enterprise? the evening? the profession?—was "rather like a Caucus Race."

And Hargreaves? Said nothing. Kept mum, as he later reminded himself, looking for ways to exculpate himself. He let it pass, as he had learned to let all such references pass, as if he had never had anything to do with the Cheshire Cat or the Tweedledee-and-Tweedledum pair. He sipped at the sweetish wine, put the delicate flute down on the marble tabletop before him, and folded his hands in his lap.

But Glenda Fenwick picked up the reference. Hargreaves heard her making some claim which he didn't quite get, having been studying the tips of his shoes. No doubt it was about having read *Alice in Wonderland.* But who in blazes hadn't?

"No, no," she corrected. "I knew him. Carroll."

He stared at her, startled, even—he feared—looking wounded. But she took it as a compliment, and his look as one of admiration.

Again, he said nothing, betrayed nothing of the connection he so deeply despised. He not only kept his mouth closed but could feel the muscles of his jaw like bands, could feel his clenched teeth so tight as to be painful. But one of the girls—Gwendolyn, the redhead—asked the inevitable question: "Tell us about him. What was he like?"

"He liked little girls," Glenda replied. "He loved little girls, I should say. He liked to photograph them and to draw them in the altogether." Glenda laughed, an ingratiating, unmistakably earthy laugh that Hargreaves recognized as fundamental to her life: that was how she survived in this business without turning depressed or crazy. She found the whole business of sex amusing, awkward, absurd, but finally funny. He admired her pluck and spirit.

He also found, in this moment of spontaneous sympathy,

that he was forced to recognize the authenticity of her claim
—she actually must have known the old goat, must have
had some experience of his company, must have perceived
more than the conventional nonsense of the dear old don
and kindly writer of children's books.

"Yes, so I've heard," he agreed, encouraging her. He
owed it to her to draw her out a little. And he was curious.
"Were you one of the young girls he photographed?"

"Would I admit to such a thing?" she asked, lowering her
eyes in a mockery of maidenly embarrassment. He supposed it was a mockery. "Even assuming that it were true
. . ."

"I have no idea," Hargreaves confessed. "I suppose
there might be a kind of distinction in it?" The inflection
was that of a question, the thought having occurred to him
for the first time.

"I should hate for that to be my only claim to distinction," she answered. She seemed inclined to terminate the
discussion. And Hargreaves felt a glimmer of self-congrat-
ulation for getting through this potentially awkward moment. It was like a tired swimmer's glimpse of shore.

"Where did you know him?" Gwendolyn asked. She
wasn't really pushing but seemed impressed by her employer's connection with the famous man.

"On the beach at Eastbourne," Glenda said. "He vaca-
tioned there sometimes."

"There and on the Isle of Wight," Hargreaves said,
agreeing, imagining how it must have been, how Carroll
must have picked her up on the beach . . . It was tawdry
and sad.

"You knew him too?" Glenda asked.

That glimpse of shore receded. He could not lie to her.
She'd know it as a lie, know that he was unwilling to discuss
Carroll with her, and assume that it was because of her
profession.

"Yes, I was at the House."

"The House?" Gwendolyn asked. She was a girl from the country and didn't understand these things.

"Christ Church," Glenda explained. "That's what they call it." But there was a look that cut off further inquiries on this tangential subject.

Hargreaves thought—and remembered thinking—how the gaffe might yet be retrieved. His own connection with Dodgson was innocuous. If he could contrive to limit the discussion to that . . .

"You were friendly, then?" Glenda asked him.

"No, not really. He was a cold fish. None of us liked him much, I'm afraid. Nor did he seem particularly friendly or comfortable with us. He was . . ."

"A frightened little man," Glenda suggested.

"Yes," Hargreaves agreed.

"I was . . . somewhat beneath what he generally preferred, I think."

"Oh?"

"In age, you mean, ma'am?" Gwendolyn asked. "Ma'am" was what they called her, as if she were the Queen.

"No, not in age. I was the perfect age for him. I must have been eight or nine. In social class, I meant."

"A snob then?" Gwendolyn asked, not quite laughing.

"Oh, yes, but for good reason."

"I don't understand," Hargreaves said, leaning forward a little but keeping from his voice any evidence of his particular interest in the subject.

"Well," she said, drawing out the syllable as one does before disclosing a delicious secret, "I suppose it may still be true today, but it was more widely true then that girls of a certain class were kept peculiarly ignorant about certain matters. Or innocent. It was the custom. And Carroll understood that this made it safer for him to restrict his attentions to young ladies of this class, who were less likely to understand and therefore less likely to object . . .''

"Yes, I see that," he said. Not only did he see it but he saw its obviousness. How could he have failed before to grasp so fundamental a point?

He was not only impressed by this advance in understanding but also tantalized. Were there further possible revelations and connections? Was it idle to hope that so unlikely a figure as Glenda Fenwick, bordello keeper, might lead him to other and more useful insights? He was tempted to confide in her, take advantage of her pariah status, and rely upon her demonstrable capacity for discretion.

He rejected it as a fond and absurd idea. Did he seriously expect to have his whole life put into some new perspective, to have some missing information supplied so that the great hurt—in his own life and Alice's—could at last be healed? It was preposterous to think so. He resolved to keep his mouth closed and his secret to himself. Alice's secret! Until now, he had not had the feeling that his visits to Glenda were a real disloyalty to Alice, but to talk about Alice here, with Glenda . . . That would be a betrayal. Besides, there were no answers. There could be no soothing of that old wound.

Still, he was unsettled by Glenda's disclosure and disarmed by her attitude—which conformed to his own—on the painful subject of that man's reputation. Perhaps distracted by the effort it cost him to say nothing more to Glenda about Alice, he drank more than he should have, drained glass after glass of the sweetish champagne, defying it to deaden the hurt. Eventually, they had to put him to bed.

He could not blame them. It was, on their part, considerate and kind. Glenda could have called a taxicab and poured him into it, but she did not.

He must have said something. A man is not to be held responsible for what he lets slip when his shoes are off his feet.

He could not actually remember what he told her. He could remember his thoughts, but he'd supposed they were merely thoughts, whirling about in his head's darkness, bats disturbed from their dangling drowse by the untoward torchlight of Glenda's observation. But out of the mouth of the cave something or other had flown, some observation or connection Glenda was able to use to hypothecate further. He honestly didn't remember. He must have mentioned Alice's name. That was almost inevitable. And he must have mentioned Carroll—or Dodgson. Perhaps that was all she needed. If the tone was right, angry enough or sad enough, she would have been able to leap to the not so difficult conclusion that his Alice was Carroll's Alice.

Glenda already knew that his forty-odd years of married life had been less than perfect. His visits to her establishment had been too regular to be merely diversionary. For him, it wasn't a condiment but the meal itself.

She was certainly clever enough so that, inclined to think about the matter, she could have put the pieces together in a fairly close approximation of the truth. But that in no way excused him from culpability in letting the secret out. If anything, it made his fault the worse—knowing how sharp she was, he should have been all the more careful. And up until the end he had been. But when they were putting him to bed to sleep off the wine and he'd been—in both senses —unbuttoned, he'd mentioned Alice's name. And wept.

Glenda had seen into his heart as she had never before been able to do, even in that intimate setting.

And now, curiously, a letter. Asking him to come to London. Commanding him, one might say. At the little writing table in the orangery, where he made notes on the success or failure of his specimens, he wrote a few lines to let her know when to expect him and tucked the note into his pocket next to his billfold, where he'd find it later, when he was in town. He'd mail it himself, that afternoon.

IT DOES NO GOOD to anticipate. He knew that, but he had to construct some interim attitude for himself, some posture of anticipation. What he contrived was a cautious defense against assault. He knew or thought he knew Glenda and believed her to be a friend. But for whatever motives, even kindly ones, she seemed intent on meddling. And it was his primary object to protect Alice. That was the main thing.

He loved her. He had loved her for a long time. In a way, as they had subsided into elderliness, sharing their losses and diminutions, more and more private in the face of increasing frailties and their ever greater intimacy with the idea of mortality, he had come to admire and love her more. She was a decent woman, sturdy, sound, and . . . all those things one never actually discussed.

It seemed all the more unfair, then, that they should get entangled by this random association—Glenda's with Carroll. What could that have to do with Alice's connection with Carroll or with Alice's life with Reginald? Nothing! And it was his duty to keep it that way.

He had nothing to fear on his own account and nothing in particular to hope for. Just so long as he managed to keep the damage from spreading, he supposed it was going to be all right. And he was mildly curious. Otherwise, he fought off any particular kind of anticipation. When he got to London he telephoned from the station, to let her know he'd arrived and to find out when she wanted to see him.

"Now," she said. "Come right over."

"It's very early," he said. He supposed that her establishment disappeared in the morning hours, and reappeared only around dusk. It was not yet lunchtime.

"That's all right," Glenda told him. "Come straight round."

It was a contradiction in terms, wasn't it? Still, he promised to do as she'd said.

ISA BOWMAN?

He suppressed a laugh. He would refuse, of course. It would be a further disloyalty to Alice even to consider meeting such a person.

"You know her?" Glenda asked.

"I know of her," Hargreaves said, as flatly as he could manage.

"But you've never met. Is that not right?"

"That's correct."

"I think you might enjoy meeting her. It could, indeed, be interesting for you."

"Interesting?"

"I think."

And then there ensued a kind of cat-and-mouse game in which both parties were as intent on concealing information as on revealing it. He did not want to let her know how Alice despised Isa Bowman, considering her to be an upstart and a pretender. For one thing, that was Alice's business. For another, it betrayed the way in which Alice still cared about Carroll, was still sufficiently involved with his memory to be jealous of another woman who, years later, had also been one of Carroll's playmates. Finally, he did not want anyone to know—and especially Glenda, who knew too much already—how distressed he was, himself, at that jealousy Alice could display on Isa Bowman's account. So, from him, even though Isa was officially connected with Carroll by the dedication of *Sylvie and Bruno* as well as by her own deplorable memoir, there should be as little forthcoming as possible.

"I can't imagine how," he told her.

"I can," Glenda said. And she proceeded to explain to him how she had met Isa Bowman.

"I don't see how this bears upon me," he said.

"But it does. If it turns out to be irrelevant, then you'll have wasted a few hours. An evening. It is not so much to gamble, is it? To indulge me?"

"Her experience is . . ."

"Fascinating!" Glenda insisted.

SOME OF THE INFORMATION Glenda gave him about Isa Bowman, Hargreaves already had. He knew, for instance, that Isa was a theatrical person, of no particular class or family (which is, perhaps, why we distrust people in the theater?), whose life not only ignored but positively flouted convention. Her life was even more irregular than Glenda's. Isa had walked away from a husband, was living openly with a lover, and continued to see old admirers from her earlier days.

"Indeed," Hargreaves said. "But what has any of this to do with me?"

"Perhaps nothing. Perhaps a great deal. I have assumed that you disapprove of Carroll. That you condemn him."

"I despise him."

"I have also assumed that Alice does not feel as you do. Is that correct?"

"I will not discuss Alice. Or her feelings. Or our relationship. It was most improper of me to have alluded to her connection with Carroll the last time I visited you."

"Do you think so?" she asked, an edge to her voice.

He did not believe it was necessary to reply.

She waited a moment, then continued, "Am I not a friend? Am I not an intimate friend? Do I not deserve your confidence? Am I wrong to suppose that friendship is ever possible between me and a few of my visitors?"

He was puzzled for a moment by the vehemence of her

attack. But when he perceived that it was not an attack so much as a plaint, that he had inadvertently struck her in a tender place, that she was questioning the very foundation of her life and career, he felt obliged to reassure her. "I didn't mean it that way," he said. "I . . . I am afraid I was not thinking of you, but of Alice."

"Yes, of course. I'm sorry."

"On any other subject, you know, I've always confided in you. And I do think of you as a friend. You know that." These things seemed to be true as he said them. The alternative was quite clear—to affront her terribly, to leave her with no shred of self-esteem. Reginald Hargreaves had been taught not only to be polite to women, opening doors for them and holding their chairs, but really to care for them. And Glenda had been kind to him over the years.

The result of all this was that he felt obliged to listen and let Glenda tell him about Isa Bowman's irregular life, however little it bore upon his own or Alice's.

"She came here, you know."

"Here? To your apartment?" Hargreaves asked. It was a flat on the top floor of the house that she kept for herself and in which she sometimes received her special friends. It was separate from the business establishment.

"No, no. Downstairs."

"A woman?" Hargreaves asked.

"It happens," she said, not condescending. He was grateful for that.

He'd heard such stories, but never quite believed them. Respectable women, fascinated by the prostitute's life, making arrangements with some madam so that they could experience the intellectual pleasure of sex with a stranger. He'd always supposed it was a man's fantasy, invented by someone who had been visiting a brothel and needed to dream up some long-odds fiction that might equalize the encounter, thereby redeeming it a little.

Perhaps there were, from time to time, such women.
How very odd. He wondered if they enjoyed themselves.

"She liked to watch," Glenda explained.

"She?" Hargreaves asked. "Oh yes. Of course." He'd
forgotten for a moment that they'd been discussing Isa
Bowman. Liked to watch? He'd heard about that, too.

"Not *of course*," Glenda corrected him. "It was her first
time, I think. She had expressed—or confessed?—an interest in watching. Or, for all I know, she had invented it as a
kind of intimacy she could share with an old friend without
being unfaithful to a newer friend. I have no idea. Anything
is possible."

"It sounds complicated."

"It was quite simple, actually. He—her old friend—is an
old friend of mine. He arranged it for Miss Bowman, as a
kind of a dare perhaps, or a joke. And she couldn't very well
back down."

"To watch? Here?"

"There is one room with a peephole arrangement.
You've not been in it, I promise you."

"But some have! How . . . underhanded!"

"Who's harmed? There are, I assure you, those who'd be
pleased if they knew. Delighted!"

"That's not the point, is it? There are those who'd be
dismayed."

"Only if they knew."

"Why would you do such a thing?" he asked. The answer
occurred to him even before she pronounced it.

"For the money, of course. I get more for the peephole
than for the room, believe me."

"I dare say."

"That was how we met. A couple of weeks ago. And it
occurred to me that it was such a great coincidence, that all
of us had had, as it were, a mutual friend . . . I thought we
might get together, that it might be a useful thing to do."

"Useful?" he asked, warily.

"Useful for you—if I'm guessing right."

"I appreciate your concern," he said, as affably as he could manage. "Still, I have arrived at a time of life when I do not expect change, don't look for it or welcome it. I am accustomed to my life. I think it fair to say that Alice is accustomed to hers. That equilibrium we have achieved is not something to trifle with. For the time we have left, I think it will do quite nicely. I understand that you are motivated by kindly feelings toward me, and I'm grateful. But I have very serious reservations."

"I'm not asking you to change your life or expecting any great result. All I want is for you to meet an interesting woman. I found her interesting, and thought of you and how you might be impressed by her. It's nothing to be afraid of, certainly . . ."

It was a dare. He understood that he could get up and leave, right then. It might not do much for his friendship with Glenda, but neither would it rupture that friendship. They would contrive some way of getting on.

That was all quite clear to him. It was also clear that if he was to perform the duty he'd set himself in the days between the arrival of the letter from Glenda and this interview, it was now, at this moment, that he had to act. If he was to protect Alice, then the means were at hand—that simple soldierly gesture of coming to attention, thanking Glenda for her interest, and leaving the room and the building.

But as long as he protected Alice from knowing about any of this, there was nothing to fear. That was the closest to bedrock he could come.

And somehow managing to intuit that the decision had been made, and in her favor, Glenda offered, "There's some sherry over there on the sideboard. You might get us a little."

"All right," he said, and they both knew he was agreeing to more than the sherry. "Why not?"

"That's the spirit," she said.

"Sherry? It's a fortified wine, actually."

Glenda raised an eyebrow. "She's in a play," she said. "We'll go to the play and then have supper afterwards. So, you see, it's not such a burdensome thing I'm asking you to do, is it?"

"No, I expect not," he conceded. He poured the two sherries and brought one over to Glenda.

"To our evening, then," she said, and drank.

"To your kindness," he said, because he had never doubted her fundamental motives. He thought they had led her astray, perhaps, but they had been good to begin with.

The sherry anyway was first rate. "Tell me," he asked, "does the girl know? In that room with the peephole?"

"Of course, the girl knows," Glenda told him. "It makes for a much better show if the girl knows."

AFTER HE LEFT GLENDA, his confidence ebbed. He could not imagine—let alone justify—how he had agreed to spend an evening in the manner that Glenda had proposed. Isa Bowman—who, as it turned out, was far worse than anything Alice had ever imagined! The idea that a woman could come to a brothel in the company of an ex-lover to look through a peephole at the spectacle of a man having intercourse with a prostitute was something so foreign to Alice that she would hardly be able to understand it, let alone conjure it up as an imaginative possibility.

Of course, her quarrel with Isa Bowman—whom she had never met—was founded on other grounds. That dreadful little memoir the woman had published, billing herself as "the real Alice" and trivializing the man . . .

Hargreaves didn't mind seeing Dodgson trivialized. But he hated for Alice to be slighted, especially in a public way.

And he had had to argue with her, telling her—rightly, he still believed—that it was unnecessary to make any reply. She ought not condescend to take notice of Miss Bowman, resting securely on what she and everyone else knew to be the truth.

Not that it was such an enviable truth, after all.

But the merits of his wife's position were not in question. His loyalty was the only issue. And he had agreed to meet the one woman in England of whom Alice might have used the word "enemy." It was Glenda's doing. She had manipulated him. It was his own fault for being so manipulable.

He consoled himself by going to his tailor's, where he allowed himself to be fitted for a new Norfolk jacket of an attractive rough tweed in a dull green and brown.

If the physicians were right, it might well be his last. He ran his hand appreciatively over the fabric, not quite sure whether he was saying hello to it or good-bye.

REGINALD HARGREAVES AROSE. He had spent the early afternoon at his club but then had gone to Brown's, where he generally took a room on his London visits. It was his habit to protect himself by having a receipted bill from the hotel, which was in any event convenient to Mrs. Fenwick's house. He also found it beneficial to take advantage of the opportunity for a few hours' rest before the exertions of the night. He had no such carnal expectations this evening, but he wanted to have his wits about him. A tranquil and collected mind was the best means of protection . . . Against attack? But it wasn't an attack. Glenda was trying to help him, in whatever way and for whatever reason. For all he knew, both Glenda and Isa Bowman felt some odd kind of sorority with Alice, in which case their motive might be no more sinister than that of a group of old guards meeting at a reunion to talk over past battles and mourn the deaths of comrades.

There was a golden light of late afternoon that matched Hargreaves' mood. He drew a bath for himself in the lovely outsized tub, and got in to soak and continue the self-indulgence to which he felt himself entitled. What harm could there be in meeting Isa Bowman? It might even be interesting. If he felt threatened he could always excuse himself, pleading illness.

Or, no, he didn't have to plead anything at all. He was a grown man. He could, if it seemed necessary, simply get up at any time and leave.

He pulled himself up and rose like a great whale breaching, the water sluicing down his sides. He stood, a little dizzy for a moment, and steadied himself, holding the chrome bar that was attached to the wall. He grabbed the rim of the tub and climbed out. A large bath towel had been warming on the heated rack. He wrapped himself in it.

There was a pink gin with ice waiting to cool and soothe him. He took a swallow and began to comb his hair.

GLENDA WAS WAITING in the theater lobby, the tickets in her gloved hand. She gave them to him to give to the ticket taker. After they had been seated and he had tipped the usher and helped her with her wrap, he gave her a program and pretended to study his own. He also glanced around the house, wondering whether he might recognize anyone —or, more to the point, whether anyone might recognize him. He felt like a regency buck, going to the theater with a woman of the town. Seated, he was safe enough. But at the intervals? There was a low level of risk, but risk there was. London could turn at any moment into a small village. But there was nothing to be done for it now. He looked again at the program. The play was one of those light comedies in which youngsters run in and out of French doors, looking attractive and saying witty things, while their elders, appearing to be calmer and wiser, behave just as stupidly, so

that the youngsters come in at the end to surprise themselves and the audience by restoring order to the world and
getting the audience safely to their trains to the suburbs.
He had read the notices and had decided to miss this one.

So much for decisions. Of all kinds.

The lights dimmed. The curtain went up. The play began. Isa Bowman did not make her entrance until well into
the first act. She was the infatuated, rather dithery aunt, an
elder stateswoman of the boudoir, full of earthy wisdom
and kindness but still susceptible, herself, to folly. Hargreaves realized that this was merely a role, but the evidence of his eyes and ears conspired with what he had been
told about the woman. He found himself wondering
whether she hadn't been cast in this particular role because
there was a certain truth in her the producer or director
wanted for the plausibility it brought to the flimsy dramatic
construction. Quite possibly the play was nonsense, but her
character was entirely real, correctly and honestly revealed.

Hargreaves was not ordinarily given to such speculations
about the truth of art and the truth of real life. He thought
of himself as a down-to-earth kind of man, literally as well
as figuratively, taking pleasure in the physical processes of
growing things—his seedlings and trees. The rest was in-
substantial.

On stage, Miss Bowman was pronouncing some apo-
thegm about romance being like gin—in that neither was
appropriate before eleven in the morning.

It was witty enough, but more and more difficult to endure, Hargreaves thought. There was less and less time to
waste. Waste was disagreeable, like a lamp left burning in
an empty room or a tap left running in a sink where no one
is using the water.

"OYSTERS, oysters, oysters. Colchesters and Whitstables
and . . . and champagne!"

It was Glenda's treat, her evening, she insisted. She would brook no discussion. She had booked a table at the Savoy Grill and that was that. They were to enjoy themselves.

They were in Isa Bowman's tiny dressing room. Isa ("Do call me Isa!"), visible only from the neck up, was behind one of those changing-screens that had been put up so she could have visitors in her dressing room. It had a pretty frame in some dark wood, mahogany or gumwood, in three panels. There was a shiny fabric, almost certainly silk, showing Chinese scenes in a vivid blue-green. The panels were asymmetrical, getting slightly taller from left to right, to make a nice sweep toward the top of the screen. The only trouble was that there was a tiny space between the panels to allow for movement on the delicate brass hinges. Through these two vertical interstices, Hargreaves could not help noticing flashes of Isa Bowman's pink flesh about thigh-high. Or perhaps not flesh but some slip or camisole?

He averted his eyes, then looked back, wondering whether the arrangement was inadvertent or deliberately provocative—not for his benefit or Glenda's, but in a more general way. The woman had, undeniably, a most latitudinarian outlook.

Perhaps it was a kind of game—a test—allowing her to judge the style with which her visitors admitted or refused to admit that they could see glimpses of her through the screen.

If so, he refused to play.

Isa was saying that she adored oysters.

Hargreaves supposed that he might argue with Glenda about whose treat it was. Then he decided to let her pay. He would not play that game either.

"An agreeable little play," Glenda was saying. "Do you enjoy it?"

"Parts of it," Isa said. "I have a few good moments. It

does get talky in the second act, and we must keep it moving. But it has its moments."

"You were very good, I thought," Glenda said.

"Oh, yes," Hargreaves chimed in. He recognized that he had to say something. There were proprieties to observe. "Very." It is far saner, he thought, to make polite remarks of a conventional kind than to stare while trying not to appear to stare through a crack in a screen.

There was nothing coy, though, in the way Isa Bowman peeled off her camisole and draped it over the top of the screen. It was as bold an announcement as could be made that she was, from the waist upward, quite naked. He looked at Glenda.

"Don't mind me," Isa said. "I'll be ready in a moment."

"No hurry," Glenda said politely.

"Of course there's a hurry," Isa replied. "I'm starving. Besides, one can't really talk this way."

She had another camisole on, this one black. In a matter of minutes she came out from behind her screen to announce, "All done," and extend her hand for him to shake. He took it. "It is a pleasure," she said. "I've been looking forward to it."

"The pleasure is mine," he said. He knew his lines.

With a minimum of logistical bustle, they contrived to shift the scene from the theater dressing room to a table at the Savoy where, obeying instructions, Hargreaves ordered the oysters and asked the sommelier for champagne.

Isa took the initiative: "Glenda tells me your wife disapproves of me."

Hargreaves hesitated. It was pointless to deny it. But he was less than happy about discussing Alice. Still, why not? "I believe she was distressed by your book. And some of its claims," he suggested, as gently as he could manage.

"The publisher's claims, I assure you. Not mine," Isa

said. "I couldn't very well argue. I needed the money. I'd have said anything."

"I see."

"It was an awkward moment for me. I was too old to be an *ingénue* and not quite old enough for character parts. Like the mule between the two haystacks, I was starving."

"I understand," Hargreaves said.

"I mean literally. Can you imagine what that's like?"

It was not helpful to have the wine steward appear with the champagne at that instant. With a flourish, he offered the bottle for inspection, wrapped its neck in a towel, and popped the cork.

"No," Hargreaves admitted. "I'm not sure that I can."

His very recognition that it had been something of a trick compelled him to admire the boldness required to perform it. Still on his guard, he couldn't help liking her a little.

One of the ways to be on guard, in fact, was to admit some liking for her. He realized this and allowed himself to relax a little. As long as he knew what he was doing, why not enjoy himself?

THERE WAS NO QUESTION about Isa's enjoying herself. For years, she had resented Alice's primacy of time and place, the success of the *Alice* books, so much greater than that of her own *Sylvie and Bruno,* the comfort and security Alice enjoyed as the daughter of Dean Liddell and wife of Reginald Hargreaves. She had thought of Alice as a snob, a woman who had no idea how lucky she was—almost as a sister who had turned away from her.

She may not have been altogether fair in her condemnation, but from a distance she felt no obligation to fairness. Now that the distance was closing, she was delighted to be gracious to Hargreaves, to repay his wife's and presumably his own condescension with kindness, and to prove herself their better if not their equal.

That some of what she had to say might distress Hargreaves, and eventually Alice when he brought home the message of what she'd told him, seemed to Isa Bowman just so much icing on a delectable cake.

Alice did not, after all, own Lewis Carroll!

The waiter brought the platters of oysters and a dish of lemon wedges wrapped in cheesecloth.

"To our meeting?" Glenda proposed, raising her glass.

They all drank to that and then tasted the oysters, fresh with the tang of seawater and salt air.

"Tell Reginald what you told me," Glenda prompted.

"I suppose," Isa replied, as if she were undecided. "You have suggested that Alice was distressed by my publishers' distortion of the truth. By their exaggeration. Is that not so?"

Hargreaves nodded.

"I think both you and she might have had more cause for distress had I told the truth."

"How is that?" Hargreaves asked.

"He used me to remind him of Alice. As I believe he used quite a number of young girls. He used to dress me in the kind of clothing she wore. He even said as much."

"I see."

"And this went on for a long time. Until I was sixteen or seventeen, I could appear girlish. I used to be able to play young girls on the stage. I was short—still am, as you see. That was what enabled our relationship to continue as long as it did. Usually, he detested girls after they had developed. But I don't have much bosom. And if I wore my hair a certain way and held my body a certain way, he could fool himself. It wasn't that I was fooling him. I was only cooperating in his own self-deception."

She paused. There seemed to be some comment necessary. "I understand," he said, but warily, wondering whether she'd pounce on him again and ask if he *really* understood.

"The point," she said, "is that I was older than most of the girls who were his 'child friends.' That's what he used to call us. Older, and I knew him over a longer period of time. I also have reason to believe that I was the last of them."

"But tell him what it was like," Glenda said. "Tell him what you told me."

"All the lurid details?" Isa asked, laughing, making a joke of it, or pretending to.

"I'm not sure I want to hear all the lurid details," Hargreaves said, trying to keep that same bantering tone.

"Then you're a bloody fool," Glenda told him, dead serious.

He looked at her, astonished.

"Are you not interested in finding out why I'm a madam?" Glenda asked. "And why Isa is as she is? And perhaps, by some process of integration, why Alice has come to be as she is? These things are too important for good manners. It's just hopeless! Do you want to leave?"

He was stunned.

"I'll tell you exactly what happened to me," Isa offered to him, "if you can stand it."

So it was a dare, too.

Hargreaves nodded.

"Perhaps we ought to get another bottle," Glenda said.

"That might be a very good idea," Isa agreed.

Hargreaves still didn't say anything, but he made no move to leave. He raised his finger to catch the attention of the wine steward.

So, Glenda thought, she has him. Hooked.

2

HARGREAVES sat at the writing table in his artificial jungle at Cuffnells, considering the seedlings on the shelves across from him. They would reach maturity long after he was gone. In a sense, then, he was staring into the future, more surely than any fortune teller who gazes into her cheap crystal ball. What he saw was the slow rhythm of growth and decay, an inexorability that was sometimes comforting and sometimes awesome and intimidating—depending upon his mood. He knew those plants as well as he knew his own body, had counted their leaves, had studied their venation under his glass, so that he could almost feel their strength in his own nerves. The growth of those marauder cells in his own body he could only feel indirectly. He was thinner than he used to be. His skin hung more loosely. His clothing—the older garments especially—billowed on him. Interesting, he thought.

It was warm and damp in the orangery, and that felt good. It was restorative for him simply to be there, as it was for other people who sit by the seaside and look out at the endless blue. For Hargreaves, the colors of life were green and brown.

He spent a great deal of time in his greenhouse, not only because he liked being there but also because it was a good place in which to think about that evening in London and the question it continued to pose. Or the questions, for they tended very quickly to multiply and spread, until every assumption by which he had lived his life came under new scrutiny and every principle of morality and taste was suddenly challenged. His first instinct had been to do nothing. But that decision, however easy to make, had to be remade every day. Or at least reconsidered. It was interesting to toy with the notion of telling Alice about Isa's experience, not to throw it in her face as a challenge but to use it as an instrument for exploration, like a compass or a sextant.

Not to mention the subject of Glenda Fenwick's experience (which would be awkward, if not foolhardy).

For the first time in his life, Hargreaves felt himself to have the advantage of Dodgson. He was no longer Dodgson's victim, or victim at second hand, a man suffering from Alice's suffering. Instead, he was an old man who had lived to see the outcome of three lives—Alice's, Isa's, and Glenda's—that had all been touched, as it were, by that famous paedophile. There was something interesting about being able to consider the effect of some great external event—glaciation or drastic climatic change—on three similar kinds of growth. The comparison was not heartless. Hargreaves felt deep affection and respect for his trees.

Still, let sleeping dogs lie. Let well enough alone. Why borrow trouble? Sufficient unto the day are the griefs thereof. These were the maxims by which he had lived, but they now seemed empty copybook phrases he could scarcely recognize.

The trouble was that it looked very much as though he had been wrong all those years, willfully blind, another obtuse victim of Victorian repression—that was how Isa had put it, and he suspected that she was trying to be kind. He had assumed that the liberty—whatever its sordid particulars—had resulted in a numbing of Alice's emotions, as though she had endured a wound. But if Isa Bowman was correct, he had believed this mainly because it was convenient for him to do so. It was a way of removing himself from any responsibility and of absolving Alice for her coldness. He could, instead, blame Dodgson, putting the whole burden upon his dead and detested shoulders.

"Has it been your experience that anything in life is that simple?" Isa Bowman had asked. "Is anything all that clearcut, black here and white there?"

"Some things are," he had said, defensively.

She had not made any answer. Instead, she had let him consider his own position, its likelihood, its compatibility with the rest of his world view, and his sense of how things were in human experience and in nature.

"If what he did with me was a re-enactment of what he did with Alice," she had said a little later, "then wouldn't you expect the same results in my psyche? Wouldn't you expect the same kind of thing from Glenda? Wouldn't we have more in common than we do, in the way we have developed and lived as women?"

"It isn't that simple," he had said, meaning something else.

"No, of course not."

ANOTHER TIME, although the times seemed to blur into one another. Again, at his writing table in the greenhouse, he was considering the accusation Isa had made—that he was a Victorian. Ordinarily, he'd have been proud of the description, claiming it as an honor rather than an insult or a joke. Those were not stupid or inestimable men and women, after all, nor were their standards so very wrong. Hypocrisy, it was now fashionable to say, had been the spirit of that age. But what is hypocrisy, Hargreaves wanted to know, except an attempt, however imperfect, at some lofty code of behavior? Lip service was better than none at all and frequently led the way to more profound belief.

More particularly, he remembered Dean Liddell, Alice's father, the great lexicographer and the presiding spirit at Christ Church. Lip service, for him and for the Liddell family, must have been difficult indeed, for it was a matter of keeping their lips sealed. Whatever it was that happened between Dodgson and Alice, whatever Dodgson did to Alice, the Liddells at some point found out about it. It was from that moment that they stopped seeing Dodgson—a student in the college—in a social way. Official relations, however, were maintained—in the common room, at high table, in the college, and in the university. The degree of restraint this required from all parties, but particularly from Henry and Lorina Liddell, seemed to Hargreaves nothing less than heroic. He had no doubt, though, that they had done the right thing—for their daughter's sake, first of all, but for the sake of Christ Church and their own family as well. The humiliation of any public accusation would have done as much harm as Dodgson himself had managed to do, if not more.

It went on for years, for the rest of their lives. It was one of those stupid Lewis-Carroll-like pieces of logical and mathematical trickery, Hargreaves thought: though Dean Liddell was twenty-five years older than Dodgson, their ages were very nearly equal if reckoned backward, inasmuch as they died within five days of one another. Dean Liddell enjoyed only five days of life on a Dodgson-free planet. Hargreaves compared in recollection the quality of Liddell's silence and the stutter of Dodgson's speech. Oh, that loathsome little toad!

Dodgson was not a Victorian, but a pervert and a disgrace, which time and fashion cannot affect. Achievements are marked by eponyms, styles of painting or music or literature or furniture. But crimes and sicknesses have a dreary sameness. They are, in the most fundamental sense, lacking in distinction. To look back on those two men, to remember Liddell's detestation and his correctness in public, to feel the electrical tension that was in the air whenever the two of them were in a room together was to appreciate the truth of Victorianism. It wasn't dowdy and silly and dull brown, the way Isa had suggested.

Hargreaves' instincts, then, were for silence, and his conscious predilections were for a style of behavior that would absolutely endorse the silence he had kept for all these years. But Isa's views came at a bad time. There were financial questions to be addressed—which included that damnable manuscript, the first version of *Alice's Adventures Under Ground* Dodgson had written out for Alice Liddell. Lorina, Alice's mother, had burnt all the letters Dodgson had sent. But even after the great rupture, she had preserved the manuscript. A puzzling thing for a woman like that at a moment like that to do, Hargreaves thought. It couldn't have been greed. The manuscript wouldn't have been worth much then, in the way of money. A more general sense of its literary worth? He doubted that, too. Those judgments are difficult enough to make when there is no emotional connection either of affection or of antipathy. Hargreaves himself disliked the book, considered it cute in the worst way, and thought it showed the nasty treacle of sentiment that was to ruin *Sylvie and Bruno* later but was already evident, always there, a flaw in the man's taste that somehow matched the flaw in his character and sexuality. But there were people—quite reputable, some of them—who admired *Wonderland* and *The Looking Glass,* too. Suppose, then, on the part of Lorina Liddell, a primitive respect for books, a sense of the general regard any book was entitled to, even a bad book by a bad man.

Whatever reason or prescience or prudence stayed her hand, she did not burn it. And the damned thing turned into exactly the kind of holy object that would have deserved Lorina Liddell's forbearance and respect. As the years passed and the reputation of the book grew out of all reasonable proportion—so that it was now considered a children's classic and a national treasure—the manuscript had become valuable and was worth a staggering amount of money. A dealer in London had assured Hargreaves that he could get five thousand pounds for it with no trouble. With no public notice, even, if he were disposed to keep the transaction a quiet one. On the other hand, if he were willing to put the thing up at auction—and to undergo the kind of attention from the press that such an action would necessarily entail—he could very probably double that figure.

Ten thousand bloody pounds!

There was the answer to all his prayers. The solution, at any rate, to all his problems. He had been fretting for some time over what Alice's prospects would be if he were to die and she were to live on, not just for a year or two but for some considerable period. A decade, say . . .

It would be just like Dodgson to find a way of dashing Hargreaves' most reasonable expectations, even from beyond the grave. Put the case that Alice is reduced in circumstances to the point where she ought to consider a sale of the manuscript. Will her pride allow it? Will her lifelong infatuation with that bad man permit it? Will the pretense of civility adopted by her parents constrain her to continue to pretend, so that she wastes away, unable even to put food on the table while yet unwilling to part with that dirty joke of a national treasure?

There was no doubt about Hargreaves' obligation to discuss with Alice their financial situation. He knew that. But he was aware of the difficulties that arose from one of Isa's *aperçus* about the odd ways in which people can contrive to adjust to each other, playing to each other even with the most implausible scripts. She had suggested—it was almost dawn, and they had moved on to Isa's place and were drinking chartreuse without ice, because the ice was long gone by then—that Alice might actually enjoy his jealousy of Carroll, that it might be a form of love she actually preferred, and that to insure its continuation she had to maintain at least an appearance of a continuing passion for Carroll.

"Are you suggesting," he had asked, "that she is merely

pretending? And that she is doing so in order to keep my jealousy going? That's absurd! Utterly fantastic!"

"Love is fantastic," Isa had rejoined.

"You mean you don't believe in love?" he'd asked.

"Oh, I believe in fantasy. I have devoted my life to it, one way or another. I mean that love is made up largely of fantasy, feeds on it, uses it . . ."

"Mmmhmm," Glenda agreed. She was sprawled on a sofa in a darkened corner of Isa's parlor.

"Do you mean to say that if I were to be less hostile to Dodgson that'd be the end of it? Would she stop 'pretending' to be a citizen of Wonderland and come back to the real world?" he had asked.

"Now? Who knows? It's gone on a long time this way," Isa had said, "longer than a lot of simpler love affairs. But it's possible, isn't it? Anything's possible."

There had been moments that evening when he had been absolutely confident that Isa and Glenda, between them, saw the truth, had managed to guess more about his life and Alice's than he'd ever known. There had been other moments, when he'd been convinced that they were both crazy, dangerous, meddlesome, flighty women. He'd been angry, amused, depressed, pained, delighted, and bored, one sensation giving way to the next, and one mood abruptly blossoming into another, as the long evening of fitful talk, strategic silences, and emotional outpourings had oozed on, as endless as a Wagnerian opera. Now, in the orangery, having had some days to think about it, he was left with his basic decision to make—whether to discuss the subject with Alice or continue the silence that had served them both so long.

Could he hope, in one last effort, to recoup somehow the losses of a long life together? Could he open doors they had agreed to leave closed between them? Did he have the right to any such hopes? Did he have an obligation—to let her know that it would be all right to sell the manuscript?

He supposed that she was a practical woman, that she was going to behave sensibly, that she'd sooner sell the manuscript than lose the house or go hungry or cold . . . But if Isa was right, or close to being right, and if Alice kept alive this peculiar emotional investment in Dodgson for some reason that had to do with her feelings for him—for her husband—then who could say what she'd do? And once he was gone, leaving her with some struggle of loyalties between ghosts who hated each other, what would she do then?

At the worst, he could risk her anger but still reassure himself that she'd do the right thing, if the need arose. It was a difficult bargain to have to make but it was difficult to resist. He began to formulate a plan, not at all what Isa Bowman had suggested—what did she know about their lives, anyway?—but partly based on some of the insights she had provided. He unscrewed the top of his fountain pen and made lazy circles on a piece of foolscap, circles within circles, and twists within twists. And then he reached into one of the drawers of the writing table for a small brown medicine bottle. He poured himself a capful of the contents, closed the bottle, and took a fresh piece of paper. He began outlining what his position ought to be, what he might say, and what he might better conceal in order to have Alice react in the way he wanted.

It was, after all, for her own good.

HAVING DECIDED, or having allowed the decision to form itself, he still waited, in order to see whether there might be some further transformation of his mind's disposition, or perhaps to gauge Alice's mood and the likelihood of her giving him a fair hearing. He found it quite peculiar to scrutinize her so. He had taken her more or less for granted for years, for decades, and he had been comfortable that way. They were both comfortable, living up to—or down to—one another's expectations. The intrusion of consciousness was as peculiar as would have been the turning of some simple reflex action—walking or breathing, say—into a conscious and studied exercise. He felt like an impostor. In his own house and with his own wife, he felt like a stranger.

He took a doleful pleasure in that feeling. It seemed to him a portent of his impending departure, a tempting suggestion of what it might be like, not exactly looking down through the clouds at his former existence and surviving widow, but close enough to that to be fascinating. At various times, he noticed how Alice methodically spread marmalade on her toast. Or, in the late evenings, he stared with a naturalist's attentiveness as she put her rings on the dressing table and her chased gold bracelet in its plush-lined box. Finally, small gestures were as endearing as anything he could imagine. He could see in the precision of her actions a woman half her age. A quarter.

Stolen glimpses. Glints gleaned. Prizes prised. It was utterly absurd, the opposite of any reasonable arrangement in which she might be storing up recollections of him, trying to fix him in her mind's eye for the coming years. Was she? He thought not. It was his firm belief that when she closed her eyes it was not to freeze the present but to thaw the past, to go back to that lost Eden of her girlhood, to be sucked back down into that rabbit hole . . .

He felt his mind changing again, his resolution reversing itself so that he was now likely to keep quiet, out of habit of course, but also out of anger. Let her do what she pleased about the damned manuscript! It was none of his affair—so to speak. Was it out of sympathy for her that he felt he ought to leave her undisturbed and untroubled? Or out of self-pity, because a man's twilight moments ought to be filled with a golden calm, a preparation for the eternity of peace or oblivion that was to follow, not these sordid entanglements with dead passions and jealousies?

He was annoyed with his variability of purpose and mood and unable to remember anything like these shifts and swings from the time he was an adolescent, back at Westminster. The whole idea of being an adult, of having a personality, was that there was supposed to be a consistency and steadiness, something identifiable and reliably *there*. He was all over the place, euphoric and then angry, accepting, calm, and then, for no particular reason, full of woe and scarcely able to keep his eyes from overflowing with hot tears.

Which was, of course, another reason for keeping silent. He had no way of knowing which self it would be that would speak to her. No matter how carefully he tried to plan out what he meant to say, he knew that the performance would be quite different. A letter, then? A long letter, to be left for her to read after his death? That was an idea with a considerable appeal, but he suspected it because it was appealing. Melodramatic? Sentimental? Childish?

Yes, yes. But why not? Why not indulge himself a little? Was it required that life always be disagreeable? Why should he have to be more responsible in his behavior toward the world than it was toward him? Was it not all nonsensical pretense, a result of the way one's nurse trained one to the potty? That Freudian theory—simplified, no doubt, as it was, but still derived from the work of the Viennese analyst—might or might not explain these things, but it certainly called into question the serene beliefs of an age and a lifetime. It also conspired with other voices and images. Hargreaves thought of the paintings of Gauguin that seemed to be saying—chuck it all, go to Tahiti, look at the naked breasts of natives, and nibble tidbits of breadfruit and roast pork. Why not?

There was hardly even a need to go to Tahiti. London itself had turned Tahitian, with flappers, fast motorcars, and a determined silliness that flaunted itself with a vengeance no one in Papeete could imagine. Hargreaves, however, could imagine it, could feel it himself sometimes. Did he want to be young? Or was it better to be past all that? These questions, too, brought answers that varied according to his mood.

One night later that week, after his excursion to London, lying awake and knowing that Alice too was awake, having heard her return from a quiet trip to the loo, he asked her, "What was it that happened with you and Dodgson?"

"I beg your pardon?"

"With you and Dodgson. All those years ago," he said. It was easier in the dark. He could imagine that he was imagining the conversation, which was a familiar activity by now. But it was also easier in that he didn't have to invent both sides of it.

"But you know that story," she said—as if she were talking to a child, as if he had asked to hear an old favorite tale one more time.

"I know the story," he said. "What I'm curious about is the truth. What actually happened?"

"But the story is true. The truth is the story." And then, after a brief pause, "Why do you ask?"

"I was thinking about the manuscript. I was wondering why your mother never burned it."

"Why would she have burned it?"

"Why did she burn the letters?"

"Did she? I don't know that there were so very many. And I can't actually say, for certain, what happened to them. They were lost, somehow . . . I never *saw* her burn them."

"She *might* have burned them," Hargreaves said. "You've always said you thought she did."

"It's possible."

"Why would she have done that?" he asked her.

It was not promising. She had already revised the story, cleaned it up, smoothed it down, got rid of the awkward details so that there was nothing left for attention to snag on. It was possible that she wasn't going to answer him. It wasn't impossible that she'd just fallen asleep again. For that matter, maybe he'd imagined the entire conversation, just as he'd imagined it so many times before but a little more vividly. He knew that this wasn't so—but it felt so much like the other times that he found he was explaining to himself how it didn't make any difference, finally, whether he spoke the words aloud or not. It all turned back into the same silence.

"What possible difference could it make now?" she asked.

So, he had been talking aloud, and she had been listening and thinking about her answer.

"It makes a difference," he told her.

"Why?"

"Why does anything make a difference?" he asked. "I've been wondering, that's all."

"Why?"

"Why not? I've been wondering about a good many things. I've been considering my life . . ."

"Your life? Or mine?" she asked.

"Where does one end and the other begin?"

"And you want to know what happened with Carroll?"

"With Dodgson. Why your mother burned—*might* have burned—the letters."

"I don't honestly remember. I was ten years old. It was . . . sixty-four years ago!"

"There must have been something, though," Hargreaves prompted.

"I suppose there must have been. What does it matter now?"

"I want to know." And then, after a while, he said, "I want to know how much of our lives was the result of what happened back then—of what he did to you—and how much might have been our own doing. How much was my own clumsiness, for example."

"Why worry about that now?"

"Because there isn't much time left in which to worry about it. And I find myself . . . considering these questions."

"There's no point," she said, gently but decisively. "There is no reason to think about such things. You haven't been clumsy. You've been wonderful, gentle and understanding and decent."

"Have I? I'm not so sure."

"I'm sure."

"Then I'm not so sure those were the right things to have been. Had I shown other qualities, perhaps we might have been better off, both of us."

"You're going to make me very unhappy, Regi. If you persist in this line of thought, you shall cause me distress . . ."

"Maybe I should have done that years ago," he said.

"Whatever do you mean? That's not like you at all!"

"The way a doctor does, in order to cure. Had I been less . . . What did you say—'gentle and decent'? We might have had quite different lives."

"Are you so very unhappy with the life we've had?"

"No, but I've been thinking about it. Considering it, as one considers a meal over coffee."

She didn't say anything. He couldn't blame her. He hadn't, after all, asked her a direct question. Meanwhile, he was wondering whether it was true that less gentleness—

genteel-ness—would have served them better, after all. Not that one gets to choose.

"It's an odd place to start, though, isn't it?" she asked. "What made you think of Dodgson?"

He tried to think what to say, whether to tell her about Isa. It wasn't too late to go back, to drop it. Nothing irreparable had been said, at least this far.

"You never speak of him," she prompted.

"Because I detested him," he said.

"I know," she said. "That's what makes me wonder. Why do you mention him now?"

"I've been wondering whether I might not have been wrong. After all those years, it's possible. I could have wronged him, or you. Or all of us. That's what prompts the question, actually."

"I see." Then, after a long pause in which he could hear her measured breathing, she said, "What a very extraordinary thing to say!"

"Is it?"

"It's not like you." It was neither accusation nor praise.

"Perhaps not," he agreed.

"To whom have you been talking?" she asked at last.

That was the way she had always been, able to see through him whenever she wanted to, or whenever she wanted it enough to expend the effort.

He thought about his answer. It was interesting, there at the brink, not knowing quite what awaited him, not at all sure of anything except that he was certainly going to take the irresistible next step. It was against his better judgment to do so, but he no longer believed in his better judgment. Where, after all, had it ever got him? "Isa Bowman," he said.

There was an instant's pause. Had she heard him? Would he have to pronounce the name again?

She switched on the light. She sat up in her bed. "Really!" she exclaimed. She was not at all pleased.

HE KNEW ENOUGH not to press. Instead, he waited out the first fury—the predictable accusations of disloyalty, cheapness, the vulgarity of his London friends, his betrayal. He wondered how much she knew and how far she was only guessing when she spoke of those "Mayfair people about whom I have never had any interest in hearing sordid reports." Did she know about Glenda? He noticed how Alice also became more Ciceronian when she was angry, with more elaborate dependent clauses. It had been her father's habit, Dean Liddell's, and Hargreaves had always admired it.

Eventually, she subsided. Or it subsided, for he thought of it as a fit or fever that came on and passed off, leaving her much as she had been before its onset but a little fatigued. Then she was ready to listen, or tired enough to lie back against the headboard and allow him to talk. Whether she would be truly receptive was not easy to predict. The lateness of the hour sharpened everything, distorted feelings and perceptions, made them both vulnerable. They were able to be reached and touched but they were also able to be rubbed the wrong way. Had he planned it all out, he supposed he would not have picked this dead hour in the middle of the night. But then, had he planned it all out, he might well have decided not to mention Isa's name at all.

When the opportunity presented itself, however, he began with his own apology and explanation, declaring that he had not sought the woman out but had been presented to her by a well-meaning mutual friend. "And Miss Bowman immediately expressed her regret at the extravagance of her publishers' claims. Indeed, she was frank to say that her only reason for writing the book was her dire need of money . . ."

"I should think so!"

". . . for food and for rent. She was, at that time, in actual want. Or so she said. And I believed her."

Silence. Was that a sign that Alice might be relenting? Or giving him leave to continue? That, at the least. He went on: "She was also very clear, not only to me but in her own mind, I think, about her relationship with Dodgson, that his interest in her was a re-enactment, and that he saw in her a resemblance to your original. She understood that and played to it, as she would play any theatrical role. She felt, nevertheless, a considerable affection for the man. And she believes that in his way, with a kind of double vision that saw both her and her impersonation of you, he felt affection for her. She was not at all the pushy upstart you have always imagined."

"Not with you, she wouldn't have been."

"I expect not."

"But now that you've met her, she's like a debutante who's been presented to the Queen. You've made her legitimate, haven't you? You've put the feather of respectability in her tawdry cap."

"I shouldn't think so," Hargreaves answered. "In fact, I should not have supposed anyone cared, really."

"I don't want to hear about it," Alice said. "I don't think you ought to have met her. And I don't think you ought to have told me about it."

"All right."

"All right, then," she said.

He waited. Would there be more? Would she ask further questions? She sat there, considering, balancing off her wounded pride and her curiosity, perhaps waiting for him to inflict further information upon her, so that she could receive it without having appeared to solicit it. He said nothing. She switched off the light on the nightstand between them. He listened for the slight rustle as she eased herself back under the bedclothes. Hargreaves shook his head. It would wait until morning. Or forever. He was just as happy. He could now let her decide whether to reopen the conversation or not. If she chose to let it go, he was willing to do that. It was a luxury to be relieved of the need to make that decision all alone.

He didn't resent Alice's adamant refusal to discuss Isa Bowman. Too much of her life depended on Isa Bowman's conforming to Alice's expectations. Too much was at risk if Isa Bowman, or Glenda, or all the other child friends of Dodgson's turned out to be different from what Alice needed them to be. Even if she was accusing him of being disloyal, he knew where his loyalties lay—and he couldn't blame Alice. She had made the best of it for herself and for him, whatever *it* was.

Why had he not seen that? Why had he burdened her further?

"And what was she like?" Alice asked, as if the interval had been a matter of five seconds rather than five minutes.

"I liked her, really. She's not our sort, but she's a good sort. Hearty and direct, and still with a considerable shrewdness. And warmth. Yes, I liked her."

"Does she look like me?"

"No, not really. She's smaller. But I could see a resemblance around the eyes and the cheekbones, that look you sometimes have. She has it too, sometimes."

"And she told you . . . what?"

He shook his head. He was glad she had turned out the light and could not see him. He took a breath, made sure he had control of his voice and feelings, and said, "Nothing very much, really. Her message—I took it to be a message—was that she hadn't meant to displace you, either with him or in the eyes of the world. That that would have been impossible. And that she was sorry for what she'd been forced to do."

"And that was all?"

"I don't know. The rest of it was what I gathered from her or out of the air. That Dodgson hadn't been all that bad, perhaps. Yes, something like that."

Something like that indeed. The message had been that Dodgson hadn't ruined Isa Bowman's life. Or Glenda Fenwick's. Or that of a dozen or a score of other little girls. She'd been earthy and lively and wonderfully comfortable about . . . about being a grown-up. It wasn't just sex, although that was a convenient shorthand for a whole range of other related capacities. It was more like the emergence of the butterfly from a cocoon. Isa and Glenda had managed to wriggle out, but Alice was still caught, no longer even struggling, but resigned to the confines of that childhood experience. He'd assumed it was inevitable, that she was a casualty of some awful assault. But Isa and Glenda had demonstrated that escape was possible and given the lie to what Hargreaves always used as his excuse for himself and Alice. What was worse was to suppose that Alice preferred the childhood world to that of adults, that she preferred Dodgson to himself.

Not that there was any real prospect, at this late date, of change. They were united by bonds of time and pain and loss that were stronger than those of flesh. And more real.

"And was she happy?" Alice asked.

"She seemed so," he told her, "but I think she would have made it her business to seem so—to me. Or to you. It's what you represent, I think, to most people, and to her, too."

"What I represent?"

"Happiness. Or innocence. What we remember of childhood, or what we imagine. You are the childhood everyone wishes to have had. And who can admit to one's own childhood self that one has failed to find happiness?"

No answer.

"I think she was as happy as most of us are."

A long time, and still no answer. He did not feel bad about having tailored his remarks to what he knew she wanted to hear. It had not been his intention to deceive but to comfort. To avoid pain, at least.

He heard a familiar sound as her breathing coarsened to a light snore. It was a beautiful sound. He lay there for a long while, staring up into the fathomless darkness and listening to that gentle, unselfconscious, delightfully animal sound.

3

THE NEXT MORNING, neither of them alluded to their conversation. This wasn't merely an omission, but a positive effort on both sides. Alice was chatty, remarking on items in the paper, invitations she had received, the weather, the question of whether to open the blackberry jam or the lime marmalade (she decided, as he knew she would, on the marmalade, which had no seeds in it)—or any subject under the sun except the fact that they had discussed Dodgson and Isa Bowman the night before. It was, he thought, rather like the first morning of their honeymoon when they had chattered away at the breakfast table in the hotel dining room, strenuously avoiding any reference to their exertions of the previous night.

The conspiracy of silence was a kind of bond. Hargreaves decided once more that he'd been wrong to violate their habits of reticence. He drove into Southampton that morning to pick up a couple of pruning hooks he'd left for sharpening, and on the way considered his attempt of the night before. It hadn't gone well. He should either have pushed further or not begun at all. All things considered, he'd have done better not to have begun. Assume some redistribution of blame, which he wasn't really ready to do but might conceive as possible—then the proper thing for him was to step forward and accept it, himself. He could have drawn Alice back up out of her rabbit hole, could have been the Orpheus to her Eurydice . . . more gently or more roughly than he'd done for these years. Or more insistently. Not just in bed, but in the style of their lives . . . She'd had that way of retreating to her own little world, and he'd respected that because it was what he supposed husbands ought to do. But that had meant hiding his feelings from her. He'd deprived her of indications she might have responded to, that he was lonely, that he was afraid. He was more straightforward with Glenda's girls, letting them know what he needed. Of course, they were paid to make him feel good and were supposed to cater to him, flatter him, and even lie to him about how wonderful he was, if that was what he required.

Alice had never had the chance. He hadn't trusted her. Or hadn't trusted himself? Both, both. And he'd blamed Dodgson for most of this, because it was easier than blaming Alice. Or the Liddells.

Drop it, then. The efforts of Glenda Fenwick did not oblige him to persist in any hopeless and hurtful actions on his own.

Still, her good intentions deserved more than silence. He owed it to her to explain that he'd tried but changed his mind. Or had tried and failed. That it was too late, in any event, to alter the patterns of a lifetime. He'd have to let her know, if he went back there, what had and hadn't happened. He could avoid that by not going. But even as he seized upon that possibility, he knew he'd go, that the routines of his own life and his inclination would conspire to herd him back. He'd go to London, and being there would drop by for a visit, if only to demonstrate to himself that he wasn't quite dead yet. The pleasures of the body were nothing compared to its nuisances and pains, but there they were, real enough. Only a fool declines them when they're available. He'd go, he supposed. And he'd have to tell Glenda something. The truth would do, if nothing better occurred to him, but he didn't mind lying to Glenda, if the object of the lie was to spare her feelings.

She deserved almost as much consideration as Alice. Anyway, she deserved some.

"NOTHING will come of nothing," he said.

"I beg your pardon?"

"Never mind," he said. "Actually, I beg yours."

The girl was attractive, more than willing, had tried hard with him, but nothing, nothing, nothing, nothing, nothing. To misquote King Lear. The other was from *Lear* too, Hargreaves was sure, albeit wrenched out of context. The red hair spreading out from the girl's head over his white belly made a sorry picture.

Gwendolyn was Glenda's favorite girl, heiress apparent to the business. It wasn't a business Glenda would hand on to a daughter—if she had a daughter—but to a young friend, a likely and like-minded young woman with the right toughness and flair. Oh, yes. He had been frequenting the place long enough to know these things, and therefore to appreciate that when Glenda sent Gwendolyn to him it was almost as if she had come to him herself. Gwen was a surrogate Glenda. In a house of surrogates.

"My fault," he said. "Or, certainly not yours. I've not been well."

"Poor dear," she said, giving a last farewell flick to his limp member. "Would you like some champagne? Or a brandy?"

"If you'll join me. Champagne?"

"Well, just a glassful," she said. "I'll get it." She slipped into a long filmy robe.

He lay there on the bed, considering the absurdity of his

position. The best-laid plans, etc., etc. Or worst-laid. He had decided right, though, when he'd changed his mind about pursuing that business with Alice. There was no hope for any reformation of his emotional and sexual life. He was beyond any adjustment of attitudes or understandings. It was now a much simpler matter of physical debility. He had taken another shuffling step on the path to the grave. Why not have the grace to admit it and keep still? There was no point in trying to rewrite history, not now.

It seemed funny and sad, but funnier than sad because it had accomplished Glenda's purpose instantly. He was reunited with Alice, was now in perfect harmony with her and would no longer require Glenda's services, or those of her handmaidens. Or maidens of other assorted parts. That seemed so neat as to be the outcome of one of those Feydeau plays, where everyone is properly paired off at the end with the right mate. He was properly paired off too now, at long last. And while there was much to regret, there was also some relief in it. Not to be burdened any more by the demands of the flesh? Well, there was one more, one great demand, and he'd soon have to pay it. But as the delights of the table and of the bed diminished, the leap into nothingness seemed less a cause for regret.

Gwen returned, carrying a tray with an ice bucket and a split of champagne along with two tulip-shaped glasses. "Compliments of the house," she announced.

"That's very kind," he said.

"And Glenda would like a few words with you, when it's convenient."

"Of course," he said, wondering whether Gwen had reported her failure—or his. Almost certainly, she had. He felt the impulse to protest that it was none of Glenda's business, but then he smiled, because it was, quite literally, her business.

They drank the wine, Gwen taking only a half glass for

herself. He had most of it. And he reached for his wallet and extracted a pound note for her, in the way of a tip. A farewell gift. He thought of making it a larger sum—five pounds, say—but that would have seemed less friendly. It would also be too definite a good-bye gift, and while he realized what it was, he wasn't eager for her to understand it that way. Their time together had been depressing enough.

So, a pound. And he told her to buy herself some trinket with it, something foolish. She promised she would, tucked it away, and gave him a kiss on the forehead as if he were a fond old uncle. Then she finished her wine and left him—she had a living to earn, and he had his rendezvous with Glenda. An efficient division of labor, Hargreaves supposed. Glenda did the talking and Gwen performed the sex act with those who were up to joining her. Slowly, he dressed, then went upstairs to Glenda's private apartment. It was empty. He hesitated but decided to go on in. He took a seat and waited. He got up. He walked around the room. It was a perfectly ordinary room, comfortable but not showy, and with little personal touches here and there. He noticed her fondness for Venetian glass. He looked at the photograph of a woman in an elaborate silver frame. Who could that be? He felt at home here, not only because it was Glenda's parlor but because it was the kind of room to which he had been accustomed for years. Did it represent her own private aspirations? Or was it a part of her general effort to accommodate herself to the expectations of her guests? After a while, he supposed, the line between those two motives tended to disappear.

His eye caught on a cheap little child's toy, one of those jumping-jack things with a figure of a clown on a stick. It had grommet fasteners at the shoulders, elbows, hips, and knees, so the clown could react to a twirl of the stick by flinging his limbs about in a series of amusing gestures. Hargreaves picked up the stick and idly twirled it.

"Silly, isn't it?" Glenda asked, having come into the apartment behind him. "That's what he gave me. Carroll, I mean. On the beach at Eastbourne."

Hargreaves put it down as if it were hot.

"Not that particular one, but one much like it. Long lost. I've replaced it with a series of his brothers, or grandchildren, to remind me . . ."

"Of that beautiful moment by the seaside?"

"Not to sell myself too cheaply. Not to be distracted by silly toys."

"I see."

"A drink?"

"I've just had some champagne, thanks."

"You can always have more. You'll join me?" she invited.

"Why not?"

"Indeed, why not?" she agreed. She rang for a maid and ordered another bottle to be brought up. When they were alone again, she asked how it had gone . . . "With your wife, I mean."

"It didn't. I tried. I began, but never got very far. She wasn't inclined to discuss it. And I really had no great hope of bringing about any change in our lives, not this late."

"It's never too late, is it?" Glenda asked.

"Of course it is. Those consoling phrases are almost always false. Many clouds have no silver lining at all. And it is frequently too late. It is with me, in any event. As I'm sure you must have learned from Gwendolyn."

"Oh, don't take yourself so seriously. It's perfectly common. A momentary thing. You'll be right as rain next time you come."

He shook his head, hardly even wondering what was right about rain.

"You will, you know. I've seen it happen a thousand times."

"No, you've seen something else. This is . . ." He looked down at his shoes. "I've not been well, you know. You must have noticed that I'm losing weight."

"A little, yes."

"I'm afraid I'm not going to get better. Just like that, Glenda. I shall very probably go back to the New Forest and never come to London again."

"I'm sorry to hear that, Reginald, truly." She reached out and took his hands in hers. She sat there, holding his hands, and looked him straight in the face, straight in the eyes. She was very brave, he thought. Had their positions been reversed, he didn't think he'd have been able to do as well. It wasn't the kind of thing most people were able to do. He, himself, had felt awkward and self-conscious on those occasions when friends of his had confided in him that they were terminally ill. It didn't get easier with practice, either.

He wondered whether Glenda's intimacy with sex helped her with this other kind of intimacy. The facts of life, after all, were that it began and ended.

"I shall miss you," she said.

"I wish I could have lived up to your expectations of me," he told her. "It was kind of you to think I could."

"It wasn't your fault," she said.

He thought about that for a moment. "It wasn't Alice's fault either. It was the way we were, how we were raised, old-fashioned but not altogether wrong-headed. If our attitudes about sex had been different, Alice's and mine, then I might never have come to know you so well. Or your girls."

"That's so."

"One thing does puzzle me, though."

"Yes?" she asked.

"You told me that you were once picked up by Dodgson. On the beach at Eastbourne, that was?"

"Yes, that's right."

"How did that affect you? What did it mean as far as the rest of your life was concerned? I mean, you still keep jumping jacks as souvenirs."

"What you're asking is how a nice girl like me got into a business like this, aren't you?"

"I suppose. You needn't answer if you feel disinclined."

"I know. But I don't mind. I often invent stories, more or less plausible, but of a style I think will be suitable. The truth is that it was a very ordinary sequence of events."

She stopped. Was she putting her thoughts in order? Or reconsidering her decision? Or inventing a story of a style that might be acceptable to a person like Hargreaves?

In fact, her only calculation was to wait for the maid to bring up the champagne. She wanted the wine to comfort her and to use as a prop. She didn't want her narrative interrupted. The girl did appear, put down the tray, asked if there would be anything else, and retired. Hargreaves removed the cork and poured.

"To my very good friend," he said, raising his glass to her.

"And to mine," she said, raising hers to him.

They drank.

She began her story.

IT WAS MY MOTHER who got me into the business, so the story really starts with her. We called each other sisters, even when we were alone, lest it slip out sometime when one of her gentlemen was there, listening. She was a slip of a thing, and had been only sixteen when I'd been born. So when I was eight, that summer at Eastbourne, she would have been only twenty-four and looked eighteen or nineteen perhaps. It wasn't difficult for her to pass as my sister. The point is that her pose changed our relationship. Instead of being a mother to me, she *became* a sister, which is much friendlier. We were confederates, allies, in it together, whatever it was. And we were close.

I knew what she did for a living, of course. It would have been impossible for us to be together and for me not to know. But I understood it was for us that she did these things. And she told me how it was that she first became a whore. It was in the most ordinary way—although I didn't know enough in those days to be able to judge what was usual and what wasn't. She had been in service in one of those great houses in the country where there were many servants and where sons came home from school on long vacations and had friends visit them and had nothing to do but amuse themselves without any supervision from parents who were busy, themselves, in the pursuit of the same diversions and amusements. My mother was a young girl, a country girl, and she believed the young man loved her because he said he did. And it was perfectly natural—she knew about sex, having seen the chickens and sheep and cows and dogs doing it in the fields and barnyards for as long as she could remember. It was no great mystery and no great thing. She was flattered by the young man's attentions and thought he was handsome. He made her laugh.

What she didn't expect was that he'd tire of her so quickly, or that, having tired of her, he would treat her so harshly or think of their relationship as basically funny. He did all of those things, even going so far as to require her to accept the attentions first of his younger brother and then of their school friends who came to visit, as they did with increasing eagerness. He threatened to have her dismissed if she refused, and with a bad character reference. That was the worst fate she could imagine. How could she then find another place? So she acceded to their demands, all the while continuing to discharge her duties as a kitchen servant, getting up early in the morning to light the fires, and scrubbing pots and pans and tables and floors, working fourteen-hour days, and then getting fucked three, four, or five times at night.

One of those young gentlemen, the young man of the house or his brother, or one of their friends, was my father. She never had any idea which, and I never cared. At any rate, she became pregnant, and as soon as she began to show, she was dismissed—and got that same bad character reference she'd been blackmailed with in the first place. This meant that she had to go far away to try to find another job in service so that she could lie and not have them check up on her, or at least not right away. She planned to say her husband had died. And she thought she'd put me out to a baby farm somewhere and send money from wherever she was.

She arrived in London and found nothing. She had to eat. It wasn't long before she began to ply the trade she'd learned back in that country house. It wasn't much longer before she found that there was a particular demand for women in her condition, and that the more swollen-up she got the more she was in demand. It wasn't any different from the house where she'd been in service except that she didn't have to do those twelve or fourteen hours of scullery work on top of everything else.

She had been a streetwalker at first, the way country girls start out, but then she was recruited for a house, because she was pregnant and valuable. They promised her they'd have a midwife for her and help her find a place for me. She was lucky, or we both were, because they actually did what they promised. They worked her up to the last day, but when she went into labor there was a midwife. And I was boarded out to a baby farmer in St. John's Wood where my mother would come to visit me once a month or so. Or so she said. I have no recollection of the place or of her visits, her comings or her goings away. It's supposed to be those first years that make you what you're going to be. But who remembers them? All I remember is that she came for me one day and took me away. I do remember that. It was raining. I had a doll and a bundle with my clothes in it. There was a carriage and a gray horse. I've always thought gray horses were lucky. Of course, it's possible that I only remember her telling me about it, remember imagining it . . . I can't tell the difference any more.

What had happened was that she'd been taken out of the house. She'd met a gentleman who was interested in her, a protector. He was a marmalade maker. All over the world, he sent his little crocks of marmalades and jams and jellies. They're famous.

He was a Scotsman, and I guess he was like a lot of them up there, passionate but frugal. He set her up in a flat in Kensington and he'd visit her himself. Or he'd have her entertain some of the marmalade buyers of the world who came to London to be entertained and buy marmalade. It happens in all businesses, I suppose, and this one happened to be marmalade. But she had a joke about it. In the mornings, when we were having breakfast, or at tea time, there'd be these crocks of marmalade, and she'd remind me that my mum was laid for it. She wasn't asking me to be grateful or anything like that. She wanted me to know how it was, I think. She was proud of herself. She'd managed, better than a lot of girls who were still in a house or walking the streets.

What she was proud of now seems perfectly clear and reasonable to me. That we had a settled life. That I could be with her and go to school. That we could be a family together, in a recognizable way. People take that for granted, but it's a luxury—the difficulty and the luck involved in that condition being apparent only to those who don't enjoy it, can't even allow themselves to imagine it, much less hope for it. But for some years, we were fortunate enough to have most of the things that people mean when they talk of

a respectable life—everything, that is, but the respectability.

What difference did that make? None, one might think.
But it made all the difference. For eventually the marmalade magnate sickened and died of pneumonia. The firm
was taken over by his younger brother, a priggish Presbyte-
rian who terminated our arrangement immediately. I have
no idea whether marmalade sales were depressed at all, but
we were thrown back upon our own resources. The furniture, my mother sold, and some of the jewelry. We went to
Eastbourne to seek a new protector. It was the season,
there, and my mother supposed that only the well-to-do
would be lounging by the seaside. And that there might be
a more relaxed, more festive mood there.

That was when I met Lewis Carroll. My part then, when
we were starting out, was simply to act as an occasion for
the start of conversations. The gentlemen might be shy,
might not be able to address a young woman directly, but
could comment on what a pretty child I was . . . They
could offer me sweets or invite us both for ice cream. By
pretending to be sisters, we seemed respectable, and it
made my mother seem very young.

Lewis Carroll wasn't interested in my sister, though; he
was interested in me. It was as if I had somehow been
promoted. All that friendliness and intimacy that had been
the result of our pretending to be sisters had, as the other
side of the same coin, a prompting toward parity, toward
equality of effort on behalf of our survival. Here was my
first opportunity to make a contribution.

Carroll, of course, had no idea what was going on. All he
knew was that there were two sisters, one of them young
enough to suit his tastes, and the other apparently simple-
minded enough not to understand what might be at risk.
She understood very well, and because of her experience
was able to interpret his subtle messages and provide for

him exactly what he hoped to find. He was suave enough, had had ample opportunity to practice his line of patter and seduction, was very good with jokes and little games . . . But he was nervous, furtive, aware of the dangers of the undertaking—the dangers to himself, I mean.

How do you know that?

(Hargreaves, eager to hear, brightened, focused his attention, and leaned forward. Of course, hating Carroll as much as he did, he was eager for demonstrations of Carroll's own suffering, any evidence of Carroll's discomfort being balm to his troubled spirit.)

It wasn't so much what I knew as what my sister knew. She could read these things better than I, and I took my cues from her. He wanted to separate us, but she resisted that. So I resisted too. And he hesitated, clearly nervous about what the older sister might think or say or do. The pickings may have been slim that season. Or he may have been particularly taken with me, having a predilection for children at exactly my stage of development. I don't take credit for it, recognizing that it was a coincidence. He was torn between caution and desire. What tipped the scale was my sister's act as something very close to simple. She had no objections to his taking photographs. *"Au naturel?"* he asked. She didn't know what that meant. Or said she didn't. So he explained, with some belligerence and discomfort, that it meant *naked.* And she laughed but made no objections, so that he saw his way to violating what I understand was his general rule about never allowing mothers or other older relatives along for these sessions.

He dithered. He fussed. He chattered all the time as we walked back to the house where he'd taken rooms. He had a bed-sitting-room and another room he'd turned into a studio with all sorts of toys and puzzles. There were props and costumes for the photographs. It was a game, really, an elaborate masquerade, dressing up as a Chinaman, an In-

dian, a beggar, a gypsy, an acrobat . . . or wearing nothing at all. That, too, was a part of the game.

All the while, my sister sat in a corner looking at picture
books as if she were the same age as I, mentally at least,
which was exactly what Carroll needed to believe. It was a
reckless game for him, with enormous risks of which he was
perfectly well aware. I only realized it later on, when my
sister explained to me how much he was crazed by his
passion for little girls, an ideal of which I was the embodi-
ment at that particular moment. I sensed his adoration, felt
it the way I felt the prickle of the velvet under my bare skin
as I lay upon the sofa while he hid behind the black cloth
that was part of his camera, getting the image right in the
ground glass, almost crooning, and telling me how beautiful I was, how very lovely, how perfect.

I remember thinking how he looked like a bird, the way
his hands fluttered around me, around the camera, around
the room. It took him a long time to get everything the way
he wanted, the pose, the camera, and the light. It was part
of his routine, a way of stretching out the experience then
and later, because he had a picture at the end of it, something to go back to. Finally he stuck his head under the
black cloth, popped out for a moment to fuss with my hair
and adjust the bend of my knee, and then back under the
cloth . . . where he remained for a long time.

My sister seemed not to notice, but she did notice, was
acute enough to realize soon that I was in no great danger
from this man but that he was our victim. She didn't react at
all, but only sat there on the window seat, slowly turning
the pages of the picture books and smiling, as she had every
reason to do. Here was money. Here was power over someone of the kind the young man back at that country house
had once exercised over her. Not revenge actually, but a
way of getting her own back, a way of balancing out the
books . . . A recognition that this was the way the game

was played, that this was how people treated one another. It is better to be needed than to need. It is better to be powerful than powerless. It isn't so much a question of male and female as it is of pursuer and pursued. All those things were tied into it. She sat there, looking simple-minded, turning the pages of the book and smiling to herself, thinking the thoughts that were to govern our lives for years, understanding how the world was and how to succeed. His croonings were to her the sounds of nature, but nature harnessed and working benevolently.

Eventually, the picture was made. It was finished. Or he was. They both were. He offered us little cakes and made tea. He was odd about making the tea, swinging the teapot about the way a priest swings a censer, trying to get the leaves all properly swished and whirled about. Or so he said. One never knew what was serious and what wasn't. He said, "Little girls have a choice of tea, cocoa, lemonade, vinegar, or ink. No one I can remember has chosen either of the last two. You may have what you prefer."

"Tea, please," I said.

"Tea, it is. And I shall join you. You are an extraordinary little girl. A good girl. I like little girls who say 'please' and 'thank you very much.' "

"Thank you very much," I said.

He laughed, kissed me on the forehead, and gave me a robe to put on. He offered my sister tea, and she said, "Thank you very much," which made him happy.

It made him less happy when my sister asked him for fifty pounds. He should have laughed, but he didn't. He realized at once that her simplicity had been an act. He had no idea how tough she was or what she knew about him. He recovered himself and tried to tough it out, but she'd seen his look of fear and knew that she had him if she was strong enough.

He threatened to call the police. She invited him to do

exactly that. He didn't, and she knew she'd won. There were unpleasant words about blackmail, child whoring, powerful friends, self-abuse, entrapment, and so on, charges on both sides, all of them true enough, none of them particularly serious. After all, there I sat, wearing the prettiest robe I'd ever seen in my life, drinking tea and nibbling biscuits, and I was perfectly content. He could have brazened it out. He could have tried at any rate, had he been a different kind of person. But he was ashamed of himself, aware of his own weak position, and ready to agree with my sister that he ought to be made to pay. He offered ten pounds and then they bargained. I think the final figure might have been twenty-five pounds, which was a considerable sum to us, enough to keep us both for quite some while. He paid, and my sister told me to get dressed, which I did. Then, surprisingly, he kissed me good-bye, a wistful little kiss on the forehead, and stroked my hair. As I think of it now, he was making the claim that I'd had nothing to do with that sordid haggling, and therefore that his feelings for me were unchanged. It was a nice gesture. Then he gave me the little jumping jack. I kept that for a long time.

Yes, yes, but how did that influence your choice of career?

It was the realization of the power we had. An ordinary whore has no chance in the world because there is so much competition from so many other whores exactly like herself, offering the same thing to the same clientele. And the laws are all arranged to favor respectable customers and punish the whore. What my sister wanted to find was a situation like that in Eastbourne in which there might be more equality, respect on both sides, if not actual fear. More need on the customer's side than ours. She was thinking, at first, of finding those gentlemen with a taste for young girls, like Carroll. But that was dangerous. Some of them, like him, were gentle and timid men. Others were much less gentle. But the principle was more important than the particular details. What she came up with, after a time, was cripples. Lunatics. Spastics. Idiots. All over England there were heavy doors with passageways behind them, leading to cellars or attics that hid the family disgraces, the poor malformed creatures of the world. A lot of the girls will do almost anything else but won't go near those people. But my sister got herself a nurse's uniform and built up a list of faithful and grateful customers who were willing to pay quite handsomely for her services. She developed a set of influential friends, patrons really, who were eager to protect her and to whom she could turn for help when she needed it.

It wasn't his twenty-five pounds that mattered. As my sister explained to me, he'd risked his whole life, his past and future, forgetting himself entirely and thinking only of how pretty I was and how much he wanted me. For that little while, he lived only for me. How many women have that happen to them, even once in a lifetime? Some of those who marry, I suppose, have that moment to look back on, when their husbands proposed to them. But that isn't quite the same as the risk of utter ruin. That's what Carroll did. And the cripples and idiots in those tower rooms lived entirely for my sister's appearance as she made her rounds, dispensing physical release and a little human warmth and contact.

Her mooncalves, she called them. The more intelligent they were, the worse off they were, for those were the people who understood their predicament and were most tortured by it. The others were sad to behold, but not sad themselves. Carroll was a mooncalf. And he knew it.

And you? You did what your sister did? What your mother did?

Eventually, yes. But not for some years. My mother put me into a school so I'd learn the social graces and know how to talk to gentlemen of quality. It was part of her plan to set me up as you see me now, with a house of my own, with protection and a degree of financial security few women in our profession achieve. She could afford to do this, once she had begun to specialize. And I contributed, myself. My virginity was sold at auction—I'm sure you've heard of such things—for a hundred and eighty-eight pounds, bid by a Canadian sea captain who enjoyed my pain and blood more than my body.

Awful!

Not really so awful. Girls give up their maidenheads every day and night for less, as my mother had done, you'll recall. And men have killed for less than a hundred and eighty-eight pounds. I believe there are livings in the church that pay no more for a year's work. The Canadian was through with me in half an hour. I had the money—or my mother and I had it—for good and all. Again, I had a sense of my great worth—what I'd had from Carroll.

Most of all, I think the result of that first encounter was that I saw through a number of illusions. Reality may not be pretty but isn't especially ugly either, once one has grown up enough to be able to confront it honestly and stare back at it. That all men are more or less driven, are more or less mooncalves, bawling for relief in their locked rooms . . . that was the great lesson. Having learned that, I have been able to feel for them, to be friendly with them, as I've been able to be friendly with you over the years. I owe it all to Carroll—and to my sister. My mother.

What happened to her? Is she still alive?

We were recruited by a countess—who may even have *been* a countess, claiming she had once been married to an Italian with a papal title—who was trying to find a mother-and-daughter team for a Portuguese vintner visiting in London and doing business here. The Portuguese was most particular about wanting an authentic mother and daughter to share his bed. We had posed as sisters and had performed a similar service, if under false colors. The truth hardly seemed a challenge. We let the countess know we were available. The price was two hundred pounds to her, of which a hundred and fifty pounds would be paid to us. It was to be a kind of farewell performance, after which my mother was going to take a long sea voyage, see something of the world, and enjoy herself a little.

We agreed. And it was all going well enough, until at one point she forgot herself, forgot we were not trying to fool anyone, and referred to me as her sister. The port maker was furious. He threw us out of bed with such a force that . . . Well, it was bad luck, too. My sister—mother—hit her head on the side of a marble mantel. I thought she was just stunned. She was dead. So the money went for her funeral instead.

You sound almost cheerful about it.

Not cheerful, perhaps, but realistic. Do you suppose she'd have enjoyed the cruise as much as she enjoyed looking forward to it? She couldn't have. That thought was a comfort to me. As was the related thought that she'd died doing what she had done well all her life. She hadn't retreated into some fantasy. Fantasy is what she and I had both been dealing with, catering to, wringing money from, all our lives. Fantasy is a much greater part of the business than sex. But for all its appeal, fantasy is very dangerous. It's what people hide in who don't have the courage to see the world as it is, or admit that they've seen it, or live in it and make the best of it.

That's what Carroll's writing was all about. It was a way of closing his eyes to what was there and inventing something else, something charming but dead. Irrelevant.

What killed my mother was that she allowed herself to believe the lie we'd made up. She called me her sister and I wasn't. I was her daughter.

THE BOTTLE WAS EMPTY but Glenda hardly felt like ringing for the maid. "I have a happy idea," she said. "There's something better than champagne, anyway, for this hour of the night."

"What's that?"

"Absinthe. From Paris. If you don't mind licorice."

"I adore licorice," Hargreaves said. "Always have."

She rummaged for a bottle that was not quite hidden in the back of a cabinet. There were small glasses out on the sideboard. She helped herself to small pieces of ice that were floating in the wine cooler, dropped them into the little glasses, and then poured a dollop of absinthe into each glass. "To your very bad health," she said.

"Ah, yes, this is supposed to be bad for you, isn't it?"

She nodded. He laughed and took half of his little portion in one small sip. "Very good," he said.

"Isn't it?"

"It's surprising at this stage of things to be discovering new pleasures," he admitted.

"I'm glad."

"And to be rid of old pains."

"Oh?" she asked.

"I've always hated him. But it's just not worth it any more, not at this stage. And not at all, considering how it must have been for him."

"Alice doesn't hate him, I take it?"

He shook his head.

"Then there's no reason for you. Not for her sake and certainly not for your own."

"I suppose not," Hargreaves agreed. "But it has been annoying. All her life, that random association has followed her around, turned her from a private person into a public curiosity, as if she were an actress or a film star."

"She's enjoyed it?"

"I wouldn't say that."

"Grown accustomed to it, then?"

"Oh, yes," he said.

"Then why let it bother you?"

He thought a moment, finished off the absinthe, and then admitted, "I was jealous, I expect."

"No reason to be jealous of him," she said.

"No," he agreed. "I suppose not."

"I wish there were some way I could have met her," Glenda said. "That's the worst of this profession. It cuts one off from so many people."

"She's become a bit crusty, I'm afraid. She's had to put up with a good deal. We lost two of our sons in the war . . ."

"People put up with what they have to. Still, I should have liked to meet her. On a train, perhaps. Or wherever strangers get to meet, just for a little while."

"You mean, because she was Carroll's Alice?"

"No, no. Because she was your Alice. I've always been fond of you, Regi, don't you know that? You're a decent, good, kind, sensible man. I like you."

"I'm touched."

"And if Alice had been different, if your lives together had been different, I'd never have enjoyed your friendship, would I?"

"Nor I yours," he said.

"So, you see. Some clouds do have silver linings."

"Yes, I expect so. It's kind of you to say so."

"Another sip?" He nodded. She poured him a little more of the yellowy liquid, clear as it went into the glass and then cloudy as it hit the ice.

He swirled the glass to speed that clouding process and then drained it off. "It has a kick, this stuff."

"Oh, yes."

"Do you mind if I loosen my tie?"

"Not at all."

He did so, and then, as if it were no more than a logical extension of that first gesture of informality, put down the little glass, slipped off his shoes, and stretched out upon the sofa, resting his head in Glenda's lap.

She didn't mind. His stamina wasn't what it had been. And the impact of these various discoveries and self-discoveries had been taxing. She stroked his brow with her fingertips and smoothed his fine silvery hair.

It made a pretty picture, of which she was aware. For that reason, she held the pose, even though his head was heavy on her thigh. It would only be a matter of time before the weight of Hargreaves' head would cut off her circulation and cause her real annoyance. Still, she let him lie there and every so often flexed the large muscle in her leg to shift the burden ever so slightly. He looked like a little boy. Or, more accurately, in the dim light she could perceive something boyish in the way he lay there. Innocent? Yes, but it was only the guilty who made such a great issue of innocence. As far as Glenda was concerned, they were beyond all that nonsense of guilt and innocence. She was, at any rate. And he soon would be.

His head was getting bothersome. She eased herself out from under him and gently lowered his head onto the sofa, sliding a small pillow under his cheek so as to keep him from getting a stiff neck. She turned off the light nearest the sofa. From a closet in the hallway, she brought out a crocheted afghan with which to cover him.

On the floor, near the sofa, she saw the jumping jack he'd dropped—or thrown down. She knelt and retrieved it. A dumb thing to hold onto, but one had to hold onto something. At least she understood that it was silly. She sat down and looked at Regi Hargreaves, trying to summon up some feeling, or to force that feeling she had into a rivulet of tears, but they wouldn't come. He'd had a good life, an easy enough life, with every comfort and privilege. He'd lost two sons, but he hadn't been alone in that. The war had been hard on everyone. And all men were mortal.

She realized she was twirling the stick of the jumping jack. Its little clown was dancing. That was the trick she'd learned from Carroll, to make the little men dance. To hold the small sceptres and manipulate them to make the clowns jump and dance. And, when one of them broke or got mislaid, to replace it with another without wasting tears over it.

She was dry-eyed, still. But there was a pang of regret as she put the jumping jack back on the table and turned out the light upon the drunken, sleeping, dying man.

One could replace them, but they were never quite the same.

FOR THE FIRST FEW DAYS back at Cuffnells, Hargreaves felt no particular difference in how things were. His habit was one of reticence and he saw no particular reason for departing from that very good practice. Or not at first. It was only toward the end of that first week, however, that he began to take it in. There really was not going to be another trip to London to prepare for. There were no appointments to coordinate, friends to notify, tradesmen to write to. And he wouldn't be seeing Glenda, either.

It was perfectly ridiculous, but that turned out to be a temptation to speech. Why not tell Alice, now that he'd finally turned the new leaf, that it was over and that she'd won? Or that they had won. An absurd idea, of course. It would accomplish nothing and cause only pain, which was a very good reason to reject the notion, as of course he had to do. But he could still feel—and had to acknowledge—an effervescence, a cheerful feeling of keeping a good joke to himself, almost a physical pressure to blurt out that his gallivanting days were over.

Or that he'd heard fascinating things about Alice's old

friend, Dodgson. It was impossible to hate a man like that—
who simply wasn't worth it. The poor, helpless, desperate
sod! It was liberating to be rid of him. Hargreaves could
remember—was pretty sure he remembered—Glenda getting his head off her lap as she slid out from under him and
put a pillow there for him to lie on. He'd pretended to
sleep. Maybe he had been asleep, but in that case he pretended not to have woken up. She'd fetched a coverlet for
him and then turned out the light near the sofa, and he'd
opened his eyes just a little to see if she had gone. But she'd
sat down in a chair across the room and mused for a while,
playing with that damned toy.

So, clearly, whatever she had said to Hargreaves, even if
it was all true, hadn't been the whole truth. Beyond the sad
and ugly facts of the case, there remained the irrational part
of it—that Glenda still felt something for old Dodgson. As
Alice did. And as Isa Bowman did. Why else would Glenda
have gone to such trouble? Why else would Isa have devoted so much time to him?

It was because of his connection with Alice, and because
of hers with Lewis Carroll. There the old sod was, with the
last laugh or anyway the smug smile Hargreaves could remember with such vividness, the eyes half-closed, the lips
upturned, the face pale and smooth and round. Like a
child's face. But whatever it was, some kind of arrested
development or other weird quirk, it had allowed Dodgson
to be Carroll, to think like a child, to speak to children in a
way they could recognize as authentic, to speak even to the
child in other adults and summon up a vestige of whatever
they had believed to be lost. It was not an exchange Hargreaves would have cared to make if some angel had come
to offer it to him.

Nevertheless, it was mildly vexing to have to admit he
was still a little jealous of whatever Glenda had felt for the

man as she'd sat there in her parlor, playing with her little toy and looking so melancholy.

It would have been a pleasant thing to have someone look that way for his sake.

He supposed that self-pity would be the last ordeal, the temptation to such self-indulgence getting stronger as he grew weaker and weaker. It would be a tough siege, he believed.

In fact, he was luckier than he'd expected. He pottered around, losing a little weight and feeling not too bad, but sufficiently weakened by his cancer so that when he contracted a mild case of influenza it was enough to carry him off, relatively painlessly and very quickly.

1926–1928

LETTERS OF CONDOLENCE continued to arrive at Cuffnells for some weeks after Reginald's death. There was a dreamy quality to the way in which the news of the death rippled out, the notice in the *Times* reaching into tea plantations in Ceylon, rubber plantations in Sumatra, coffee plantations in Java, and mining towns in South America. From these remote places, his fellow botanists sat down at their rough tables or high desks or elegant Chinese writing stands, to dispatch letters attesting to their friendship, their respect, and their sense of loss.

Alice had always assumed that the arboretum was a lonely place and that his cultivation of trees was a solitary pleasure, an excuse to get out of the house, sit in the damp heat, and think his thoughts. She was surprised to discover that he had been a member of a far-flung network of planters, foremen, remittance men, and company agents, as various in backgrounds as they were in handwriting and style of condolence. But all of them were quite sincere in their respect for each other and their fondness for trees. It was a comfort, then, for her to collect their letters and tie them together with a black grosgrain ribbon, realizing that Reginald's life had been a little brighter and warmer than she'd supposed. She was happy for him and proud that he was the kind of man to inspire such long-standing, long-distance friendships. *He was a good man with trees, but a good man with people too. It gets awful lonely here sometimes, and a man's only companions are strong drink, native women, and trees* (a man from the Philippines wrote). *Your husband gave a big boost to the trees and made them as good a bet as the other two; and they were always a lot cheaper.* The letter was stained with sweat, either from the effort of its composition or the heat of Palawan— which she looked up in an atlas. But its profession of friendship was more persuasive than much of what she'd heard from the neighbors in Lyndhurst.

Her sister, Rhoda, came to stay with her, to get her through the difficult time. And Caryl was there, more useful than Alice could have expected—because of his uselessness. He didn't offer help so much as demand it, needing her and thereby restoring her to a feeling of indispensability that was familiar and comforting. He was drinking more than was usual even for him, so that she worried about him —which was a welcome change from such worries about herself as whether she had been, after all, a good enough wife to Reginald. She had seized upon that question as less uncomfortable than other more selfish but nagging concerns. It was not easy to admit to herself that she was afraid of being lonely and alone. Reginald had been so reliably there, ready to listen, to take care of her and provide for her. She had no idea whether they had been well fixed, just barely balanced, or even in want. Regi had always seen to the money.

The simple truth of the matter was that she missed him, could hardly imagine life without him, kept thinking to find him in the next room, sitting in one of his accustomed chairs, or coming through a doorway, exclaiming "Ah, Alice!" with what always sounded like delight. She could not yet look at it directly, but only at the shadows cast by the fact of his death. She was being foolish and even cowardly, but she was tired of pretending to be brave. Without Reginald as an audience, there seemed little reason to struggle any further. She had endured the deaths of two sons with fortitude, but now she could feel whatever she felt like feeling.

This included rage, when she realized that one of the condolence letters she had received and was now reading was from that woman. To use Reginald's death as an excuse for an approach! She very nearly tore the letter up, could all but feel the satisfying sensation in her fingertips that would come when she ripped it into bits and then allowed the snowflake-size pieces to sprinkle onto the fire. But for Reginald's sake, she forbore. He had defended the woman, had spoken charitably of her.

Besides, if she tore up the letter she might have to explain to Rhoda, who was sitting across the room, why she'd done such a peculiar thing, from whom the letter had come, and what it meant. And she might have to defend herself or else admit to being overwrought and even silly. The gesture was not what one could make, anyway, after all this tiresome calculation. One had to do a thing like that spontaneously and instantly or not at all.

She smoothed the paper on the table and read it again, more carefully this time.

My dear Mrs. Hargreaves:

It was with great sadness that I read of the death of your husband. I had the pleasure of meeting him not long ago and, knowing what an extraordinary man he was, I can appreciate your loss that, in a small way, I share.

I do hope he explained to you my reasons for having written the book about our other mutual friend, and that he conveyed to you my regret at any displeasure or annoyance it may have occasioned for you. The exaggeration of my claims upon Lewis Carroll's friendship was that of the publisher. We both know the truth about the matter, what my relationship was, and how it was at best a faint echo of his friendship with you.

It is not my intention to impose upon your grief. My only purpose

*in writing is to offer what comfort and solace I can, however slight,
and to let you know that I share your sorrow.*

*Unless I have your express invitation, I shall not impose upon you
further. But know that you have my friendliest warm feelings.*

Most sincerely,
ISA BOWMAN

Alice put the letter back into its envelope. Astonishing!
"Unless I have your express invitation," indeed! What the
woman was doing was angling for such an invitation, trying
to get Alice's permission to call at Cuffnells. She wanted to
legitimize her old claims. Still!

"What's the matter?" Rhoda asked.

"Nothing."

"Something's the matter. You look like that only when
you're upset."

"I'm not upset."

"Then you're coming down with lockjaw."

Alice opened her mouth and closed it, lightly. "I don't
know what you mean."

"Who was the letter from?"

"What letter?"

"The letter in your lap."

"Isa Bowman."

"Do you still care?" Rhoda asked.

Alice didn't answer, couldn't answer. The question, nevertheless, reverberated. Now that Reginald was gone, what
difference did it make? Now that there was no one to feel
jealousy or resentment, as he had always done, so sweetly
and so gallantly, was Rhoda's question answerable?

She thought of showing Rhoda the note, letting her see
the smarmy and ingratiating text, but thought again and
rejected the idea. Rhoda might take it at its face value.
Rhoda prided herself on being a sensible, down-to-earth,
realistic woman, and in many respects was all those things.
But a sixty-year-old spinster had lacunae that were perhaps

predictable. She knew a great deal about suffering of a physical kind, having been a nurse, but the subtleties and refinements of human emotions were outside her purview. She had, moreover, the fatal illusion that she was free of illusions.

Was it possible that no one cared any more? Carroll was gone. Alice's parents were gone. Reginald was gone too, now. Rhoda was younger, hadn't been born in those days when Carroll had entertained Alice, Edith, Ina, and on occasion their older brother Harry. Rhoda was therefore a part of the rest of the world, the outsiders who had heard at second hand about that day on the river and the story Carroll had made up for the little Liddells. Alice sometimes wished they'd never asked him to write it down. Then it would still be her story, not shared with anyone.

She looked down at Isa Bowman's letter. It lay there in its envelope, hot enough to burst into flame. She could feel it through the cloth of her skirt.

Isa Bowman still cared. She cared at least enough to manufacture pleasant lies.

"Do you still care?" Rhoda asked again.

"Yes," Alice admitted.

"Nonsense!"

"Nonsense is a vital part of life," Alice said, allowing herself a wistful smile.

CARYL HAD BEEN LIVING in London in a flat just off Sloane Square and coming down to Cuffnells for weekend visits. It was a way of living that seemed suitable for all concerned, or had seemed so while his father was alive. There were questions now that had to be faced, and unspoken assumptions that would have to be examined and openly discussed. Not the least of these was the gentleman's freedom that Reginald Hargreaves had always enjoyed and that, up until now, Caryl had found so congenial. Caryl's expectations were guarded. The deaths of his brothers in the war had left him as the sole heir. Cuffnells, however, had not been maintained in recent years in quite the old style. This was either an indication of his father's declining interest and energies or else it was evidence of a decline in his father's fortune. A place like this was wonderful but its upkeep was an expensive proposition, even with a reduced staff.

How much money was there? Enough for his mother's lifetime? Enough for his own lifetime as well? These were grubby questions to be worrying about, but they were also that practical side of things—to which he had always given insufficient attention. The interview with the solicitor in Southampton loomed as large in Caryl's mind as a trial would have done if he'd been a criminal. Like a criminal, he knew himself to be guilty—of laziness, of nervous inability to apply himself to onerous tasks or keep long-range goals in mind. He didn't care enough, didn't trust the ambitions and resolutions by which so many other people seemed to govern their lives, had seen enough in the war to know how provisional life could be. At any rate, he couldn't take it seriously, couldn't bring himself to believe that the great concerns of London and the nation weren't fundamentally a hoax, a grim joke delivered in the most deadpan manner but all the more mordant for that.

This is not to say that he believed in nothing at all. He had his standards and his private code. He did not like to be unkind to his friends. He believed in decent behavior and, within reasonable limits, trying to keep one's promises. He was intelligent enough to understand that this code was essentially that of a schoolboy, with little intellectual justification. It was more an emotional, even a sentimental attachment for what had once seemed good and right. The playing fields of Eton and all that. But that's exactly what he was, and he was neither proud of it nor ashamed.

So, guilty as charged, or guiltier than anyone had ever dared charge him. But there was still the hope that the sentence would be light. A rap on the knuckles, or a mild warning that it was time to reform. He'd heard enough of those warnings to be quite comfortable with them, but the possibility of real punishment always lurked in the shadows somewhere. He remembered his father, the weekend before he died, and the command the old man had laid upon him: "Protect your mother. Promise me that you'll protect her . . ."

"Yes, father."

"Good. Good lad."

It had seemed, at the time, a merely conventional formula, one of those unexamined and all but meaningless pieties by which his father's generation lived. They'd been lucky, perhaps, and had been able to get through their lives without having to scrutinize those unenunciated principles of decency and honor, without having them too severely tested. Caryl's generation knew better, or understood how far they fell short of the standards by which they, too, would have liked to live. "Protect your mother." Who wouldn't at least try? What scoundrel would even have to be told to do such a thing?

And that was when Caryl began to reconsider what his father might actually have meant. The intention had to be more specific, with some particular danger that he had in mind and against which Caryl was to try to protect her. Money, he assumed. And the meeting with the solicitor would let him know how bad the situation was and what he might have to protect her from.

He was down in the wine cellar, sitting on a case of Clos-Vougeot, looking at the mostly empty bins on the wall in front of him. He had come down to sit in the cool dimness of the place and try to get some solace from the quiet presence of his old friends. These vintages had been friends, hadn't they? Greater love hath no man than to lay down his life for his friend. There had been a lot of dead soldiers coming back from this front. But so many?

Clearly, his father had worried about money. There was no other explanation for his failure to restock. Unless, of course, he had realized that he was dying and had therefore decided to let Caryl make the decisions. Different palate, different tastes. But how far wrong can one go with Clos-Vougeot?

He wasn't at all panicked. At worst, he thought it was another of life's beastly ironies that his father, who had a perfectly well suited temperament for work, should have been left to drift through life more or less idle, while he, quite unsuited to its demands and unprepared for its disciplines and inconveniences, should be forced to it. His father, left to his own devices, had applied himself to the study and cultivation of trees as though it had been a business. He, on the other hand, would go from business to business, in a series of diminishingly promising opportunities, and no doubt an increasing imposition upon the patience and kindness of friends. But he would protect his mother, having promised to do that.

Unless, of course, the old man had meant something else altogether. He had been such a private man and he'd had so polished a surface that Caryl had never been sure what lay beneath. It was not easy to raise such personal questions with Reginald Hargreaves. It would have been bad form, not to say impertinent. Still, there was an image in Caryl's mind of that near encounter, that non-meeting, on the street in Mayfair two years earlier. Caryl had seen a tall, distinguished looking man, well tailored and of the same general carriage as his father. The same hat at the same angle. Of course, it could have been someone else, but Caryl's first impression—that it was his father there—had been by no means tentative. And he'd been about to call out, to greet him, when he'd checked himself, realizing that the doorway from which the man had stepped out was that of a brothel. What to do? He had knelt down as if to retie a shoelace.

And standing up again, he had looked once more and seen no one. The man was gone.

Well, it could have been his father, and then again it might have been someone else for whom there would have been nothing unusual, nothing noteworthy in the way a younger man had bent down to retie a shoelace. But assuming that his first instinctive recognition had been correct, and assuming that his father had similarly recognized him and then, gracefully turning back, had managed simply to disappear, it was as much a mutual show of consideration as an avoidance of unpleasantness. Why should the son subject the father to embarrassment, or the father cause the son a pang of awkwardness and chagrin?

There had never been any reference to this non-meeting. Caryl had put it with the other secret in that limbo of his of questions that could neither be posed nor entirely forgotten. He had learned patience from the puzzle about his mother's connection with Lewis Carroll. This one was rather easier to manage because he was older and could afford to be more tolerant, even of his own parents. Indeed, it once or twice crossed his mind that there might even be a connection between the two mysteries.

Anything was possible. But it seemed in the last analysis unlikely to Caryl that his father could have been referring to this curious semi-incident, for such a reference would necessarily involve a fundamental doubt about Caryl's good sense and gentlemanliness. Any man of whom such a question must be asked is not a man of whom the question can be asked. He did not suppose his father hated him. The meaning, if there was any particular meaning, had to lie elsewhere.

Here and there, Caryl found a few bottles, some of them very old and dusty and rare, some of them not yet ready to be drunk. He picked a Medoc that seemed neither too young nor too venerable for the occasion, and looked about him one last time. It was sad to see now, but it must have been sadder for the old man, watching what had once been a great cellar diminish over the course of . . . it must have been several years. He'd never referred to it. And Caryl had never had occasion to come down here in recent years. It had been his father's domain, like the orangery or his father's dressing room, private space.

He pulled the cord that killed the light. He closed the heavy oak door and locked it.

At dinner that evening, he asked his mother whether his father had expressed any particular opinions about the state of the family finances.

"Certainly not," his mother said. "Whatever for?"

Money, then, Caryl decided. He poured himself a little more of the Medoc and reflected that it wasn't half bad for a *cru bourgeois*.

Later that week, at the solicitor's office in Southampton, Caryl's fears proved to be accurate. The estate, the solicitor ventured to guess, was worth something in the neighborhood of twenty-five thousand pounds, a handsome if not princely sum. The difficulty was not Reginald Hargreaves' will but that of Caryl's paternal grandfather, Jonathan Hargreaves, by whose instruction Cuffnells was to pass, upon Reginald's death, to his eldest surviving son. So Caryl had Cuffnells to keep up, as well as his flat in London. He was entitled to evict his mother, should he feel disposed to do such a thing. He could put Cuffnells up for sale or at least rent it. The income he could derive from it, one way or another, would be ample to keep both him and his mother in more than decent comfort.

But it was an unthinkable idea. It was what he had unwittingly promised his father he would not do. Instead, he would protect her, even if it meant a slow, inexorable decline from independence to penury. He could always get a job, he supposed. Or try some long-shot speculative venture in the City. He had all sorts of friends who had made killings or claimed to have done. The prices of shares made headlines all the time, going up and up to set new records every week and challenge the nerve as well as the greed of the most sportsmanlike investor. With the right advice and a little luck, he'd be able to improve his position just enough to allow his mother to continue on at Cuffnells for as long as she liked and still keep himself in some style in London. Most of all, he'd be fulfilling his obligation to his father.

The solicitor was rambling on, and his technical explanations were increasingly depressing. Caryl learned that his mother owned all the wines, the jewelry, the cars, the furniture, and so on, provided only that she insure it and that she pass it on to Caryl at her death. She also was entitled to the income of eight thousand pounds which had been her marriage settlement. This last "technicality" reduced Caryl's working capital to seventeen thousand pounds. He had a little money of his own, but only a little. It wasn't going to be easy.

Back at the house that evening, he assured his mother, however, that it was all right. She needn't concern herself. He'd take care of everything for her. There was nothing to worry about, he promised her.

He could make some money on the stock market, or get a job, or, if all else failed, marry money.

THE FLOWERS WERE DYING, but then the light was also dying. Isa looked at the arrangement in its large Art Nouveau vase, tried to decide whether to let it go a day longer, actually turned away from it, but then turned back. It wouldn't do. Her habits were stronger than any impulse toward . . . economy? And thrift was far down on the list of her concerns, particularly with so highly charged a question as whether to keep flowers another day or throw them away. The language of flowers is eloquent, but it can say unpleasant things.

Worth preserving as an epigram?

It would reappear or not. It was beneath her deliberately to try to remember some fortunate formulation like that. She didn't like to appear to be studied. Still, the question of the flowers posed itself, stupidly insistent, in the vase on the hall table. She picked up the vase and took it into the kitchen where she could pluck out the blossoms that did not withstand the most unkind scrutiny. In the right light— dim enough, that is—the flowers could pretend to the youth and vigor of their debut. As Isa herself, for so much of her life, had pretended, playing young in the theater, playing young to Carroll, and playing young to Frank Barclay, her common-law husband, who at the moment was out of town.

He was often out of town, legitimately or not. His business, as a mechanical engineer, took him all over Great Britain in the pursuit of defective machinery and inefficient manufacturing processes. He also used these trips as an excuse for the pursuit of younger women. The awful truth was arithmetical—he was forty-five and she was fifty-two. These ages were not so far apart; but inasmuch as they were different sexes, Frank and Isa experienced them as separated by a great chasm. For a man, forty-five was the very prime of life, the peak he ought to enjoy of achievement, respect, health, mature good looks, and all the fine things to which these blessings in turn entitled him. For a woman, fifty-two was . . . of a certain age. She could play young, exercising a little art as she did with the flowers in the vase.

But she knew. And she knew that anyone with an eye in his head could also tell, if he chose.

It was no mere metaphor. The flowers were a deliberate gesture. Isa kept flowers around her as a matter of habit which had begun as an exercise in prudence. An admirer might, at any time, send a woman flowers, and the sudden appearance of some floral tribute in a room that had not hitherto been so graced might be the occasion of awkward explanations, jealousy, and other unseemly displays. As an older character actress—now deceased—had taught her, a woman should be in the habit of having flowers around. They should not be objects of particular notice or inquiry.

In her younger days, then, after the breakup of her marriage to George Bacchus, she had kept herself in flowers. No one admirer might wonder about the expressions of affection, admiration, or delight that might be blooming in a bowl or vase or—in one lovely instance—in a silver epergne that had arrived to grace her dining table. And now, now that she was in her older years, she found that the charade had somehow reversed itself. She kept flowers around her so that Frank might not suppose she was no longer able to attract such tributes.

Having winnowed down the healthy-looking blossoms to a mere handful, she decided upon another vase with a narrower neck. She went out to the pantry and was delighted and surprised to find an impressive display of fresh flowers in her largest vase, placed there by her charwoman. The card was in its envelope on the countertop. She opened it. "Sweets to the sweet," it said, "and flowers to the deflowered. Regards, Breezy."

She smiled, but the smile was one of recognition rather than amusement. Breezy—Arthur Brisbane, Lord Langley—had taken her to Glenda Fenwick's house to spy. Five months ago? Six? Early spring, it had to have been. And now he was back from Antibes, and the flowers were to

announce his return to London for the season. There was a
kind of caring in their friendship, a peculiar sort of intimacy
that can exist between ex-lovers. He remembered her remark—about never having done this kind of thing before.
And he'd replied, at supper afterwards, raising his glass,
that it was a great discovery at his time of life how many
kinds of virginity there were to take. Isa had smiled, a little
flattered. Surely he had meant it to be flattery.

His allusion in the card was to that exchange. Perhaps it
extended to other areas of that same conversation. He'd
asked how she and Frank Barclay were getting on. She'd
confessed that Frank's travels kept him away more than she
liked. Breezy had immediately thought of sexual infidelity
—which was his hobby now, more than his passion—and
raised an inquiring eyebrow.

"There are advantages and disadvantages," she had explained, "to a connection with a younger man. They are
vigorous and giving. But they are also easily bored. When I
was forty and he was thirty-three, it didn't matter so much.
But ten years later . . ."

She had waved an airy gesture. "His nights are errant?"
Breezy had asked.

"I fear so. I assume so."

"Then that explains why I am favored again with the
pleasure of your company!"

"It's not just that," she'd protested.

"But the immediate prompting?"

She had confessed with a sweet smile. It was an expression she did very well, having used it in several plays and on
innumerable occasions off stage.

"I'm flattered nonetheless," Breezy had told her, "that of
all the various escorts among whom you had to choose, you
selected me."

"My dear loving friend," she had said, raising her glass to
him. And that, too, had been a reference to their first pas-

sage at arms, when he'd used the term, meaning by it that he was not a lover—not a candidate for matrimony or even for the serious taking of a mistress. She was not to count on him. And yet, over the long run, she had been able to count on him for certain things—a cheerful lewdness, a comradeship, the kind of relationship that obtains among veterans of some old campaign, with that shared surprise at having survived.

This bouquet was to let her know that he was still available for strategic use. If she wanted to have an admirer, someone to spirit her away and keep her out until all hours, he would be available. If Frank's jealousy—or her own pride—made such forays useful or desirable, he was willing to oblige. And she could rely upon him for as much or as little discretion as she found convenient, good food, good drink, good cheer, and no risk of misunderstandings or emotional excess. And, not incidentally, occasions for sex if she felt like it, either with Breezy or with any number of the bright young things who flocked about him, of various tastes and persuasions, but all of them eager as bears for honey. The great thing about Breezy's parties was that one was reasonably safe there. Breezy himself was beyond criticism, and he had enough money and shrewdness to intimidate anyone foolish or desperate enough to try to exploit the informalities of Langley House, not to speak of actual violations of the law.

Her habits of thrift having been too well learned to be abandoned now, Isa took the flowers that were still good from the old arrangement and stuck them in a posy pot with some fresh water, having trimmed their stems a bit. They'd last another day or two, surely. They could serve in her bedroom. Breezy's more impressive offering she could put in the parlor, prominent in isolation on a cherrywood side table. It looked very grand, she thought.

The truth of the matter was that she felt a good deal

closer to the fading flowers in the bedroom. It was self-indulgence, even self-pity, but knowing that didn't change her feelings: they were still there, gloomy as ever. It would have been unnatural not to have such feelings, with Frank away up in Manchester, entertaining himself, no doubt. She had decided, long before, that the important thing was how he came back after each of these jobs, returning to her as if he had been absolutely faithful. As if they were legally married. As if . . .

The trouble was that she wasn't so sure she would come back if their positions were reversed. If she were the younger man, what would bring her home each time? The furniture? The flat? The piles of shirts in the highboy and the books on the shelves in the library? These were the trivial things that held most domestic lives together, the amber in which men and women got stuck. Habit, really, but these hanks of cloth and bits of wood and glass were the raiment of habit, the props of a life. In order to transcend these mere things, one needed the indifference that only the wealthy and the poor could afford. Breezy had it. As did some of the demimondaines he collected about him. And Glenda's girls, but probably not Glenda herself. Isa knew herself to be vulnerable that way. She only hoped Frank was, too. And that he continued to be. That nothing came along to nudge him from his not very deep groove.

And if the worst happened and she were left alone? She would survive. She could continue to earn a living, more likely than not. She could keep on with the character parts for which she had earned a reputation in the business if not among the general public. She had her sisters and her younger brother to whom she could turn, if she were in real need. There were a great many women who were worse off. But it was not a prospect she was eager to explore.

Slowly, thoughtfully, she undressed and put on her flannel robe, old and faded but comfortable. She often wore it when she was alone. She went to the kitchen, took a cucumber from the ice chest, sliced it, and brought it back to her bedroom. She lay down and put the slices of cucumber over her eyes as a mild astringent and restorative. It was cheaper than a facial and did more good. The idea of it was attractive as well, suggesting that the health and freshness of the country might in this way be available to a woman of the city, and that the crisp cleanliness of youth might be retrieved by a woman no longer young.

She lay there for some time. Indeed, she may have drifted off into a light drowse, a pleasant cucumber slumber.

She woke in the dark, having no idea what time it was. The cucumber slices had fallen off her eyelids. She got up, switched on the lights, looked at the clock—it was going on nine—and, retrieving the bits of cucumber from the bed, took them back to the kitchen, where she decided to have a piece of cheese and some crackers. It was too late to bother with a meal and too early just to go to bed for the night. An odd time. Which was the problem with her life, too. Get through the next ten years, she told herself, and Frank will be safe enough. A grown-up, at long last. She put that threshold at fifty, but was willing to concede that not everyone attained maturity at the half-century mark. Not Breezy, surely. He'd never grow up. Old, perhaps, but not up. Not as long as he could still get it up.

The likelihood was that she'd receive an invitation within the next day or two. She could amuse herself, if she chose, by toying with the idea of accepting. To go and be silly and self-indulgent, wearing a domino, a peignoir, and nothing else, and play his elaborate parlor games that inevitably spilled over into the bedrooms . . . She probably wouldn't, but there was no harm in keeping the question open, a possibility for fantasy more than for action. She knew that once she decided against going, the fantasies would dry up, deprived of the nourishment they managed to extract from the merest wisp of connection to the world.

She tidied up after herself, put the plate into the sink, and returned to the bedroom. It was early yet, but there was no reason to stay up. She didn't feel like reading. She certainly wasn't going to do any mending. She had no expectation that Frank would telephone. Or anyone else. She supposed that a good night's sleep would be not only beneficial but a way of getting through the long desert of an evening. She turned out her light, got into bed, and lay there, daring her mind to wander, curious as to what direction it would take. Breezy's extravagances? Or Frank's? Or her own accommodations to their demands? Surprisingly, she found herself imagining Frank's death, the word arriving, the sudden change to widowhood, or something as close to it as her living arrangement was close to marriage. To be left alone would not be so bad, perhaps. To have no one to whom she had to adjust, about whom she had to worry, or by whom she might be betrayed. There was something fine about it, something secure. If he died, she'd have him at last. She supposed that was a mean thing to think, but she knew herself well enough not to be surprised. There was a satisfaction in touching bottom, or at any rate in imagining it, facing the worst and surviving it. She drifted off into a sleep that may or may not have been dreamless but which left her no shreds or fragments in the morning.

She woke to the sounds of crockery. The char had shown up on time and made tea. A little while later, when Isa was emerging from her bath, the woman brought in the morning post—with its predictable invitation from Breezy. There was also a note in a small but well-made envelope, addressed to Miss Isa Bowman in an unfamiliar hand. A feminine hand, perhaps. Isa opened it first and looked at the signature.

Alice Hargreaves. Of all people.

My dear Miss Bowman,

Thank you for your kind note. It was good of you to take the trouble.

I find that I shall be coming to London within the next week or ten days. If it is convenient for you, I should like to pay you a call. I am curious to know about your meeting with my late husband. He did mention that encounter, and I must say I was pleased to learn that the pretensions of your book were those of your publisher rather than your own.

I look forward to our meeting.

Very sincerely,
ALICE HARGREAVES

She put it down on the counterpane, opened Breezy's card, glanced at that, and put it down beside the letter. It was an unlikely conjunction, she thought, those two pieces of paper together on her bed. She remembered that other conjunction, the delight Glenda had taken in bringing her together with Reginald Hargreaves. Isa had not supposed anything would be accomplished by it but had played along —quite literally. She had rather enjoyed the chance of playing a lead instead of one of her inevitable character roles. And Glenda had invested so much of herself into the meeting that Isa could not refuse. She thought, looking back on it, that it had been surprisingly sweet. Not that Glenda was the whore with the heart of gold, exactly, but there might be a little truth in that sentimental convention. One wanted a woman in her profession to have some soft spot, to betray some sign of human vulnerability. Isa supposed that Glenda and her sisters represented the most extreme kind of realism anyone could imagine, and that the need to imagine their having hearts of gold was a way of excusing that same tendency in oneself. If even prostitutes can occasionally forget their own self-interest, then the rest of the world need not reproach itself for its infrequent lapses into altruism and generosity.

Isa could understand the pleasure of that self-important feeling Glenda must have experienced: the possession of a secret is wonderfully soothing to one's self-esteem, and Isa was experiencing that pleasure now. She was not really the proprietor of any secret, but she could at least amuse herself by imagining the reaction of her correspondents if each of them were aware of the part the other played in Isa's life. That she balanced deliciously between Alice's ethereality and Breezy's fleshliness was pleasing. Each quality needed the other. And dreaded the other?

Breezy would not be put off by Alice so much as Alice might be by the crew generally to be found at Langley House. Nonetheless, Isa was not content to classify herself simply as one of Breezy's people. Her range was greater than that. Indeed, her obligation, aesthetic and moral, was to extend herself as far as she could so as to include all possible aspects of womanhood, from Alice's extreme to that of Breezy's playmates. Not to be limited by one set of preconceptions or another.

She had tried to do that for much of her life and had pretty well succeeded. It was unfair, then, that her success had not been better rewarded. She had slept alone last night and almost certainly she would be lying down to sleep alone when night came again.

Annoyed with herself for dwelling on unpleasantness, she flung back the coverlet and got out of bed. She didn't want to deepen her frown lines any further. A few minutes before the mirror and a judicious selection from her wardrobe, and she'd look like something. Then, inevitably, she'd begin to feel like something. She knew how to take her cues from the external world, the lighting, the furniture, her clothes and makeup.

She knew she was fooling herself but didn't mind that. In

fact, she was rather proud of herself for knowing how to do it so well.

2

CARYL SPRAWLED on a chaise longue with a pitcher of perfect martinis beside him on the floor. He didn't like them much, but that was what Madeleine was drinking this week. She liked to change cocktails the way other women change their hair. But they were better than the sidecars she had been drinking the month before.

Madeleine lit a cigarette, shook the match with the ferocity a terrier might show a rat, and took a deep drag. "So," she said, forming the word entirely of smoke, "you have to sup with your mother. You're quite impossible, you know that, I hope! For a forty-year-old man to be obliged to dine with his mother . . . I'd rather you were lying to me than that lame excuse. That you really had another girl . . ."

"I'm sorry to disappoint you."

"About the girl? Or about the dinner?" she asked, waving her cigarette.

"Both," he told her. "Mother comes to town only rarely, and she asks very little of me. This is the first time she's come since father died."

"Well, if you insist on being reasonable and responsible," she said, looking at him over the rim of her glass, "I shall have to excuse you. But you are the most unreliable of all my lovers, and the most vexing."

"I'm pleased, then, not to have been dismissed."

"You should be. But don't push me too far. My patience is limited, you know."

"Yes, I know. Your patience, or your attention," he teased.

"Now, don't be nasty. I'm not being nasty. I'm being

almost sweet. And what do I get in return? I ask you, now! It just isn't fair."

"No, perhaps not," Caryl admitted.

"Why don't we all have dinner, the three of us together? You think your mother would like me?"

"If I weren't there, she might very well like you. But it would be misleading, wouldn't it? It'd look as though I were taking you to meet my mother, which is the first step down a very tricky path. We'd look to be on the verge of an engagement."

"And you don't want to disappoint her, is that it?"

"Or you. Or myself."

"Caryl, how sweet. You can be a dear sometimes."

"It's true. We're such good friends. And we'd make such awful spouses for each other. We have to be careful."

"I don't think it's that at all," Madeleine said. "I think it's just that you have an allergy to the idea of matrimony. It makes you break out in an awful rash. I knew a girl once who broke out that way whenever she rode horses. Or ate tomatoes."

"Or both together."

"No one I know eats tomatoes on horseback."

"Well, you may be right. I mean, about me and matrimony."

Madeleine swooped down from the window seat, did a kind of arabesque across the room so that the loose peach silk of her dressing gown billowed nicely, and she turned, dipped, and snatched up the martini pitcher. It looked like the maneuver of a seabird darting down to grab a fish, impressive in its accuracy and grace.

"I can understand about me," she said. "After Felix was killed, I swore I'd never tie myself that way, never invest that much of myself in any one person again. But that's old news now. I've become a cliché. There is a whole generation of women like me, and we're all destroying ourselves as stylishly as possible. But you? How have you stayed single in this cut-throat market? For a heterosexual, you have great strength of character."

"Not at all," he said, taking another sip of his too warm and too sweet cocktail. "It's another cliché. The unhappy childhood."

"You had a perfect childhood!"

"You think?" Caryl asked. "You must know that there's no such thing."

She was waiting. He thought of what to tell her, or what the point was of telling her anything. He thought of that encounter at Glenda Fenwick's door with the man he was 90 percent sure was his father. He thought of the later connections he'd made—how little his parents had hugged one another, not to mention their three sons. He would have liked to discuss these things with someone, and it would have to be a woman. One simply didn't speak of such matters with a man. But he was reluctant to put his friendship with Madeleine at risk. He didn't want to regret having gone too far in his revelations. And then, there was the more recent consideration, improbable but by no means impossible—of matrimony. If his speculations on the market failed utterly, if everything went sour and all the shares he'd bought on margin tumbled into the depths, he might have to review his position about matrimony. In that event, Madeleine would be a plausible candidate. Her late husband, Felix, had been poor as a churchmouse, but her father was well fixed. The general had enough and to spare for all of them. And Caryl could stand good old Mad. He could be comfortable with her, he imagined. He could at least imagine being comfortable with her.

"Cat caught your tongue?" she asked.

"Not really. I was trying to sort out whether I wanted to tell you any of the sordid details . . ."

"I love sordid details."

"Yes, I know," he said, smiling. "But I realized that I might need you one day. If everything else goes bust and I have to put myself on the market, you're one of the very few women I can imagine myself actually marrying."

"Is that a proposal?"

"I hope not. But if the choice is between you and the soup-lines, I'd expect I'd come to you. And you'd take me in."

"I might. But I wouldn't be faithful to you. You know that."

"I rely on it."

"And we'd be polite to each other and boring."

"Not very polite, I think. And never boring."

"Would you be faithful to me?"

"I might be, but I'd never let you know about it."

"That's what I like about you—your stupidity."

He laughed. "And that's why I can't take you to supper with mother. I really have had idle thoughts about marrying you."

"A shame to spoil a lovely friendship," she said.

"Yes, but it's not likely to happen. The market has been behaving ridiculously well these days. The stupidest men in London are making fortunes. I doubt that it'll come to that."

"And would you take me in if Daddy's money disappeared and you made your stupid fortune?"

"Take you in? Of course. But not as a wife. You'd be a mistress, and you'd wear those filmy things all the time. Maybe we'd move to Venice and live in crumbling splendor the way all really wicked English people do."

"Good! Want another of those?" she offered.

"They're disgusting."

"I know. I may never make another pitcher of them again."

"Perhaps a straight gin? At the distillery, they know what they're doing."

"Be a dear and dump that, would you? And bring me one as well."

He went out to the pantry where there was a small sink, and where he found an opened bottle of Booth's. Tell her more? She'd taken this last very well indeed, but then, he'd expected her to. Their habit was to engage in this mock banter, where they slipped truths into their jokes in as subtle a fashion as possible. It was like filling cream puffs. There was only so much *crème patissière* they could take.

His instinct had been not to tell her more. He'd go with that. He brought the gin in and poured a generous splash into each of their glasses, put the gin bottle on the floor, and sprawled again on the chaise. For a while, neither of them spoke.

"You're very quiet," he said, at last. "Bowled over by my proposal?"

"Yes, a little. Or by my reaction to it."

"You mean, you'd have me?"

"Probably."

"Good old Mad."

"Not good. Only old. And mad." She drained her glass. "You'd better get out or I shall get maudlin."

"I wouldn't want that," he said. "You'd ruin your mascara."

"Yes. Besides, you have to change for dinner, don't you?"

"You want to come?" he asked, rather surprising himself.

"Another time, perhaps," she said.

"Perhaps."

He drank a little of his drink, put the glass down, and got to his feet. He gave her a rather chaste peck on the forehead that only later on, as he was walking back to his flat, seemed to him to have been husbandly. He undressed, showered, and began to dress for dinner with his mother.

He had not been able to decide whether to be annoyed with her or grateful to her for this novelty. Never before had she come to town and stayed in a hotel. He had a spare bedroom, and he could have put her up. But she had been quite clear and firm in her intentions. She wanted to stay at Brown's, where Regi had always stayed. (Or had said he stayed. Caryl wasn't certain.) It was conceivable that she simply refused to recognize that the Sloane Square flat was in fact Caryl's home, preferring to cling to the notion that he still lived at Cuffnells but more or less camped out in London—even after all these years. It was also possible that she just didn't want to get in his way, either out of consideration for him or out of concern for herself, trying to remain ignorant of the details of his London life. That seemed the likeliest explanation. The converse—that she might have business in London of which she hoped to keep him ignorant—did not seem probable.

He'd keep his eyes and ears open, though. As was only right and proper in an attentive son. And he'd try to see to it that she had a reasonably pleasant dinner. He'd have to work at it, of course.

What he hadn't told Madeleine, and what he only told himself at certain times, when he was strong enough to stand it or in the right mood for a certain kind of pain, was that he and his mother were conspirators in the suppression of a number of unpleasant truths. He felt bad about his father's death. The old man had collapsed at the news of Rex and Alan dying in the war, had just lost all interest in life, withering away—as though Caryl's being alive counted for nothing. And that was because of his blasted name, which not only required to be spelled out all the time, but which his father had always detested. It was his mother's last act of defiance, he supposed.

His mother was always particularly nice to him, not only because he was the youngest but because he was his father's least favorite. And knowing that, he'd always wanted more than anything his father's approval and love.

None of this could be discussed, ever. It just hung over them, like a foul haze over some northern industrial city. What would they talk about, then? How would he contrive to keep the conversation going? Would he mention Madeleine? Probably not. Not yet, anyway. Not until he knew whether he was likely to please her or disappoint her—and until he knew which of those he'd rather do.

ALICE HAD COME TO LONDON with a schedule of appointments and an agenda all of which had to do with the manuscript. Her first interview had already taken place, back in Southampton, where she had consulted with the same solicitor Caryl had visited. The failure of Caryl to report to her on the depressing subject of their financial position seemed to Alice capable of different interpretations. It could have been Caryl's quite typical way of postponing whatever was demanding, unpleasant, or otherwise unwelcome. Or, putting the matter in a kindlier light, she supposed it was possible to allow him a certain feeling of consideration for her age, her recent bereavement, her position as his mother. He might perfectly well be trying to protect her, to make whatever other inquiries and arrangements he could think of to soften the blow. She doubted that, but it was conceivable.

Meanwhile, left to her own devices, she saw nothing to prevent her from at least exploring the next obvious and reasonable steps, which pointed to the sale of the manuscript. It was said to be valuable. That was what she had for many years been given to believe. She would now find a particular figure, at least a rough estimate of the price it might fetch, and she'd be able then to decide whether to proceed. Or how.

She was surprised, although she managed not to betray this, when Mr. Osborne in his small office at Sotheby's alluded to her late husband's earlier visit on the same subject. It had, in fact, been fairly recent, only a few months before his death.

"And what was the conclusion of that interview?" Alice asked.

"Surely, he must have told you . . ." Osborne looked down at his interwoven fingers on the polished surface of the desk as if he were appraising *objets de virtu.*

"We rarely discussed money," Alice hastened to explain.

"I see," Osborne said. It was, Alice realized, a thing people say when they do not see at all. She did not feel obliged to enlighten him. She could play the *grande dame* and let him assume what he liked.

"What I told him was that the amounts that could be realized from the sale of the manuscript depended upon the conditions of the sale."

"I'm sorry? I don't understand."

"If it were to be a private sale, negotiated without any of the publicity one might expect in a transaction involving so interesting an item as this, there might be a certain sum. At a public auction, with its attendant brouhaha, that sum might very probably double. One could propose a floor price for a private sale, in other words, but the auction price could be considerably higher. Very considerably higher."

"And the floor price?"

He unclasped his hands, unscrewed a gold fountain pen, and wrote a figure on a scratch pad. He turned the pad about so that Alice could see it.

Was this his ordinary custom, she wondered, or was it for her benefit, as if he were eager to observe whatever proprieties she had maintained with her late husband? He was not even going to risk mouthing the words. Alice found it hard to suppress a smile. And she realized that he now supposed she was smiling at the figure—four thousand pounds.

"And if I wait?" she asked.

"Difficult to say," Osborne said. "From a strictly business point of view, the appreciation in value of the manuscript is likely enough, but there are certainly other investments just as safe that also produce income as you hold them. Your own business advisers can make that kind of judgment far better than I. The market in manuscript items and association items—this is both those things at once—has been healthy. I see no reason to expect any sudden change."

"I appreciate your candor," she said.

"It has been my pleasure," he assured her.

Back at the hotel, she lay down for a bit, physically tired but mentally alert and even overactive. She found herself wondering whether Regi might not have stayed at one time or another in this very room. A mysterious man. He had known enough to understand that the money was running out. He had made inquiries about the value of the manuscript. But he had never discussed either the money or the manuscript with her. Had he supposed that she was sentimentally attached to it? Or was it simply his natural distaste for anything that had to do with Carroll? As likely as not, he had simply left it to her and to Caryl, having satisfied himself that there was value there and that they would be able to convert the manuscript to pounds sterling if the occasion required. A kind of tact, really, that was quite in character and comforting for her to remember, even now.

Caryl, she thought, was unlikely to make any objection to her selling the manuscript. Her concern, really, was that he'd be too eager, would be inclined to inflate the value to some absurdly large figure and take it as an excuse to shirk his own responsibilities, either to cut down on his own expenses or to contrive to find a way of bringing in some money. Alice didn't see why he found it necessary to keep a flat in London when there was so much room at Cuffnells. It was simply a place to bring his disreputable friends, or to keep from her the depressing details of the life he was leading. In any event, it represented a distance between them that was more than geographical.

At dinner, he surprised her, striking exactly the right balance between excessive eagerness for her to sell the manuscript and excessive pride. It seemed to him to be a matter of no great personal importance. She could do what she liked with it, and whatever she decided would be fine with him. About London, though, he was less flexible. "Everything you say is quite true, mother, but beside the point. What it really amounts to, I believe, is that you don't like London, don't really approve of it. It isn't quiet and calm and orderly the way things are at Cuffnells or the way they were at Oxford when you were young. There's bustle and noise here. But that's just why I do like it. Fortunately, I can get home almost every weekend, as I've been doing. And it isn't very expensive. I'm comfortable here. You're comfortable there. Why should either of us impose on the other's tastes?"

He could be like that, cutting through to something that she had to admit was at least close to her basic objection to London. It had been where Regi had gone for all those years, either to a mistress—or a series of them—or to prostitutes. She had assumed so, at any rate. She had admitted to herself that this was a natural and almost inevitable thing in men, and she had been scrupulously fair about not blaming him any more than she had blamed herself. But she hadn't found it attractive or admirable. And there was a feeling that London, in a vague but nonetheless real way, was her rival, her enemy.

She decided to let the question of Caryl's flat in London go, at least for the moment, and concentrate on the more pressing matter of money. His attitude about the manuscript was perfectly correct. Perhaps she could move him along to what she saw as the next necessary step. He had to find some source of income. Tactfully, almost diffidently, she alluded to his need for money, leaving it to him to strike whatever attitude he would. "I agree," he told her. "I've been giving that very question a great deal of thought. I'm conferring with several friends in the City and I hope to make certain improvements in my circumstances within the coming months. I'll let you know when the picture clarifies a little, but I am paying attention."

"I'm glad to hear that," she said. "The money from the sale—when I do decide to sell—will be considerable, but hardly infinite. It won't fundamentally change anything. For you."

"But for you?"

"I won't live forever."

"You mustn't worry about me, mother. I'll be able to fend for myself, one way or another."

"I certainly hope so."

"Besides, if I am to provide for myself, there are many more opportunities here in London than there are down at Cuffnells. Isn't that so?"

"All right, you've made your point."

"A brandy?" he offered. "To celebrate our evening?"

"None for me, but you have one."

"I believe I shall," he said. And when the sommelier brought him his armagnac, he raised it toward her and told her, "I'm really proud of you, mother. You've been a wonder. I think, now that there are just the two of us left, we're likely to be good friends."

"Well, of course we are, my dear."

Later, upstairs, alone, she wondered if she hadn't underestimated him for all those years. It would be pleasant to discover she had been wrong. She could think of nothing she'd rather have as a present from the grudging gods. Was it possible? Regi had kept the practical details of life from her, and in the same way she had kept them from Caryl, their youngest and most soulful child, out of habit and the desire to protect him.

What she wanted was to be protected, herself. It was unfair that she should have to be the mother and Caryl had to be the child. It was an arbitrary and stupid arrangement, having to do with their chronological ages and their blood relationship. But where is the soul? Hers was hiding somewhere, had been hiding for years as if in a game, and the game was long over, all the players having given it up to do other things. A far better system would be one in which people picked their best moments, grew into them, and then simply stayed there. Regi could have been somewhere in his late twenties forever. And Caryl? Perhaps eighteen.

And she herself would be ten again. But with a kindness that ten-year-olds don't often have. To be ten and at the same time kind, and to stay that way forever . . .

She lay down on the bed to rest, but more to give way to the indulgence of daydream, to baby herself a little, as one was allowed to do again when one reached the seventies. Bland foods and naps in the afternoons. Oh yes, indeed. The time of day when the body rests and the mind ranges, frolicsome and free, the way it has always done for as long as one can recall. The only imperfection is that one sometimes has appointments, an agenda to remember. She still had to call on Isa Bowman to take the measure of that woman. In fairness, if Caryl was going to be eighteen, then someone would have to make provision for him. And Alice had to decide what threat there might be from Isa Bowman, what spite of jealousy or envy or blind rage that could make a mess of the sale of the manuscript. The words of the man from Sotheby's had been clear enough—the price it would fetch at public auction would be greater than what might be realized in a private sale, but the possibilities for mischief were greater too.

Isa Bowman could cause a deal of harm—to herself and Caryl, and to her late father, the Dean, and to Regi. And not least to Lewis Carroll.

It wasn't just babies that turned into pigs. That could happen at any time, to almost anyone. And often did.

ALICE HARGREAVES WORE BLACK, presumably as a sign of mourning, but also, as Isa was quick to see, because it was becoming. Either way, it was a reminder of who and what she was—as if Isa needed one.

"How good of you to call," she said. "Do come in."

"It was good of you to have written."

"I was sorry to hear the news . . ."

"He was a wonderful man."

"Do, please, sit down," Isa offered. She felt from Alice not so much hostility as a trying-out, a scrutiny of appraisal. "Tea?"

"Please," Alice consented.

Isa rang. She was happy to be able to show off not only her tea service, which was good Georgian silver, but her style. She could preside at a tea tray with impressive authority. The girl appeared. "The tea cart, please," Isa ordered.

The girl went off to fetch it. Isa had supervised the setting out of the tea things to be sure that it was *comme il faut.*

"When you knew him," Alice asked, "did he still wave the teapot about to steep the leaves thoroughly?"

He of course was Carroll.

"Oh yes. His habits were quite fixed," Isa replied. "As were his tastes. You're taller than I'd have expected."

"I grew late. I was small when I knew him."

"Yes, of course."

Alice looked about the parlor. The room was large enough, and clean, but there were traces—worn spots in

the upholstery of the furniture, faded places on the rugs—
of the owner's failure to achieve that perfect transcendence
over material things that came with large sums of money.
Isa often pretended to indifference, but not now, not with
Alice Hargreaves. She could make her own announce-
ments, letting the worn plush reply to the shiny black of
Alice's dress.

"Your journey was pleasant, I trust?"

"Thank you, yes. I don't come to town often. Reginald
came up regularly and attended to those few errands I
needed run."

"If there is ever anything I can do," Isa offered, "you
have only to write or telephone."

"You're very kind," Alice said, without a thought of accepting.

The girl brought in the tea cart. Isa performed with it
beautifully, as always. She was aware of Alice Hargreaves'
attention and enjoyed it. She was playing to an audience as
surely as she had played to an audience that other time,
with Reginald and Glenda, each of them looking at her in
the hope of some hint that might at last explain everything,
might tell them secret truths about their own lives. Or
Alice's.

And now Alice was here with altogether different questions, wanting to know about Reginald more likely than
not. Unless she already knew about his London life . . .
Did she?

Alice accepted the teacup and said, "My late husband was
not quite himself the last months of his life. I fear it may
have been the result of his efforts to comport himself cheerfully and carry on in a normal way, for my sake and for the
sake of his idea of decorum—even though he knew he was
dying."

"It must have been difficult for you both."

"More difficult for him, I think. I was entitled to cry, if I was so disposed. He felt obliged to keep up a brave front, even to me."

"Yes, I can see that."

"I allowed it, of course. I didn't want to take his pride away from him. Almost until the end, he carried on as if nothing were changed, as if there were no end in sight."

"I see."

"It is for that reason that I have been thinking these past few days about his meeting with you. It seems . . ."

"Out of character?" Isa offered.

"Yes."

Isa was amused to realize that Alice's own word might have been stronger. Isa wasn't afraid of strong words or strong feelings, however, and she let Alice know that, rephrasing the question. "You want to know under what possible circumstances Reginald Hargreaves would have consented to meet a person like me?"

"I was wrong to have thought badly of you," Alice said, "as I've made clear. And as you have made clear about the responsibility for the claims of your book . . ."

"Did you read the book?"

"No."

"Had you done so," Isa pointed out, "you'd have seen that I gave you and your family proper credit. There was never any question in anyone's mind as to who was the real Alice. And had there been such a question, my book would have answered it correctly."

"I know that now. But I hadn't read the book, having been put off by the cover, and there was, I confess, a degree of animosity I felt. Reginald knew this and had to have disregarded it. That was what I thought to have been so uncharacteristic."

"Unless of course he believed that you might in some way benefit by the interview," Isa suggested.

"Oh?" Alice lowered her cup and put it on a small table beside her. "Is that what he told you?"

"No. It was a friend we had in common who led me to believe he might have had such a motive. I'm not altogether certain whether I believed her or not."

"And who was this friend, if I may ask?"

"Actually, she was a friend of a friend of mine. An acquaintance, at any rate, of Lord Langley's."

The name meant nothing to Alice. Or, if it did, she showed no reaction. But then, Alice hardly looked as though she kept up with London's fast set. "She knew Lewis Carroll briefly."

"Indeed?" Alice prompted.

"I believe he made her acquaintance on the beach at Eastbourne, as he was evidently in the habit of doing."

Alice gave Isa a look of frank disapproval. "I have heard that kind of imputation before."

"And disbelieve it?" Isa asked, more amused than intimidated. "It's perfectly true. I know it to be true."

"You know what to be true?"

"Those imputations, of course."

"I know no such thing."

"Then you may believe me or not, as you prefer."

Alice said nothing.

"Reginald believed me. And Glenda. He believed her, too. I don't think there was any question in his mind."

"Glenda?"

"The friend of Lord Langley's."

"I see," Alice said.

Did she? Isa wasn't sure what to think. It was perfectly possible that Alice knew all about her husband's forays to the brothel. But it was just as likely that she had contrived to blind herself to it, to avoid facing it somehow, as she had avoided facing any of the unpleasant truths about Carroll. It was tiresome and dishonest, but if that was the way Alice

Hargreaves chose to live, then Isa was inclined to let her think whatever she liked. Or, if Alice preferred, not to think at all. It was none of Isa's concern. She could understand, however, how Reginald could have been driven crazy by it.

"And the two of you told Reginald what, exactly?" Alice asked.

"About Lewis Carroll's fondness for young girls, his liking to take their clothes off and photograph them or draw them, the physical attraction they had for him."

"And is that all?"

"And the consequences of our experience," Isa said.

"I'm not sure I follow you."

"What it meant for us, for Glenda and me at any rate, to have been admired in that way by such a man at such an early and—as they used to say—tender age."

Alice picked up the teacup and sipped. She was very steady, very good, but Isa knew enough about stage business to recognize a pretext for a pause when she saw one, and she picked up on how carefully Alice was concentrating on what otherwise might have been an almost unconscious series of gestures. Alice, then, was an intelligent woman. Isa could see that. She'd always assumed so. Carroll never liked dull children. But Alice had remained quick after all those years. And she'd now realized what the purpose was of Reginald's inquiry.

Isa's delight at the prospect of getting her own back seemed quite rapidly to diminish. What possible satisfaction could there be in causing discomfort to this delicately featured, magisterial, frail, somewhat rigid, somehow admirable, rather sad old woman?

"I should imagine," Alice said, "that our experiences were different and that our lives have been different. And therefore that the consequences have been quite different."

"Oh, yes," Isa agreed.

There was a pause in which Alice considered her next question. Isa wondered why there should be so much caution on both sides. It was extremely unlikely that the two women would become friends. It was improbable that they'd even see one another again. Why not put aside pretense and caution? But Isa felt as much on her guard as she could ever remember being, and had to assume that her guest's mood was not much easier.

"My late husband didn't initiate these meetings, I take it?" Alice asked at last.

"No, I think not. I believe it was Glenda's idea originally. She persuaded him to meet me. He was apparently reluctant."

"I see."

"He was curious to hear about Carroll, whom he disliked."

"I know."

"He wanted to know whether he had perhaps misjudged the man. Or that was my impression. He listened very intently to what we had to say."

"What did he decide?"

"He didn't make that clear to us," Isa said. "He spoke very little about himself and not at all about you. He just listened, asked questions from time to time, and seemed . . . regretful. But I couldn't tell whether he was sad about Carroll or about himself or about us . . ."

"Us?"

"All of us. Glenda, you, me, and all those other child friends Carroll had."

"I'm not sure we have that much in common. He may have behaved differently with each of us. He could have changed over the years."

"Yes, that's possible," Isa agreed, "but it was my impression that he was carefully re-enacting the experience he'd had with you. There were differences, of course . . ."

"What did happen?" Alice asked. "What was this experience of yours Reginald was so curious about, that made him so regretful?"

"It's a long story," Isa said. "Do you really want to hear it?"

"Yes," Alice said. "Yes, I do."

It was the acknowledgment Isa had been waiting for. She took her time and savored the moment. It wasn't what she had anticipated. She had enjoyed it more when she'd had Reginald and Glenda as an audience.

Still, there was some degree of achievement in the fact that Alice had come to call and had asked the question. Isa moved to a more comfortable chair and began.

MOTHER ALWAYS LIED ABOUT MY AGE. She was looking forward to a time when it would make a difference for my career. One must establish the numbers early on. It isn't how you look so much as how producers think of you when they look at you, casting their plays. You have to help them see what you really do look like. Twenty-nine can be worlds away from thirty-two.

It was a reasonable enough thing for a stage mother to do, even though it didn't quite work out. What she couldn't have known was that I was never going to be much good as an *ingénue*. I would only become successful—relatively speaking—later on, as I got to do character parts. But I can't blame her for that. She was a mother, not a gypsy.

So what she said when Lewis Carroll appeared that day was that I was eleven. I was older than that, but we shaved it.

I'd been in his play. Or the play Henry Savile Clarke had made from *Alice*. I'd been the caterpillar, having just the one scene, but Carroll had seen the production and noticed me, so that when he came backstage afterwards to say something to the cast and meet us all, he spoke to me and my mother and asked my age. She told him I was eleven. It was habit.

But it was lucky, too. Or a coincidence. He liked eleven-year-olds. Younger than nine, he thought was too scrawny; older than eleven was too coarse. He said, "coarse," but meant developed. I hadn't developed much, yet. Haven't developed much, really, ever. Even at my age, I have this China-doll face and these little child's breasts. Abrupt puffs. Meringues, someone once called them.

He wanted to know if he could borrow me for the day. I remember he used that word, as if I were a toy, an object. But it wasn't insulting. There was a playful tone in the way he said it so that I was keen. Which was important, because my mother looked at me and I nodded. If I'd objected, I don't think she'd have forced me to go with him. She was ambitious for me and saw the opportunity, as I think I must have glimpsed it, myself. But she consulted me, and I did nod ever so slightly. She agreed I could be lent.

What she had in mind was no more than what I had in mind—that I ought to be nice to the gentleman who had been kind enough to take special notice of me and was in a position to do me a lot of good. He was a famous man, after all, and a famous author can help a young actress. Father was gone, had died the year before. There were the five of us and mother, all depending on one another. The good fortune that happened to one of us happened to all. That didn't have to be said; it was the way we always thought.

I suppose there were risks, but they hardly seemed as weighty as the security we had in the way we were connected. He was the friend of Mr. Henry Savile Clarke who was our employer . . . It may have crossed my mother's mind to worry about me, but she would almost certainly have thought of these protections she and I could count on. If the man were some sort of child molester, he'd pick on strangers' children. Or he would if he were smart—and Mr. Carroll—Mr. Dodgson—was an Oxford don.

We spent the day together. I remember we went to a picture gallery and then a restaurant for lunch. For my lunch. He never ate much at midday. No more than a small piece of cheese and a glass of sherry. But that impression is from later on. I remember walking on Bond Street, holding his hand. He told me I could call him Uncle—which I thought was a great privilege—although I see it now as his way of obviating people's questions.

We must have got on well enough. He talked nonsense, child-talk. I don't remember it clearly, can't distinguish it from other times I spent with him later on. What was happening, I believe, was that I was on display. It was as if he were purchasing an automobile—not that there were automobiles then—and wanted to drive it around the block as a kind of test. If I'd understood what was happening, I'm sure I should have been nervous and unsatisfactory. But I was so proud of myself for having been picked out of all the children in the cast for such an honor that I was—not relaxed, really, but on my mettle. Excited and enjoying myself. Which is the best way to be if one is trying to make an impression. I was on my best behavior, of course, and he liked that. He liked little girls whose manners were good and who were agreeable.

When he brought me home, I thought that would be the end of it. He hadn't indicated anything about a further excursion. But then, he was being cautious. He was inspecting the household too, I can see now. He was looking at the flat, which was clean enough, if modest. It was a walk-up in East London. And my sisters and my brother were there, all dressed up for him to inspect. And no father . . .

He accepted tea. He and my mother talked. About her life and how difficult it was bringing up a family of that size, and yet how fortunate that I was an actress and that Nellie and Maggie acted too. Empsie was still very young, and Charlie was a baby . . .

It wouldn't have been difficult to figure out a way of suggesting that I'd been a good girl and deserved a rest. A treat. A few days at the seaside.

My mother was agreeable, having already entrusted me to his care. What was the difference between hours in London and days at the seaside? Just so long as he brought me safely home.

He made himself clearer, though. He explained, or at least he hinted, about what he wanted. He liked, he said, to sketch. To draw from life. He liked little girls as his models. He had once photographed them but he now contented himself with pencils and charcoal . . . My mother had no objections? No apprehensions?

I don't want to choose between stupidity and wickedness in her motives. I reject all that, because it worked out differently from anything she could have imagined, let alone planned for or counted on. So that entire question, now, is beside the point. I believe she assumed there would be pretty much what Carroll said there would be—some modeling and sketching. If he had intended anything more serious, he would not have mentioned the modeling at all, would he? And if anything happened that he hadn't mentioned, she had her weapons and could hold him accountable. His Studentship, for instance, was tenable for life, but only so long as his behavior was good. A complaint from the mother of a girl he had assaulted would, at the very least, have deprived him of his living.

I expect she knew this, or knew that something like it could result from a public complaint. I just don't *know*. She thought for a moment, perhaps so as not to appear too eager. And he assured her that no harm would come to me.

Which was what she had been waiting for. She looked at him, looked at me, and this time it was with even greater eagerness that I nodded, signaling to her my willingness to accompany the man to the seaside. She agreed.

He finished his tea, thanked her, spoke briefly to the other children, praised the delicacy of our features, and took his leave.

I expect she must have thought about it during the week that followed. There were all sorts of ways she could have got out of it, or got me out of it. She could have invented an illness, I imagine. Mine, or even Nellie's or Empsie's, so that there was a reasonable fear I'd soon be taken sick too. Maybe she lay awake thinking of such excuses, preparing them, and taking from that preparation a kind of comfort because it meant nothing was yet final, no die had been cast.

But of course it had. The opportunity was so exciting, the favors he could do for me were so great . . . And it wasn't unthinkable. There were child brothels all over London, and not all the children in those establishments had been kidnapped. Many of them had been sold, the way the Chinese sell their daughters. For rent or food, or more likely gin. It was not uncommon in our part of the town. A few blocks farther east and closer to the river, there were people much worse off than we, much more desperate. Not that one wants to emulate such people, but the possibility was there, always. It wasn't unimaginable.

This was anyway a considerable cut above that kind of transaction. The other, the business of selling young girls, I mention only to put the question in some kind of perspective. The man was famous, after all, and had much more to lose than your ordinary gentleman, your stranger from out of town, say. And could do us more good, too. She must have gone over these things in her mind, over and over again, at night after we were asleep. She never let me know what she was thinking or that she was worried for my sake—if she was worried. But the night before my departure she explained to me that, for the purposes of our deception about my age, we had better shave off those hairs that had grown like a wispy mustache over my sex.

The women in Japan do this, I'm told, as a matter of course. The experience was quite new to me, however. I remember it with some clarity—the feeling that I was so much meat being prepared and served up. Men shave every day and, I expect, get used to it. But for a girl . . . It was a way of preparing me for what was to come. It made me conscious of myself, of my body. The area was quite sensitive and I had . . . razor-burn. Is that the word? Yes, obviously. Later on, the next couple of days, there was a mild tingling feeling he would have adored, if he'd known about it.

But most of all, I think, it was an expression of my mother's complicity, which is to say her approval. It is unusual, still, for girls to feel their mothers are kindly disposed toward expressions of their sexuality, particularly their earliest experiments and explorations. It was even more unusual, not to say peculiar, back then in Victoria's reign. It was of inestimable value for me to have that burden of guilt so efficiently lifted from my frail shoulders. Indeed, it sometimes occurs to me that the one I ought primarily to thank for my good fortune in sexual matters is not Lewis Carroll at all but my mother, whose preparation and support were there to help me when I needed them. And are still there, and always will be.

He was clearly a snob. One got that right away from the way he talked and held himself. It was a defense for him, or even a weapon, to disdain what was threatening to him. Or, for all I know, he was actually convinced of his superiority —as a lot of Christ Church men are said to be.

My mother, then, prepared me with a wardrobe of new clothes and new underwear. It was an investment, but it had a personal quality, too. These were things for me to wear, to be pretty in . . . Later on, I came to realize, as many women do, that an investment in clothing and jewelry and underwear, particularly underwear, can be exactly that—an investment made with the confident expectation of a profitable return.

But to continue, he picked me up at the appointed time and took me by train to Eastbourne where he had engaged rooms for the season, in a house on Lushington Road. It was close to the seaside, I remember. We arrived late in the evening. The beach I only saw the next day and, because that was a Sunday, I didn't get to step into the water and actually feel it until Monday. I was terribly disappointed and had to conceal my impatience. I think now that it worked out extremely well for me, much better than I could have known at the time. He was a gentle man, kind—fundamentally—and because we were so late in getting there on Saturday evening, he helped me unpack, gave me something to eat, and put me to bed, leaving me alone. The next day, the worst attentions I had to endure were his insistence that I accompany him to two church services. It was the Lord's day, and he took that most seriously, leaving me alone again afterwards.

As a matter of fact, I suppose he must have planned it that way, working out in advance how the circumstances would compel him to be as circumspect and gradual as he intended to be. I'm sure of it. He always planned ahead that way, putting coins in various pockets and in various compartments, in exactly the right denominations for all the eventualities of a journey. He treated a simple trip from Oxford down to London with a kind of forethought and planning that seemed almost compulsive. So in an encounter to which he had probably given particular attention, it is only reasonable to expect that the same sort of intelligence was operating. I'm convinced the timing had been worked out way ahead, during that week . . . Or long before he had ever met me, on other occasions, with other young girls.

For all I know, the entire routine had been developing for years, evolving with each performance as he modified and improved his moves according to the reactions of his audience. But I doubt it. In order to think that, it is necessary to suppose a flexibility and a range I don't believe he had. He found his possibilities more constricted and limited than most people do. His fascination with dentistry, for instance, was unlikely to have been worked out for its effect on young female friends, but there it was. He believed in oral hygiene, care of the teeth and gums . . . It sounds funny, but he wasn't funny about it at all. And I expect that some of his young ladies may really have required dental care. Perhaps this had shocked him so much that he repeated the visits to the dentist with all his subsequent child friends. I don't think I ever visited him at Eastbourne without his taking me to the dentist.

Penetration? Was that what he liked to watch? He came into the room, stood there, and gazed as the dentist put those tools into our little mouths, stuck in his fingers, peered with mirrors. Lewis Carroll stood quietly against the wall, watching the examination and the treatment, barely symbolic proceedings. Still, there may have been a number of girls whose cavities he caused to be discovered and filled, whose teeth he helped to preserve . . . Maybe one little girl had some kind of bad breath because of dental neglect . . .

But whatever interpretation you want to put on the dentistry, there were other kinds of attention that could not have been seductive or deliberately planned to get around our objections or fears. His churchgoing was stern and serious. The walks which he made us take with him, for very great distances, all the way to Hastings once to see the battleground . . . There was nothing seductive about those walks. On those long, rather dull exercises, done for their physical benefits, he never stopped to admire a tree or flower or picturesque building. We were quite exhausted. At any rate, I was. I ached; my feet and legs were in torment.

And the lessons. He was a mathematician, of course, and he insisted on sharing his mathematical skills with us. He treated it as if it were a game, but that doesn't mean he didn't take it seriously. He was as serious about games as about anything in life. He used to teach me theorems from Euclid, making me learn the proofs and making sure that I understood the logic by which they had been reached. The effect of this teaching, combined with the dentistry and the exercise and the prayers, was to assert his authority and to establish my acceptance of that authority.

Whether it was part of a whole choreographed routine or not (and I don't think it was), it did have its effect. More particularly, it had a very considerable effect on those of us who were susceptible to what you might call the schoolgirl crush, the kind of emotion—very strong sometimes—a girl may feel for a teacher in school, or for a director in a theater. The object of this emotional outpouring is invariably older, old enough to be the girl's father. And the emotion is some sort of halfway thing between the love one feels for a father and that one feels for a lover. It is as if he had the secret of changing size, the way Alice does early on in the book. He could be grown-up and fatherly, and he could shrink suddenly to the playfulness and spontaneity of a child.

Not that he was alone in this. He was the first man I knew to have that talent, but I've met others, since then. Indeed, I look for that quality, the ability to be boyish, to be infantile even, particularly in bed. Frank Barclay, the man I live with now, continually delights by being whatever age he feels like, matching my mood or contrasting with it, surprising me. But that is perhaps beside the point. Or beyond the point, several points down the line. (Carroll was a stickler for accuracy, particularly when it came to geometry.)

What woman, what girl, what female of any age or condition does not dream of having the question taken from her, her responsibilities for choosing this man or that assumed for her? The cliché about the handsome man who sweeps you off your feet means just that, that he takes the choice from you and exercises it himself, while you are thrilled, liberated, and delighted!

That was what Lewis Carroll was able to do, not even aware of what he was doing or how he was managing it. He exercised that grand authority. And my mother had pretty much endorsed his authority, hadn't she? So that when he asked me to pose for him, so that he could sketch, I agreed. Of course I agreed. He had taken me to walk on the beach, to church, to the dentist's . . . And each of these was a kind of whimsical choice of his that I didn't think to question. Why should I question his request that I get dressed as a Chinaman? He had costumes, not so many as he had at Oxford, but a few, for me to change into. And that was, I believe, deliberate, the result of experience and calculation. He established that we were play-acting, that it was a kind of game of dress-up. Or undress-up. For he had me change from one costume to another, as he sat there. And he helped me with some of the buttons that went up and down the back and were very tiny indeed. It was hardly a great step from one costume to another. Or from costume to no costume.

And as far as I can remember, he hardly touched me during the first couple of sessions. He might arrange the disposition of an arm or adjust my posture or the way my head was held, but that all seemed to be a part of the proper business of sketching. I used to think that this restraint was for my benefit, or in a more general way a calculated gradualness, so as not to frighten his models, whoever we were. But I have come to understand that he was the greater beneficiary of this policy. He was pleasing himself, as some exquisite sensualists learn to do, getting the greatest possible delight from each deliberate step in the increasingly familiar pattern. He had been there before, knew what to look forward to, understood that it would happen, and therefore could afford to give his full attention to each of these preliminary phases. He liked to look at us, adored the sight of our bodies, was happy staring at us in much the same way that a connoisseur of paintings or miniature bronzes is happy caressing a favorite object with his eyes.

I posed, held the pose he wanted, and of course was glad when he took a break. He intended this, I'm sure. That part, I am quite certain, was the result of practice—that there should be a break which should be the occasion of biscuits and milk, the reward for those long dull minutes of holding the pose. The self-consciousness some of his young models might have felt at the beginning would be gone by this time, as mine was; there was nothing more natural than to wander over from the little platform he'd set up for the pose to the table where the biscuits were, without any detour for a robe or a dress . . . It was the most natural thing to forget about clothes, as one does after a remarkably short time, and just go and eat those lovely biscuits in the shape of leaves with a thin coating of chocolate over them . . .

And to sit on his lap while eating? That, too, seemed altogether natural to a little child whose whole life had been spent being caressed and hugged and petted. Little children have this ease, and some of us regain it when we grow older, having lost it when we wanted it most. And what we regain is only an imperfect copy of that spontaneity that once blessed our lives, a faint likeness of that easiness of being in the world of bodies . . . Girls of better families would have been even more at ease than I, having been kept in more of a state of ignorance about sexual matters, so that it wouldn't even occur to them to question the propriety of what they were doing or the motives of the man who had invited them to climb onto his lap.

I might not have known, myself, or might not have made the connection if I had not been through that peculiar ritual before setting out for this excursion—I mean my having been shaved. I knew rather more than some of you protected young ladies would have known, having had the chance to witness more in the greenrooms and behind the flats of some of the theaters. It is not quite the orgy people of fashion generally suppose, but the theater does have its interestingly uninhibited participants. Even a child hears and occasionally sees things. So I knew a little more than some girls of the age I was pretending to be. I knew enough to be able to identify an erection. More important, I knew enough to be flattered by one.

"REALLY!"

Isa wasn't actually surprised. But exasperated. The two of them were alone. There was no reason for pretense any more. How could this old woman continue to behave as though she were still the little girl of the storybook? Or as if Queen Victoria were still sitting on the throne.

"Yes, really."

"You seem to take a perverse pleasure in turning everything sordid. Your relationship with Carroll and, by extension, mine. It's just not so."

"It's all perfectly true, whether you're willing to face it or not. What Glenda Fenwick and I experienced may or may not have anything to do with your dealings with the man. But it was the same man. And this was what Reginald wanted to hear about. He thought it was interesting enough and that it somehow bore on his own perception of Carroll.

If nothing else, it illuminates something about his partiality for young girls."

"I don't see," said Alice, "that there is any absolute necessity for such physicality in your account."

"We live physical lives. We experience the world and each other in physical ways. I don't see any particular reason to avoid or deny that."

"You wouldn't, would you."

"And yet, if it is truly too disagreeable for you to hear, I could invent something more palatable. Or terminate the account?"

Alice thought for only a moment. "No, no. Go on."

I AM NAKED, YES? Sitting on his lap, I am naked and feel his erection under me. Isn't that where I was? But it is difficult to remember what I thought and felt back then because there were so many other occasions, so many re-enactments at other times over the years. We conspired in our imposture, he and I. I continued to play an eleven-year-old girl, long after it was obvious that I was a young woman, and Carroll went along, conspiring in the deception. It was a willing suspension of disbelief—isn't that the phrase? I remember sitting on his lap later on, and feeling that same rigidity, but knowing how complicated a combination of joy and shame it produced in him. I'd have been glad to soothe his hurts, to assure him that it was all right, that it wasn't terrible. But he couldn't ever have accepted such assurance from a little girl. I would have projected myself into the role of a mature woman, even of a motherly woman, had I attempted to say such things to him. And that would have broken the fragile threads of fantasy and deceit by which we were connected to each other.

My impression of that original moment is blurred by later moments, but I must have behaved properly—I mean in a way that accorded with his wishes or needs. My recollection is clear enough about realizing the condition in which he found himself. And I think that he put me down again, back onto the posing platform. Or I think so. He might have told me to get dressed. At any rate, he disappeared into the next room for a fresh piece of charcoal. Some such pretext. It was almost certainly to masturbate.

I assume so, basing my assumption on later experience. For most of the girls he managed to get to pose for him, either for his photographs or for his sketches, I think that was pretty much the extent of his molestation—getting the little girl to disrobe, kissing and holding her as she sat on his lap, and then going off to another room. It was hardly likely to cause much of a psychological disturbance. Some of the girls might not even have known what was going on. I was aware because I was older than most of his child friends and because I'd led a different kind of life. And I was aware of the possibilities, because my own mother had shaved me.

Otherwise, that week, that first visit to Eastbourne was a great treat for me. He behaved oddly, walking a lot and having this obsession with dentistry, but most children will tell you that most adults are odd. They do curious things for improbable reasons or no reasons at all. Children are very logical; having no experience in the world to go on, they rely on logic. The logician in Carroll was therefore bound to appeal to children. He understood that they use logic all the time, needing it, and delighting in it when it works. Or, without understanding that, he was merely lucky, fortunate that his peculiarity happened to fit the requirements of his peculiar audience. That would be the Darwinian explanation, wouldn't it? They'd consider him a strange mutant who had a useful adaptation for his unusual environmental requirements.

I couldn't begin to guess, and it wouldn't matter anyway. The point is that he was perfectly well fitted, either by luck or design or mere ardor, to talk to young girls in their own language. I felt as though I had a best friend, a person who was both a playmate and, by some funny imposture, large enough to pass for grown-up in the outside world.

The posing and the extremely diffident sexual advances did not take up that much of our time or of my attention. I'd expect he thought more of this aspect of our friendship than I did. It would have been like a subtle wash of rose-colored light on the stage to give a warmth and set the mood . . . What I told my mother, then, was largely about the parts of the week that had meant most to me. The seashore and the expanse of all that sand and water, the way it stretched off as far as one could see . . . That was new to me. And the fireworks at night, they were fun. I'd seen fireworks before, but not often, and these were very good. And Carroll's harmless peculiarities—the trips to the dentist and the long walks. I told her much of that. Toward the end of my recitation, I mentioned the sketching—which I had to do in order to avoid arousing her suspicions. After all, Mr. Carroll had told her in advance that he planned to draw me from life.

"He didn't bother you in any way?" my mother asked me.

"No, not at all," I said, quite truthfully.

She was relieved, absolved from complicity in any misfortune. I expect she had been more worried than she let on to me. But she had what she wanted, if it came to that. She had something to bargain with, not necessarily to use as blackmail but something that could be used . . . That would be in the back of her mind and in the back of his, later on, when she would ask him for a larger part in the next production of the dramatic version of *Alice*.

That was what she had had in mind from the beginning, from the first sign of Lewis Carroll's interest in me. I didn't have this in mind, myself, or wasn't aware of it in the way she was. I expected . . . good things, a good time and a good future. Nothing particular either way. I never defined my expectations, but there was a kind of confidence, an assurance that something good would happen, that good meals, interesting amusements, and the rest of it would be somehow provided, that I was entitled to them. This is the secret of the successful courtesan or demimondaine . . . Whatever you like to call these women. The best of them have no set price, but a more general confidence that tribute will be paid, a sense of their own worth that never wavers.

It isn't stupidity, but a kind of innocence. These women —and I don't actually include myself in the group—are like guests at a little girl's birthday party. They are so pleased with themselves and their pretty party dresses and they know how charming they are . . .

I was never one of these women, mostly because of the turns my life has taken at critical moments. My marriage. Or my liaisons . . . These have been rather more long-term than a true courtesan would permit.

Indeed, I've paid out as often as I've been rewarded. Not in money, but in . . . jewelry, for example, that discreet currency of the *beau monde*.

Still, I think I have come close enough to that kind of life to see how it works and what it requires. And I was never so good at it or so natural about it as I was that first time I visited Lewis Carroll at Eastbourne.

Later on, we were both carefully re-creating that first time. Going beyond it in some ways, we still kept to its tones and lines, as actors will keep to the blocking and pace of their rehearsals throughout a long run.

At any rate, that's what I was doing. What he was doing may have been even more complicated. He was looking at me but seeing you—whose part I was playing, that being the reward my mother had managed to extract if not extort from him. The next Christmas, when the play was revived for its holiday run, I had the lead. I was Alice. Offstage, I was Alice, too. He called me that, sometimes. Not always, you understand. I was often Isa. But when he wanted me to be particularly his, when he wanted to be secretive or intimate, when he was like a child with a special password, then he would call me Alice.

I didn't mind. I was rather flattered by it. Only later on did I realize that there was a real-life Alice, a real girl for whom he had written the story in the first place. And only much later did I begin to wonder whether that little girl also took off her pretty party dress for him and sat on his lap while he held her in his arms and stroked the skin of her back.

I was so interested in the things I was feeling, in the way I could get excited by these things, that I hardly gave much thought to him or what he was feeling . . . Or what he was thinking about. Or whom he was thinking about.

You, of course. But after a while, me too. Both of us together. A dream creature, made up partly of you, partly of me, partly of a dozen other little girls, and partly from the fantasies and the obsessions of Carroll himself.

There was no cause, at any rate, for me to resent what he was doing. Or feel jealousy.

No real cause, then or later.

During those later meetings, those re-enactments of that first visit, we stretched as far as possible the gauzy veil of innocence, either at Eastbourne at his old rooms there, or up at Oxford where I sometimes visited him. We each pretended not to know what the other was doing. I would sit on his lap, riding his knee in a parody of a child's game of horsey. Inadvertently, accidentally, I would contrive to rub against his erect penis, not so much to excite him to a conclusion, nor even to make it clear that I was intentionally stimulating him, but . . . in a light, teasing, apparently unthinking way. That's what he liked more than anything. And to hold me, his fingers and thumbs almost girdling my waist so that he was aware of my slenderness, my youth. He closed his eyes, showing a smile of such beatitude as would look quite reasonable on a cherub's face, and was content to sit that way for . . . for as long as I'd allow it.

It was heaven for him. And I was it. So I was heaven. It sounds foolish put that way, in a syllogism, but it was in that lucid form that I made the connection, using his model for logical thinking. I have carried that conviction of my worth, my value, my power, ever since. It is a wonderful thing for a girl or a woman to have. It frees one. It freed me, certainly, allowing me the confidence to show affection without the fear of rebuff or rejection. It is exactly that kind of fear that cripples most people, forcing them to hide their feelings, to seem cold when they're warm, indifferent when they are ardent.

It is more valuable, I think, even than beauty, this self-confidence, this self-esteem. With that, one can turn one's attention, generously and affectionately, upon whatever person in whatever situation—and, more likely than not, attention is going to be reciprocated. Interest will be repaid with interest, and delight will produce delight.

Even when my acting career has been in difficult straits, when my purse has been empty and my lodgings modest, I've always had the inner wealth of knowing who I was and of liking myself, so that I could get dressed, go out into the town, and be welcomed the way people welcome a spring breeze or a bouquet of flowers.

My mother, I think, assumed he had deflowered me. By the end of the time that we spent together, when I was seventeen or so and admitting to fifteen, she drew the reasonable inference that he had finally managed to seduce me. She assumed he must have done so.

Of course, he never did. He'd have hated me and himself as well, would have turned away from me, avoiding me

. . . As he never did. He wanted to, but even more he wanted not to, was afraid of what that would require him to admit about himself. It was an issue we managed to avoid together, and our conspiracy to avoid it was one more bond between us.

It was impossible to maintain this conspiracy of deception forever. It seems remarkable that we managed to prolong it as long as we did. Toward the end, when it began to look a bit peculiar for an unaccompanied young lady to visit a single gentleman that way, he arranged for lodgings for me in town, close by Christ Church, but that was the only practical adjustment he had to make. It was a bit more complicated for me. As the years passed, the preparations I had to make became more and more elaborate. I had to shave under my arms as well as at my pubic area. I had to schedule my visits to accommodate a menstrual cycle that had begun by then to operate and would have intimidated him. All of that was acceptable, seemed a perfectly reasonable price for me to pay for the reward of his attention and affection. In a way, I think I have never been so much adored by anyone else.

Not that it was a perfect idyll. We were only human, and had our frailties. I chafed and fretted under some of the restrictions of the rules of our game. I wanted to be loved for myself—whatever that means. I wanted to be accepted for what I was, without the bother of having to oblige. It is a silly idea, and there is not much comfort in the consideration that nearly everyone else I know has been seized by it at one time or another. Even the smartest of us. Especially the smartest. Carroll was right about that, too. Love can turn theoretical and intellectual at any instant and destroy itself that way, if only you give it the chance.

I wanted him to love me as a young woman. And of course, he couldn't. So I found a way to punish him for this failure—that he couldn't help and regretted more than I did. If I regret anything at all of what happened between us, I regret only the way I punished him at the end, bringing my fiancé up to Oxford to call on him.

Not that anybody said anything. We were all much too civilized for that. Still, my intentions were unmistakable, and he saw them at once. What I was saying when I introduced George to him—that was George Bacchus, who was to become my husband and technically still is—was that we had been lying, Carroll and I. And that the lie was no good any more. I was not a little girl. In other words, I was saying he wasn't good enough for me, wasn't . . . man enough for me. Which seems now both inescapable and extremely cruel. I was taunting him for the weaknesses he knew well and had contrived to live with, just barely. I betrayed him. All the games and nonsense, all the delights of that artificial childhood he had created for both of us to hide in, I turned over, just as Alice does in the end, saying "You're nothing but a pack of cards." If I remember correctly, she has grown to her full size again, in that very sentence.

Terrible. And prophetic. Because Alice—you, the real Alice—could not possibly have done any such thing at the time he wrote that. You were still in real life a little girl.

But he could see what was coming and would have to happen, even under the most favorable conditions, assuming the most compliant kind of reality, eagerly adapting itself to his fantasies. As I was. As we tried to do.

Until the end. Even then, the thing I suppose I wanted was not really to hurt him but to . . . to nudge him, make him stand up, look at George, about whom I had mixed feelings even then, and tell George that he couldn't have me. I wanted Lewis Carroll to claim me for himself, to accept me as I was, to adapt to me as I had been adapting to him. Because I loved him. Even then, in that room at that moment, with my fiancé on my left and Lewis Carroll on the right, it was to my right that I gazed with rapt attention, understanding, concern—and with love. I absolutely loved seeing the way he had turned formal, properly Oxonian, ceremonious. It was the very opposite of what he was like— or had been like—when we had been alone together. He was a little boy playing grown-up. It was entirely convincing, except for the fact that I knew better. And he knew I knew.

George had been at Merton, and although he had heard of the Reverend Mr. Dodgson and knew who Lewis Carroll was—as everyone did—they had never met.

He gave us tea. We were in his rooms, and he made tea but didn't swing the pot around like a censer, the way he had in the old days, when we were alone. The conversation was strained and stilted, about the weather and the long vac coming up . . . If you hadn't known any of us before, it might have seemed perfectly natural. But he never looked at me. He avoided me the whole time, talking to George as if George were the old boy who'd come back to introduce the girl he'd found and was going to marry. That was the odd game they were playing, and I watched, knowing how false it was and feeling in the falsity the reverberations of what was really happening, even though no one was in a position to admit it.

His response, really, to my announcement that I had grown up was this charade by which he claimed to have grown up too. And I think it was surprising. I was surprised to see how very well he managed, almost frightened by it. As I think he expected me to be.

After a certain point, there is only the choice between hurting each other and nothing at all. Of the two, the hurting seems somehow preferable.

George, meanwhile, was infuriatingly oblivious. He sat there swilling tea and talked about rowing as if the rest of the world hardly mattered. I had the awful feeling we were all at a funeral—which of course we were—and that the conversation was all wrong, too frivolous and loud.

At the end of a visit of perhaps three quarters of an hour, I could no longer stand it. I made some excuse which George picked up on, thank God, and we made our moves to leave. The Reverend Mr. Dodgson couldn't have been more gracious. "It was so good of you to have brought your young man to see me. It was very kind of you to call. All happiness, all good wishes. Congratulations."

He shook hands with George, and made a little bow to me. By that formality he seemed to be saying that if I could pretend nothing had happened, why so could he. If he had meant so little to me, then I meant no more to him. He would forget what I seemed to want to forget.

It was as if he expected exactly this, had been waiting for it all along. Had been through it before, time after time. Perhaps he had.

But not, I think, quite in this way. I may not have been the first of his child friends, but I think our relationship went further than any of the others, developed more richly, and lasted longer. And risked more.

He died the following year. After that dreadful afternoon, I never saw him again or even exchanged letters. There was no word at all, not even when I sent him an announcement of the birth of a daughter. Nor three months later, when the little girl died. I'd called her Alice, in spite of George's objections. But if I'd called her anything else, it wouldn't have helped. She'd still have died. George would still have decided that I was . . . to use his words, "sexually voracious." He fled from that, taking to easy women. Easier than I, that is. We were already separated by the time Carroll died. I was living alone, on my own, trying to re-establish myself in the theater, trying to get those adult parts that were so difficult for me to come by. My sister Nellie always had better luck as a grown woman, even though I had been the more successful child actress. I've never been able to decide whether that reversal of fortunes was finally fair or unfair. Unfair, I think, more than not.

Of course, when they asked me to, I wrote the book. I had to, for the money, to pay for rent and clothing and other such necessities as you and Reginald never had to think about. It was difficult for me to do because I don't write easily and, as you can imagine, I had to keep more of the story out of the book than I was putting into it. The publishers were disappointed. I was afraid they'd scrap the whole project. I had to accept it, then, when they put that false claim on the cover. It never crossed my mind that you'd be offended, though. It was all so long ago—for both of us. We had a certain girlish charm once, but it goes. And if we are to be anything at all as human beings, other aspects of ourselves must come into play. Our intelligence, our taste, our sexuality, our character . . . all the things that people who love you love you for. All the things you think of as your inmost self.

I have been living with Frank Barclay now for some years, in an informal way. We have our eccentricities, but I trust him to . . . know me. As Carroll never knew me. Carroll never really knew anyone—you, me, or any of the others. There was a type he liked, and he selected it from the little girls who happened to pass by. I used to think I was imitating you, but what I was really doing was conforming to his requirements, which is what you were lucky enough to do. And we outgrew those requirements, as he never could. He couldn't grow at all.

Only surreptitiously, pretending not to notice, with a naked little girl sitting on his lap . . .

"Is it absolutely necessary to reduce all experience to a few crude drives?" Alice asked.

"Not at all," Isa answered. "But one must acknowledge that those basic drives are there, operating in however complicated a way. To deny anything so fundamental is to reduce life, I should think. To censor it."

"I know, I know. I've heard all that before. It doesn't impress me. It's supposed to be enlightened but seems to me benighted and slavish. Beastly, in the strict sense of the word."

"Why must we make any judgment at all? It was what happened. It's the truth. What Reginald wanted to know was what happened to Glenda Fenwick and to me, how it affected us, and how it influenced our lives later on. I told him. You wanted to know what I told him, so I told you. Out of friendliness, and because of the coincidence in which both of us happened to have been friends of Lewis Carroll. It doesn't give you the warrant to judge me," Isa said. "If anything, the reverse is true. I have been entirely open with you. You should appreciate that."

"The implication is that Reginald was interested in these personal revelations because he saw in them some suggestion about my experience with Carroll, isn't that so?"

"Not necessarily."

"Of course it is," Alice insisted. "Why else would he have cared?"

"Because he hated Carroll," Isa retorted. "Because of what he believed Carroll had done to you."

"And what would that be?"

"I have no idea," Isa said. "I'd have supposed that you knew. His frequent visits to Glenda Fenwick must be an indication of something less than perfect harmony that obtained between you."

"This Glenda Fenwick is . . . ?"

"A madam. A brothel keeper. Formerly, she was, herself, a prostitute. Evidently, she and your late husband were old friends."

"I'm not surprised," Alice said. "I knew, of course, that there were some such connections in my late husband's life. He never spoke of them to me. But I think he knew I was aware of that possibility. And that I had no particular objection to make."

"But *he* disliked it," Isa said. "He disliked himself for it, and resented having to go there."

"Perhaps," Alice admitted.

Isa was surprised at her visitor's refusal to flinch. Or was it a refusal to understand the challenge?

Alice touched her fingertips to her forehead. "If so," she said, "I am sorry for it. Sorry for him, I should say. As I imagine you were sorry when your husband—George?—left you. People are not necessarily suited in their appetites. But there are other things that make a marriage. Allowances must be made. Otherwise, what is to become of the family? What is to become of society?"

"I'm not sure that I care," Isa said, as brave as Alice.

"I do. Not that it makes very much difference. Finally, we do what our feelings tell us. Our convictions, I should say. There is less conscious choosing than one might like, in a reasonable world. But it isn't, is it? A reasonable world, I mean."

"No."

"I am sorry to hear what became of Carroll toward the end. He was not like that when I knew him. And I am sorry to hear that Reginald had . . . second thoughts. It always seemed to me a great convenience that Carroll was there for him to blame. It was so much easier than having to blame himself. Or me. As if blame had anything to do with it."

"I agree with you," Isa said. "Which surprises me."

"Why should it?" Alice asked sharply. "You didn't know what I think."

"I supposed, from having met Reginald . . ."

Alice waved her hand. "He was a sweet man, but he was depressed when you met him. He was dying and knew it. That casts a kind of shadow over some people's thinking."

"And then, of course, I expected you to dislike me," Isa said. "That casts a shadow, too."

"I grumped a bit when your book came out," Alice said, "but that was so long ago. It was another world. I've lost two sons and a husband since then. I have different ideas about what's important."

"I'm glad," Isa said.

"I must be going," Alice announced.

"You'll let me know when you'll be coming into town again?" Isa asked.

"Of course," Alice said. "Although these trips are not frequent."

"I understand."

Alice stood. Isa stood and showed her to the door. The two women gazed at one another. "Good-bye, then," Alice said.

"Good-bye."

After Alice had left, Isa poured herself a small glass of gin from the bottle in the kitchen, swallowed it down in two gulps, and gasped with the rawness of it. The woman had come to find out what Isa had told Reginald, yes. But also what Reginald had told Isa. And, most important, whether Isa was any sort of threat to her. Satisfied that she was safe enough, Alice had taken her leave.

Isa doubted that they'd ever see one another again.

Later that evening, thinking about it, Isa was surprised to find that she rather liked Alice—not because Alice was likeable but because she was tough. Realistic. A grown-up, free of illusion. She was more grown-up than Reginald had been, but then women, Isa believed, were generally more grown-up than men. Or was that an impression she had carried on into her adult life from that first long connection of her girlhood, her connection with Carroll? She had known him well enough to be able to understand how he could hide in nonsense, how he could fend off the importunate or distressing realities of adult life by interposing his desperate inventions, his buttered mice for breakfast, his rat-tail jelly, his boiled pelican. She had laughed at these extravagances and he had laughed with her, and it had been good fun, surely. But there was rage, too, a protest at the good manners that required of well-behaved boys and girls that they eat whatever was set before them. He felt put-upon still, one of those children to whom an enormous portion of something more or less revolting had been presented. Food, or drink, or sex . . .

She remembered her impulse, stronger and stronger toward the end, to comfort him, to mother him, in just the way he'd have found least acceptable. She had wanted to hold him as the child he kept trying to be. But he'd been afraid, unable to move forward or back, in either of which conditions he could have rested his head upon her meager bosom. She sighed. She picked up the telephone and called Breezy to accept his invitation. It would be a drunken and disreputable party, and she knew that she was accepting for the wrong reasons, but she knew, too, that such invitations do not always arrive when one needs them. That was part of being a grown-up too, being able to face unpleasant truths about the world and one's prospects.

SHE KNEW WHERE SHE WAS. She could feel with peculiar clarity every jolt of the train, had been sitting there on the plush train seat as if her compartment were a subtle instrument of torture, each weld in the rails working like a drop of that famous Chinese water torture. The ride from Waterloo Station had been an uninterrupted series of tiny assaults, but on the whole she supposed she was more grateful for them than not. They kept her mind from gnawing on itself, distracting her from the emotional distress that she otherwise would have been experiencing. She looked out of the window and saw a town, a collection of gray buildings huddled together under a lowering sky. Basingstoke, most probably. It had been about an hour since the train had left London. A lifetime, it seemed.

She had suspected that it would turn out this way. She had told herself that she was venturing forth into the enemy's lair in order to judge the seriousness of the threat Isa Bowman might one day pose, but she had been fooling herself. What had really drawn her to Isa had been curiosity, about Isa and about the last days of Regi's life. Now she knew enough to feel bereft—that was exactly the word—of both her husband and her enemy. She had no one to love, no one to hate. Her life was ebbing away, exposing the most unpredictable rock formations that for years had lain below the surface. She could take a grim satisfaction from staring at them, even though they weren't pretty.

Sooner or later, she'd be obliged to sell. She knew that. To put her trust in Caryl was absurd. He was a decent boy, a sweet young man, but with no head for practical details. And she could not trust him to resist the temptations to sentimentality or to grand gestures that were sure to arise. In order to get the money the manuscript was worth, she'd have to sell it herself. Caryl would be likely to give it away. Or to get swindled out of it somehow. Only she had the necessary toughness to make them pay. She was just like Isa, then, wasn't she? Turn it into money and let it go!

Reginald had left it for her to deal with because he knew she would rather do it alone. He had, in his very considerate way, made the necessary inquiries to satisfy himself that she would not be in actual want, but out of delicacy he had never discussed his findings with her. What a considerate and dear man he'd been! What a good person.

There were tears coursing down her face. She reached

into her soft leather handbag and found a handkerchief with which to blot them. The other passengers in the compartment were looking away, avoiding any acknowledgment of her presence, as if she had some terrible disfiguring disease. She dried her eyes, composed herself, and stared out of the window.

It *was* a disease, she thought. Or it was like a disease. One of those very complicated illnesses in which one went along for a time, unknowingly incubating whatever it was, and then, months or years later, suddenly blossomed forth with fevers and chills. That early period of silent incubation was childhood. And the rest, the fever and chills, the taint of it all—that was life.

The tears, however, were not for herself. She was weeping mostly for Reginald, whom she missed sorely. He had busied himself out there in the orangery, fussing with his seedlings and saplings, and all that time he had been showing her the very same patient care, the same attentive tact. He had hated Carroll on her behalf, and he'd never had any idea about the break that had come about between Carroll and herself. No one who was still alive knew about that.

She thought of her sisters, Lorina and Edith, and remembered how it had happened. No word of that, no reference however oblique, had she been able to detect from Isa Bowman. So Carroll had never told her. The three little Liddells were safe with their secret—or, as their father would have thought of it, their honor.

Poor Edith. She'd been dead now fifty years. She was the one Regi should have talked to. If there was a heaven with spirits in it that had anything to do with the lives they had lived on earth, perhaps her sister and Regi would have that talk after all. At last, Edith could soothe the man's mind, ease his pain, and let him understand that there had never been cause for jealousy or hatred, there had been no need for him to resent Carroll so bitterly.

It had begun to get dark. She could see her reflection in the window glass. She looked awfully old. She was tired and had been crying, of course, but that was not a sufficient explanation. Really, she was surprised each time she passed a looking glass to find that she had grown up, grown old, was no longer that young girl to whom, quite arbitrarily, Carroll had tethered her in his looking glass. She had fought it or had tried to ignore it, but there was a part of her that was really arrested there and could not let go of him or of Edith. It was the most Wonderland-ish aspect of her life, the way time had been interrupted. It was always tea time in the story, and the clocks had stopped. In Alice's life, too, there was that same suspension of the passage of time. The face she saw was that of a stranger, an imposter.

The train arrived at last at Southampton, and Odell was waiting with the Rolls. Alice supposed she might sell that, too. That or the Thorneycroft. According to Regi's will, the cars were hers to dispose of. She didn't need two of them.

Rhoda was waiting for her, had been distressed at Alice's insistence on going to London alone, even affronted by this lack of trust. Alice had tried to explain that it was simply something that had to be done by herself, like going to the bathroom.

"People sometimes have help, going to the bathroom," Rhoda had argued.

"I am not an invalid," Alice had told her, closing the subject. Now that she had completed her journey, however, she could tell Rhoda about it, at least a little of it. She recounted the essentials of her interview with the man at Sotheby's. And she told her sister that she had paid a call to Isa Bowman.

Rhoda was astonished. "Why would you do a thing like that?"

"Because Regi visited her, shortly before he died."

"Oh?"

"They talked about Carroll," Alice said.

"Well, of course they talked about Carroll. But . . . how odd! After all that time."

"Why was it odd? He was dying. He knew it."

Rhoda stared into the fireplace where a small fire was burning. "It still bothered him?"

Alice nodded.

"He loved you a great deal," Rhoda said.

Alice nodded again. "I know," she said. The tears welled up again. She rose, crossed to the doorway, and left the room.

Upstairs, she got hold of herself. She was well satisfied that she had drawn the curtain so that Rhoda's curiosity would not be troublesome. She had not actually lied to Rhoda, but the effect was much the same. The tears had even been real.

For Edith, there were no tears. That was an older and more serious difference, and it was a real question in Alice's mind whether, after all this time, she ought to be begging Edith's pardon or Edith begging hers. The trouble with the dead is that they are so intransigent. One talks and talks to them, but they will not budge, not an inch. They will not forgive or forget. They won't even acknowledge one's own forgiveness if one contrives to offer it to them, as Alice had, many times.

It was Edith, more than Lewis Carroll, who had caught her there, tethered her to that single summer's day. Not the manuscript or the story it contained, or even the teller of the tale, but little Edith. Poor dear.

Also, a bitch, of course. But one could love a bitchy sister. Had she lived, Alice thought, they might have made it up. She liked to think so.

3

IT WASN'T JUST A PIECE of rotten luck. Good breeding required one to refer to it that way, but Caryl felt it to be something more. The understated, offhanded description of bad luck did not convey anything of his sense of destiny. Englishmen weren't supposed to be creatures of destiny, which was for eastern Europeans, for the grotesques Dostoevsky and such writers loved to describe. Still, Caryl was convinced, absurdly, that his misfortunes were somehow necessary, had been fated.

He was enough of a rationalist to understand how probabilities of the future become inexorabilities of the past. But he also knew the limits of rationalism. He knew that if he blamed his broker, his banker, his friends who had passed on the tip, there would still be an insufficiency that could only be made up by his own admission that anything he tried would come to ruin, if only because there was a part of him that expected it to do so. Dame Fortune was a fickle debutante sometimes, and if you failed in self-assurance she'd turn you down flat, walk away in the middle of one of your carefully rehearsed sentences, and finish the evening with your best friend.

He'd been right, though, to plunge. People with bad luck can't assume a long run of success. The most they can hope for is a quick killing, a moment of relenting on the part of the gods or demons whose business it is to persecute them. Get in, get out, and get going. What Caryl had done, then, was to buy on margin one of those speculative issues that was supposed to go up sharply, to double in a month. The fix was in. Private information was going around. It couldn't help but be a good thing. He'd sunk eight thousand pounds into it, which on margin meant that he had eighty thousand pounds' worth of this sure thing. If it doubled, the way his friends promised, he'd have nearly ninety thousand pounds net. He'd be set for life, get out, never play the market again, live a quiet life, and hope that the displeasure of his demons might subside after his brief moment of defiance.

The demons, however, had been more vigilant than Caryl had expected. They'd allowed the issue to rise in price just enough to lend an air of probability to the assurances of his friends, but not enough to tempt Caryl to sell out. Then, suddenly, trading was suspended. Some government committee was looking into the question of manipulation—which Caryl knew to be the knell of all his hopes. There were a few warnings issued, a handful of official reprimands. Trading was resumed, but the price had fallen. There was a margin call for more money, which Caryl could not provide. Could not and would not. He was unlucky, but not stupid or suicidal. He knew it was over. The cost had been all of his eight-thousand-pound investment. A sobering thing to face, it was also oddly reassuring. He would have had trouble identifying with success, wearing it with comfort and assurance. But the ruin and the loss were his own, looked and felt like that perfect sports coat that fits as though it had been poured over one's body like the sauce over quenelles. He said as much to Madeleine, who was displeased.

"You oughtn't run yourself down that way," she said, lighting a cigarette and shaking the match as if she were angry at it.

"I'm not so sure I'm running myself down," Caryl told her. "If you want to know the truth, there's a little pride in it. It's what I've been trained to, after all."

"Failure?"

"Not exactly. Say, a kind of lofty indifference. Of course, the real test might have been success, which is much more difficult to be indifferent to. But it doesn't matter. It oughtn't matter."

"But how will you live?"

"I shan't starve. If worse comes to worse, I can always go back to Cuffnells and live with mother. There's plenty of room, God knows. And food. What else does one need?"

"Is that what you want to do?"

"No. Actually, I thought I'd propose marriage, first."

"To anyone special?"

"I've a list, but you're at the top of it."

She took a puff of her cigarette, exhaled a plume of smoke, and then began to laugh. "You're absurd, you know. Utterly and absolutely absurd."

"It's my charm. I make do with what I have."

"And you expect me to take that kind of proposal seriously?"

"Not really. If you can't, that's perfectly all right. It wouldn't have been a good idea for us to marry, in that case. But if you can, why I'd be pleased. I'd even see a peculiar rightness to the match, if you know what I mean."

"You're impossible."

"Yes, but that may be just what you need. All your other admirers are excessively possible and they bore you. Or they make you feel some sort of disloyalty to Felix's memory. I'm not that kind of threat."

She looked at him hard. It wasn't anger, but it was unmistakable as a warning that he was treading on dangerous ground.

"You mustn't be vexed with me," he said.

"Why not?"

"It would be in dreadful taste, I quite agree, if I were making jokes. But you see, I'm not. I'm perfectly serious. And if we're to have any sort of life together, we ought to be able to speak seriously to one another, at least upon rare occasions."

"You're serious?"

"Perfectly."

"I find that difficult to believe."

"Yes, I can see that. But, as I say, that's what gives us a way of living together, which we wouldn't have if I were another kind of man."

"Your proposal has nothing to do with your need for money. Are you going to try to persuade me of that, too?"

"I haven't suggested anything of the kind. On the contrary, I am driven to it by my need of money. I'm risking a valuable friendship, which I probably wouldn't do if I weren't forced to."

"Have you no shame?"

"Oh, yes. There are some things I won't do. I shouldn't try to borrow money from you, for one thing. And I shouldn't propose, even needing the money, if I didn't like you and think we could live together in reasonable happiness and cordiality."

"What about love?"

"Oh, Lord!"

"It's not a dirty word, Caryl."

"No? Probably not. But it's a highly charged word, which is very nearly the same thing. I've seen people ruin their lives with it, more than with sex or whiskey or horses. It's like one of those awful acids in a chemistry laboratory. All you have to do is forget yourself for a moment, and it blows up in your face. A bad business."

"I loved Felix."

"Yes, I know," Caryl said.

"It doesn't bother you."

"Not at all," Caryl said. He was tempted sorely to tell her why, to explain to her that he thought it was grotesque to be jealous of a dead person, that he'd spent most of his life watching his parents torture themselves with just such a ridiculous piece of emotional thuggery. His father's jealousy of Carroll had been absolutely hopeless and pointless and nonetheless painful. The name Caryl bore was evidence of his mother's complicity in the moral, mental, and emotional self-abuse that his father had indulged in for so long. But he didn't have the heart to pour himself out to Madeleine that way. He didn't think it would be fair, either. He didn't want to bludgeon her into accepting his proposal. Or to confide in her with these intimate revelations if she were going to refuse him. Another time, perhaps, Caryl decided.

"Let me think about it," Madeleine said.

"Certainly."

"My present inclination is to accept, but let me sleep on it for a night or two," she said.

"Alone? Or . . ."

"Of course, alone! It's the only way to decide anything important. One wakes up and the decision is made. One feels right about something or one doesn't, in that first clear light."

"I generally feel in dire need of a cup of Indian tea."

"You know what I mean," she said.

"Yes, yes, I do. I'll phone you, then, in a couple of days."

"Please. And . . . thank you."

It was her thanking him as much as anything else that confirmed what he'd already known, that she would accept his peculiar proposal. His luck or destiny or whatever one called it was as good in this sphere as it had been bad in the domain of finance. He was pleased but not at all surprised.

The only surprising thing was that he had not been thrown back upon his mother's largesse. That was what he'd most feared and therefore had come to consider as most likely. But he was off that hook, at least for a while. Madeleine's father, the general, was well enough fixed for him to live decently for years, certainly for as many years as his mother was likely to have left.

He supposed he'd have to go down to Cuffnells and tell her, but decided he could wait until Madeleine had given him her answer. He didn't want to jinx it.

ALICE WAS NOT PLEASED. She kept harping on Madeleine's age, which Caryl thought was bizarre. Alice might have been talking about breeding horses or cattle. Or royalty. What difference did it make whether he had offspring or not? Who cared? He tried to keep calm and to explain to her what was in any event quite true—that Madeleine was not so very old and could have another child or two if that was what the two of them decided they wanted. Only slowly did Caryl come to wonder what her real objection might be, what it was that bothered her but that she wouldn't talk about.

"She already has children, hasn't she?" his mother asked, as if it were some sort of disgrace.

"Yes, two boys. Pleasant little boys. They need a father."

"I dare say," Alice said.

Caryl wondered whether some whiff of Madeleine's reputation had not reached the nose of one of his mother's London friends. She wasn't in any way what Caryl thought of as notorious or disgraceful, but she was, by his mother's standards, perhaps a little negligent. "Felix was a friend of mine," he reminded her.

"Are you simply doing your duty?"

"Doing my duty to Felix? No, not at all. I like her, very much."

"Do you love her?"

"I never know what that means," Caryl said. It wasn't quite true, but he didn't want to get into some simplified version of the *Symposium* with his mother.

"Then you don't love her."

"I care for her," Caryl insisted. "And in the long run, that may be just as well. Even better, for all I know."

"Is it for the money?"

"Not really, no."

"Her father . . ."

"General Palmer," Caryl supplied the name she wanted.

"Yes, exactly. General Palmer is well off. And Madeleine is his only child."

"That's correct."

"But none of this has any particular connection to your decision to propose marriage?"

"It was a consideration, but not the only one," he said. "I'm forty years old, mother. I think I know my own mind by this time, at least as well as I ever shall."

"I dare say," she replied, perhaps reversing his meaning.

He waited for her to make another sign, either that she was renewing her attack or that it was over and she was willing to accept his decision.

"If it's primarily a matter of money, I can supply what you need, up to a certain point. Within reason, that is. I can do what your father would have been able to do for you."

"It's not necessary," he told her.

"I know it's not necessary. But it's available, another possible solution. I can move to Rhoda's. You can put the house up for sale. It's a great old elephant of a place anyway."

"You've always liked it here."

"I've lived a different kind of life from what I'm living now. This is extravagant and foolish."

He didn't say anything. He didn't believe for a moment that she wanted to leave Cuffnells.

"And then, there's the manuscript. It's worth rather a lot now. I can sell it, or let you have it to put up for sale."

"No."

"It doesn't do either of us a whit of good in that cabinet over there. It could give you something of a cushion."

"I don't need a cushion, mother. I'm not a lap dog."

"I'll probably sell it in any event."

"You can do as you like with it, of course. That's your affair," he said, more sharply than he'd intended. It was what his father would have said, although his father would have been more tactful. "I appreciate what you're offering, mother. I do, indeed. But money is not the primary consideration, however much it may appear that way. I get on with Madeleine. I'm comfortable with her. And the boys like me. Even the general seems more or less favorably disposed toward me. So my decision isn't going to be affected one way or another by what you do with the Carroll manuscript."

"All right."

"I am grateful for the offer . . ."

"We'll say no more about it."

"About the manuscript? Or about Madeleine? You'll get to like her, I'm sure. She's a decent woman. She's been through a lot and she's quite admirable in her way. I'd have thought the two of you would be likely to get on famously."

"I'm sure we shall get on well enough."

"A glass of sherry?" he offered.

"A whiskey, I think," she said.

He went to the table where the decanters and the glasses were set out. It was unusual for his mother to have a whiskey. It had been difficult for her, then, this interview. He felt bad, not having made it easier for her. He wished he were better at this kind of thing.

"Water?" he asked her.

"Neat, please."

He felt even worse. But that didn't mean that there had been any choice, really. He didn't see how he could have put it, or what he could have done differently that wouldn't have bothered her in just the same way. But he would not accept the benefit of that man's manuscript. If he'd learned anything from his father, if he had any character or honor or decency at all, he wouldn't accept a farthing from such a source.

He hadn't said that to his mother. But of course he hadn't needed to say it. She knew. And that was what the whiskey was for. He brought it to her. He stood there and watched while she drank it down like medicine.

SHE DECIDED AT LENGTH that if Caryl was determined to be punctilious about the manuscript, he was unlikely to have such delicacy of feeling about pound notes, which were more neutral and indistinguishable. If she went ahead and sold the thing, it would be over and done with, out of the house. It wasn't, as far as she was concerned, such a desirable keepsake anyway. She telephoned the man at Sotheby's, informed him of her decision to put the manuscript up for auction, and offered to bring it to London. They were quite willing to send someone to fetch it, which she thought was decent of them. "When do you suppose the actual sale might take place?" she asked.

She had hoped it might be in a matter of weeks. In fact, the matter was rather more complicated than that. There would have to be a sale in which other significant and valuable lots might attract a number of buyers. There would have to be catalogues printed up. The likelihood was that perhaps by April or May of the following year, 1928, there might be some opportunity of realizing the greatest potential from the manuscript.

It was disappointing. Having made the decision, Alice was impatient about the delay. On the other hand, she also had a sense that the decision had been made. The courier arrived to pick up the manuscript and, once it was out of the house, Alice could consider that she had concluded that piece of business. She knew perfectly well that it was not yet impossible to change her mind, that she could pick up the telephone and risk Mr. Osborne's annoyance by telling him that she had decided to wait a while longer. He would be unlikely to show his displeasure in any way, and he'd simply send it back. But she didn't want it back. She'd lugged it and its burdens about with her for far too long already. She felt it as one more burden that she'd been unable to do this while Regi had lived. He'd have been happy to see the thing leave the house. And he'd have been comforted by the money, their need for which must have troubled him, particularly toward the end.

But it was done now. And with each passing week she felt less and less connection to the manuscript and more curiosity about the actual figure that would be realized from its sale. The larger the sum, the more persuasively she'd be able to offer Caryl an alternative to his plan of marrying Madeleine Hanbury-Tracy. Alice felt that the match was wrong and foolish. Or, more accurately, it was too calculated and sensible to succeed. Frenchmen and Italians made marriages in that way, bartering themselves for money or land or titles. Americans, even, made matches of that kind. But it wasn't an English thing to do, and surely wasn't an enterprise of which anyone in her family or Regi's could have approved. It simply went against the grain somehow.

She'd have expected it to go against Caryl's grain, too. He was hardly the calculating, practical fellow he was pretending to be. It was so unlike him! And that, too, worried Alice. She didn't so much mind his attempt to pretend to her, or to Madeleine for that matter, but when he tried to pretend to himself, then she knew he was courting disaster. She'd tried, once or twice, to discuss the question with Madeleine, herself, but the woman apparently knew of Alice's uneasiness and made it impossible to talk frankly. Besides, she could hardly imagine herself saying, in a pleasant conversational way, "He doesn't love you at all. He's just marrying you for your family's money because he refuses to accept the help I've offered him."

Fortunately, they seemed to be in no great hurry to exchange their actual vows. Alice's only hope, then, was that the sale would take place, that the sum would be enormous, and that Caryl would then realize he wasn't forced by his own want of funds to carry out his bizarre intention. Meanwhile, she had to restrain herself and keep him from the realization that she was thinking as much of his welfare as of her own. Such a thought might force him, simply out of stubborn pride, to go ahead with the marriage, even though there was no longer any need to do so.

In fact, Alice rather liked the girl. Or young woman. She had no particular objection to Madeleine as a human being, even if she was a bit old for Caryl. She tried to keep it in mind that it wasn't Madeleine's fault that Caryl was behaving in such a ridiculous way. In the long run, it was Madeleine who would suffer for it, along with Caryl. At her age, Alice couldn't possibly be worrying about herself. Why didn't they understand that? Why couldn't Caryl see that she had no selfish motive whatever in her concern for him and his future?

She had them down to visit at Cuffnells in November, and then again for the new year. They'd spent Christmas with Madeleine's family in Lacock, probably drowning in all that butter and cheese the farmers made there. Alice was as affable as she could contrive to be under the circumstances, and she hoped that they would both make allowances for her advanced years and her conservative ways. She thought the visits went well enough. She'd intended that they enjoy themselves. She was relieved to learn that they had not yet fixed a date for their wedding, were vague and airy about it, and were comfortable in the assurance that there was plenty of time to get around to such things.

The catalogue arrived. Alice was impressed by it and

interested to see the company her manuscript was keeping: the last letter Dr. Johnson ever wrote, Lord Byron's matched dueling pistols, a manuscript of a poem by Thomas Hardy, and the prompt copy of Middleton's *A Game at Chess*. There were also other Lewis Carroll items, including various autograph letters, the original holographs of some poems he'd written to various young girls, and a copy of the rare 1865 edition of *Alice's Adventures in Wonderland*. It was what they called "an important sale."

She asked Rhoda to go with her. It wasn't something she wanted to face alone, and it didn't seem right to ask Caryl to meet her at the gallery on New Bond Street. Rhoda was willing enough. One could depend on her always. They met in London and were driven to Sotheby's, which looked like a library or a common room of one of the Oxford colleges with its oak-paneled walls and its oil paintings in heavy gilt frames. In front of the auctioneer's desk there was a large table, covered in green baize and in the shape of an open rectangle. Beyond the table there were rows of chairs, most of which were taken. Places had been saved for Alice and Rhoda, and they could feel more than hear the murmur of recognition as they entered the room and sat down.

The bidding began at five thousand pounds and rose rapidly in one-hundred-pound increments. Alice had no idea who was bidding. The auctioneer, a Mr. Des Graz, seemed to be pulling bids out of the air, hearing words that Alice could not hear or discerning signals Alice was unable to see. At twelve and a half thousand pounds, there were still two bidders left, one of them a London dealer representing an anonymous client, the other a Dr. Rosenbach from the United States. They continued to bid until they'd reached fifteen thousand, a figure Alice thought altogether impossible. No book in London had ever fetched so high a sum.

"Fifteen thousand two hundred pounds," Mr. Des Graz

intoned. He paused for a moment. "Fifteen three. And fifteen four." He paused again. "And any more? At fifteen thousand four hundred pounds, going once, and twice, and sold to Dr. Rosenbach of Philadelphia, and our congratulations, sir."

"It's wonderful," Rhoda whispered.

"Yes, isn't it," Alice said. Even after the Sotheby's commission, it was an immense amount of money. Caryl would hardly feel any necessity to sell himself now.

There were reporters in the street, asking her about her reaction to the price that had been paid for her manuscript. "It's a large sum of money," she said. No one could possibly argue about that.

"And what do you plan to do with such a sum?" one of the more enterprising reporters asked her.

She looked at him for an instant. Did he seriously expect a reply to such a question? Apparently he did. "I do not yet know what I shall do with it," she told him, and she got into the waiting automobile.

"SHE OFFERED to make good on all my losses, pay my debts, and wipe my nose, if it came to that," Caryl explained.

"Is that so terrible?"

"Yes, actually. It shows what she thinks of me."

"Does it?" Madeleine asked. "Or is she just trying to help?"

"Both, of course. But it's the way she does it. I told her I wouldn't take a penny from that manuscript. And she went ahead anyway and put it up for sale. Which she had every right to do. It was hers, after all. But then, to turn around and offer me money, as if I had no idea where the money came from, as if I hadn't read in the newspapers how she'd got it . . . Really, Madeleine! There are limits!"

"Perhaps she didn't believe you," Madeleine said. She reached across Caryl's body for the ash tray on the night stand on his side of the bed. It was awkward, the way the bed was jammed into a corner in his bedroom so that there was only the one night stand. On the other hand, what with the boys and the nanny at Madeleine's flat, there were awkwardnesses there, too. "I never know how far to believe you, myself. You do carry on."

"Only about unimportant things. On serious questions, I say rather little. And I mean what I say."

"But did she know that? Did she understand why you wouldn't accept any of the money from that source?"

"I think so. The alternative is simply too ghastly. It would mean that she had no idea about anything in my life or my father's. Or her own, for that matter. It's just impossible."

"But if she hadn't sold it, then you'd have inherited it, would you not?"

"I expect so."

"Perhaps she was worried about your just . . . giving it away."

"More likely, she didn't trust me to get the best price for it. It's one more demonstration of her contempt for me. Quite possibly, it's even a justifiable contempt, which is by far the worst kind."

"And you think that's a reason for us to set a date? To go ahead and get married?"

"Why not?"

"I suppose," she said. "You want to prove to her that her offer means nothing whatever to you. There's no way for you to back out without admitting more than you'd like."

"Something like that."

"Not exactly flattering, is it?"

"To you?" he asked. "Or to me?"

"To either of us. But I was thinking of myself."

"Good for you. A girl can never be too careful."

She laughed.

"There are other reasons, of course," he told her. "Your

flat is more comfortable than mine. And the boys like me. What better could a girl want?"

"What better indeed?" she asked. And then, after a pause, she said, "I still love Felix, you know."

"Yes, I know."

"And you don't mind?"

"No."

"You really don't? It's nothing to joke about."

"I know that. No, I don't mind. I admire it, actually. And I liked Felix myself. A lot."

She didn't push him any further. He was grateful for that, for he had already seen his way to the next step in the argument. He was comfortable about her loving Felix because, comparatively, it was a hell of a lot better than the situation his father had managed to cope with all those years. He didn't despise Felix. Felix hadn't written some damned book to make Madeleine famous. Felix wasn't some kind of sick little pervert. Felix was dead. All those things made marriage with Madeleine easy to take.

Just beyond what he was willing to admit to himself, there was a further possibility with which he was much less comfortable. It had crossed his mind, but he'd turned away from it before making any decision about its probable truth or falsity. It was also possible that Madeleine's affection for her late husband was what made her attractive to him, reproducing as it did so much of his parents' marriage, leaving him to tolerate her primary loyalty to Felix in much the way his father had contrived to tolerate his mother's primary loyalty to Lewis Carroll. It was one of those far-fetched wild ideas that come unbidden in the small hours of the night and then, in the light of day, may hide but never quite go away. Like mice in old houses, one knows they're there.

He reached over and slid a hand into Madeleine's red silk robe.

"Is there time?" she asked.

"If we don't dawdle," he told her.

They didn't dawdle. In fact, he was quick, even rough, quite unlike himself. Madeleine was surprised at how he carried her along. Afterwards, satisfied but wary, she asked, "How would next June suit you?"

"But that's almost a year away!"

"I like June weddings."

"All right, then," he said, thinking that she'd married Felix in June and wanted to duplicate that, or to see if he could stand her attempt to duplicate it. He could stand it. "June's fine, then," he told her.

It felt good. It would happen. It had already begun.

4

IT WAS AT ABOUT THAT SAME TIME, during the second week of July of 1928, that Isa Bowman and Glenda Fenwick encountered one another at Harrods. Quite naturally, they stopped to talk, discussed the news of the recent sale of the Carroll manuscript, considered the possibility of having tea together, but then realized that they might want more time and, above all, more privacy. There was a delicate ritual enacted in which invitations were exchanged, pressed, opportunities for refusal carefully provided, and then, all the signals having been given and answered, a joint resolution formally adopted that they would take a taxicab to Glenda's—where, in the privacy of her apartment, they could have a drink together and talk.

In the cab, Isa told Glenda of Alice's visit. "Of course, I realize now that she was there to find out whether I might make any trouble for her, cause any fuss that might affect the sale."

"You think?" Glenda asked.

"I rather think so, yes. She seemed very no-nonsense."

"Then the nonsense she clings to must be very important to her," Glenda suggested. "The underpinnings of all the rest."

"She's very different from us."

"Yes," Glenda agreed. "But she was different from us before she met Carroll. As we are different from each other. But she is more different."

"But not more fortunate, I think," Isa said. "I always thought of my encounter with Carroll as liberating. She seems not to have been affected in that way."

"Liberating? Really?" Glenda asked.

"Oh, yes," she said. It was not a subject she had been able to discuss with Alice, or even with Reginald Hargreaves for that matter. But to Glenda, she knew she could say anything without having to worry about offending delicate sensibilities. She could also assume good will and kindly attention, which she knew to be rare in the world. As a performer, she understood what luxuries these qualities could be.

Inside, over a dry sherry, she told Glenda what she'd said to Alice about her visit to Carroll at Eastbourne. But, in many ways, that was only the beginning.

IT CAN BE A FRIGHTENING THING. For women or, more often, for girls who have been told all the wrong things, it can be dismaying, something alien and hostile. The size is surprising. And for those of us who know in an abstract way what the mechanics must be, the idea that a piece of equipment of that size is to be inserted into our bodies can be quite dismaying. I had been surrounded by toys, by games, riddles, puzzles, and amusements, and this, too, was another puzzle. A plaything. And ever since, they have all been playthings. I was fortunate, I think, to have been introduced to an erect male organ in that way. I have a fondness for them of the kind that girls have for their pets or their dolls. There they are, to be petted, stroked, fondled, nursed, teased, and occasionally punished. If little girls were encouraged to transfer their inventiveness and tenderness from their dolls to the pricks of their lovers, mankind would be a lot better off. And womankind too, for men treat us well only if they feel good about themselves.

What guilty torment follows upon our failure to understand this fundamental truth! It never ceases to amaze me. That we are the playthings of the gods is inescapable when one considers how our attention is fixed upon what is, after all, a little inflatable toy. Or a puppet—which raises the question as to who is the puppet master. I remember an Atlantic crossing when the weather was very bad and the ship was bouncing crazily. After three days and nights, the storm abated. The sky was suddenly clear, and the sea, smooth and gentle. We all felt spared, although some of us were better equipped than others to express this feeling. I expressed it by sneaking into first class, where I thought the company might be more agreeable. I found myself an American businessman from Cleveland.

Because of the storm and that giddy feeling of freedom, I decided to play. I invented a husband back in cabin class with whom I was angry and to whom I was being deliberately unfaithful. The idea was to make my encounters with the Cleveland businessman more heightened and hurried. I would come into the first-class bar, have a quick drink, and then go with him to his stateroom, where we didn't even pause to undress. He simply lifted my skirts and came at me in a great hurry. And then I would disappear.

Having invented the story, I thought it would be amusing to elaborate on it, so in cabin class I found myself a Canadian engineer on his way to the Netherlands to study windmills—I can't think why—and told him the same story, but with the husband in first class. I had contrived an elegant machine and I was able to run up and down the stairwell that separated cabin class from first class, making my stimulating visits and then departing immediately, leaving each of them to imagine me back with my fictitious husband. Each of them confessed that this was an added excitement, jealousy in small doses being an aphrodisiac. And I imagined them being jealous and thinking of me as I spent my evenings alone in my cabin, learning the lines of a play in which I was to appear when I got to London.

A difficulty arose, however, in my trips up and down the companionway when a purser saw me and told me it was forbidden for cabin-class passengers to use the first-class accommodations. I thought the game was over. And then, with nothing much to lose, I decided to gamble and tell him what I'd been doing. I was an actress and I always liked an audience's reaction. I told him everything and offered him anything, and leered, which is not something one gets to do very often. He took my meaning and the challenge, and he agreed that I could pass back and forth, but only if he could levy a toll, as it were. I agreed to that and we went to my cabin. And then, I told each of my paramours about the randy purser I had to satisfy in order to negotiate the companionway. The effect was marvelous. It was as if each of them, knowing that I had just submitted more or less reluctantly to the demands of the purser, wanted to obliterate the experience I had just undergone. Each of them made love with more and more vigor, as if each penis were an eraser and I were a piece of paper.

This is not merely a dirty story, although it is that first of all. The point is that playing with quantities, making sex into a game with rules and a score that I could keep . . . that all came from Carroll. The game-playing and the mathematics came from him. And the making-up of stories that nobody ever quite believed. But most of all, my attitude toward those poor, fragile, throbbing little things, standing up and demanding attention like so many baby birds . . .

that was from him. And the great satisfaction I took from the absurdity of it was from him. I remember how it was when I was on his lap that first time, the glass of milk on the edge of the table and the leaf-shaped chocolate biscuit in my hand, and how I felt this funny thing moving under my bare bottom. I thought it was a great silliness. I can't imagine a more fortunate way for a young girl to discover the delights of sex. I don't mean just the absence of fear and disgust, but the positive association of another of Carroll's ridiculous children's games.

I suppose, though, it also had a good deal to do with my mother. If she had not been the extraordinary woman she was, so full of life and sure of herself, I might have reacted differently. I realize that no life can be quite so uncomplicated as hers seemed at the time. She had her children, her husband, her lovers, and seemed to be able to balance us all so gracefully that we never questioned her. My father simply adored her and was willing to put up with whatever she did because he was so smitten with her. There must have been some period of adjustment, but that would have been before I was born or when I was still too young to notice what was happening.

After he died, mother's admirers were often men of great wealth and power who could do things for her and for us. Just for a weekend in the country, she could be given a bauble worth enough to keep us all in food and shelter for a year or more. But I never supposed she went just for the bauble. No one could come home with that glow of pleasure who had been disagreeably occupied for three days in the country somewhere. I think her great secret was finally no secret at all. She was so open and aboveboard in everything she did. It was her nature. She recognized her nature and insisted upon it, expecting people around her to recognize it as well.

In the end, I think what we inherit is a set of attitudes.

One is either forgiving or condemning, generous or mean, sympathetic or not. And one supposes that these are matters of choice, or logic. But one acquires such attitudes from one's family. I was lucky to grow up with a special kind of love for me to learn the habit of.

My father died young, a year or so before I met Carroll. His legacy to me was an odd kind of freedom. I understand now that he indulged my mother or overlooked her deviations from the ordinary behavior of married women because he had his own irregularities. He was able, I think, to relate sexually to male as well as to female partners, and he could be comfortable with mother because she was indulgent with him, while he was able to project himself into her life and share with her the power of her attractiveness. I didn't understand these things at the time, but that permissiveness, the delight he took in my mother's adventures got through to me. So I always had that feeling of possibility, of not being oppressed by convention, even before I met Carroll. I wasn't bound by the same received ideas that so many other children were subjected to. The morality of the Victorian age was the morality of bank clerks. Victoria's own family—I think of the Prince of Wales—never felt themselves to be limited in that way, nor did most of the aristocrats my mother knew. Most of morality is snobbery anyway, people pretending to behave like their betters—whom they don't even know well enough to imitate. So they ask and are told all kinds of nonsense, which they believe and adopt as their own code of morals. It's funny, really, but mother was in on the joke. And so was I. Her only morality was the effort to avoid causing other people pain.

It was to that fortunate family that Lewis Carroll returned me after our excursion to Eastbourne, depositing me with my mother and then taking his leave because his hack was waiting for him. My mother asked me how the weekend at the shore had been.

"Fine," I told her. "He was very nice."

I had expected to be grilled. I'd been looking forward to that feeling of importance that comes of having information someone else wants very much to know. But she was cleverer than I'd expected—parents often are. She opened the door with her general question and then let me decide what I wanted to tell her. If I'd been upset or hurt, that would have come out immediately. I'd have complained or asked for comfort or protection. The fact that my answer to her general question was favorable must have been reassuring. I'd not been disturbed in any deep way.

As for the details of the week at Eastbourne, she knew that I could manage to wait only a few minutes for further questions, in the absence of which I'd volunteer. The time had been so interesting and I'd been fascinated by the strangeness of the man. I was also trying to figure out my own story for myself, and one of the best ways of doing that, even now, is to tell it to someone else, to try to organize and explain it. She let me do that, offering me an interested ear. I could tell her what I needed to tell and keep back what I thought was unnecessary or was uncomfortable with. That thirteen-year-old girls need their privacy ought to be obvious to everyone, but it isn't. They need it more than grown women do. Everything is so new to them, so very vivid.

This is perhaps what Lewis Carroll liked about me—if there was anything more than an accidental coincidence of how I happened to look and what he happened to require. That vividness, that sharpness, which I think of as having to do with my character at the time, matched his timidity. It was like the photographs he took, where one can compensate for a softness of contrast by doing certain things in the darkroom. I'm not sure of the details, but there are ways one can fiddle. Or emphasize. He found in me what he was looking for and was therefore willing to overlook my age as the years passed by and it became more and more evident that I was beyond his ordinary range. He was a frightened little man, but I didn't frighten him—which was nothing more than a return of the favor, inasmuch as he hadn't frightened me with his furtive and minimal molestations. I think I owed him more than I gave.

That business of the mad rutting on the transatlantic crossing was unusual for me. Unique, I should say. But it was always possible, always there for me to do if I ever felt like going a bit wild. The physical coupling was nothing at all compared to the feeling I've always had that it was there if I wanted or needed it—like money in the bank. Frank had left me—I thought for good, although that turned out not to be the case. It was the first of a number of separations. Or diversions. He is younger than I am, and thinks himself entitled, and has discovered that I am likely to tolerate these interludes. Or he believes I have no choice. And he may be right.

This fling, then, was to enable myself to forgive him, to restore the necessary feeling of balance, and it was also pure wicked fun. All those things worked together, as they hadn't ever done before or since. There have been some desultory imitations, casual re-enactments, but nothing like that. Still, how many times must one repeat a pleasure in order to believe in it?

That's the question I keep coming back to. About Carroll's life, and about my own, now, as well. What he had decided was that his life with young girls was the only real living he'd ever known. The alternative was death, I suppose. So each of us was another temporary fending-off of the inevitable. Coming at the end, as I did, I had more of an opportunity to see how grim and determined that gaiety had become. It marred the book—*Sylvie and Bruno*—which is why it hasn't ever been popular. Even children sense the woe that lurks behind it.

Look, how dark it has got. I had no idea how the time has flown . . .

INDEED, IT HAD GROWN DARK. From the floors below, there were indistinct sounds of conversation punctuated occasionally by laughter. The girls were getting ready for their evening's work. Smells of cooking and of perfume combined agreeably.

"Another sherry?" Glenda offered. "Or a whiskey, perhaps?"

"A whiskey? Why not?"

"You never had children?"

"No."

"By design?"

"Partly." Isa accepted the whiskey, took a sip, and put the glass down beside her. "At first, I was waiting for the right moment. Then I had an abortion and developed an infection. I was lucky to have lived. But I couldn't have children."

"That was with Frank? The abortion?"

Isa nodded.

"He didn't want the child?"

"He never knew about it. I'd thought of telling him but I hadn't quite made up my mind whether to have it or not. It was something I was still turning over in my own mind, whether I trusted Frank enough to become as dependent on him as I'd have to be, at least for a while. Whether I wanted to give up my career, or dared to. What it would mean to me and to us . . . And he left. So I took the first job that was offered me. It was in New York."

"Ah, I see."

"About the crossing? Yes, I see too. I saw it then. It was a way of asserting that I was still a woman, a way of proving that I was still attractive. I see all that. I had a wonderful time, nevertheless."

"I don't doubt it," Glenda said.

"It was . . . there when I needed it."

"So you said. But was it quite as free as you've been saying?"

"What's free? You look back on anything in the past, and there's no way to change it. It all seems gossamer at the time, and then suddenly those light threads turn to steel. There's no escape."

"But there is," Glenda said. "Time may not heal all wounds, but it does change things for us. Problems transform themselves or just go away sometimes."

Isa drained the last of her whiskey, put the glass down, and said, "I keep telling myself so, but it doesn't help much. Actually, I'm terrified. I have no idea whether Frank is coming back or not. Or whether I want him back. Or whether it was worth the effort to go out and raise hell with Breezy so I could feel like taking Frank back, up to it or down to it . . . I'm so tired of thinking about it. The trouble with sex as a subject for thought is that it's interesting but one never gets anywhere."

"Your feelings will clarify themselves," Glenda assured her. "A decision will form."

"I wish I could be as sure of myself as you are."

"We have in common an instinct for self-preservation," Glenda said. "That's what I'm sure of. If you've described Alice correctly, that's what we all have in common."

"Self-preservation?"

"Self-esteem. The rest flows from that."

"From Carroll, do you mean?"

"Probably not. Except incidentally. He liked bright and attractive girls. Playful ones."

"Smart enough to recognize their own worth?"

Glenda nodded. "Not that you're obliged to take my word for it," she said.

"Oh, no. I do take your word for a great deal. You're a

realist. I suppose you have to be. And when one is trying to make decisions and has lost sight of what matters, there's a terrible uncertainty about everything one has always taken for granted. What do I want? What's real? Those questions suddenly echo in a dismal vacancy."

"Have I helped?"

"You've helped me understand some things about the past. But what to do now?"

It was a rhetorical question. They both knew that.

ISA LIVED. She coped. She got a small part in a silly play that nevertheless worked well in rehearsal and opened to indulgent notices. It helped keep her busy. But she thought a great deal, particularly during the second act, when she had nothing to do but sit in her dressing room and wait for the time to pass. She had to reappear in the third act, not dead after all, and ready with witty explanations. But what explanations did she have for her own life? For one, she decided that Alice had in her way been faithful to Carroll. It was stupid, but admirable nonetheless. The long years of marriage had done nothing to violate the little shrine she had made for herself (and of herself) to the memory of that man. Hargreaves had felt it and resented it, up to the very end.

The only trouble was that Isa didn't believe life was so neat. She might have preferred it that way: as it was in plays, when the last lines rang out and the actors froze while the curtain rapidly descended and the applause—it was to be hoped—sounded back. But then there were curtain calls. And then supper. And the moment of balance and stasis, so carefully contrived, dissolved in the flow of living. She had seen enough of that to know that it might bring Frank back. If anything was going to, that was what it would be, life's inherent tendency toward messiness.

Nothing was that logical. The appeal of Lewis Carroll's

alternatives to real life was their neatness, but the real world seemed to Isa to have been so constructed as to frustrate the mind and keep it from making any satisfying formulation. Worse, it suggested formulations all the time and then showed them up as inadequate. She had thought she was being so very clever when Frank had been away, going out to Breezy's that way for a little guilty fun, but Frank hadn't cared. It hadn't made a damned bit of difference. He had been enraptured by his find in Manchester, and was merely grateful to have been spared a tirade.

Isa, alone, read a great deal. She took in a cat, which was diverting. A cat was a good thing for an old lady to have, a preparation for the role that would get to be less and less a performance as the reality caught up with her. It was a big lazy tabby that liked to lie in the sun and sleep. Or Isa thought it was asleep. In fact, it seemed to be engaged in a kind of voluntary reverie from which it could rouse itself at the slightest prospect of food. Lazy and greedy, it seemed to have a good understanding of the intricacies of philosophy.

Frank returned, after all, about five months later, when the job was completed. He had had a falling-out with his Manchester companion months before, had been living alone, and had been taking the time to consider his life and prospects, and their future together. He said, "We suit each other," and defied her to disagree. He didn't like the cat, thought it homely and aloof, seemed to resent it—but Isa insisted that the cat must stay. Frank would have to put up with it. Frank did, tolerating the animal until its death in 1933.

Frank and Isa remained together until she died in 1958, in her eighty-fourth year.

1932

THE BLINDS ARE LOWERED, but there is a slice of sunlight that slants in between the bottom of the louvers and the top of the sill, animating the dust motes in a way that seems to Alice at once familiar and terrifying. She has seen the phenomenon before and knows that she ought not find in it anything remarkable. Fatigued as she is from the academic exercises of the morning, she sees in that swirl some suggestion of the dance of matter, the wild whirl of atoms of which all things are composed. Even something as inert and harmless, as lifeless as a writing desk . . . How is a raven like a writing desk? They both dance.

She cannot get away from it. Even if she closes her eyes, there is the same dance. She has seen this before too, in bright light, and understands it to be nothing more than imperfections in the aqueous humor. But it looks like a primordial swarming of gnat-like energy. And she is susceptible to such suggestions now, particularly, because that exercise, that innocent reunion of manuscript, writing desk, and little girl (the girl more battered by time than the other two) brings back—with more vividness than she might like—recollections of that other sunlit afternoon, the famous excursion all those people in the crowd were trying to lay claim to, trying to wrest from her along with the manuscript.

They are welcome to it. What a blessing it would be simply to be rid of it!

One of the mercies of life is forgetfulness. The reward of old age ought to be the choking off of the faculty of memory, but of course it doesn't work that way at all. One may forget one's appointments, one's errands, where books or glasses or a fountain pen were put down, but the events of years before remain undiminished in their clarity and detail. Alice often wondered whether the real reason her father had devoted himself so strenuously and so long to the lexicon was the hope that by filling every last cranny of his mind with infrequent Greek words and their sources in the ancient writers he might seal himself off from memories of other kinds, displacing his own experience with relics of the Greek language. Oh, not literally, perhaps, but in some vague way. Surely there was a devotion to it, a dedication to an activity that was an alternative to the torments of living.

With the three of them, Lorina, Alice, and Edith, were Dodgson, and Robinson Duckworth, his friend from Trinity. The Dodo and the Duck. They boated out to Godstow to have tea on the bank there, and on the way the Dodo made up the story, as he had made up other stories on other days. It was that day's story, though, a little more elaborate, a little luckier in the way it took things and turned them around, that prompted her to ask him if he might write it down. She and Edith wanted it to keep, to go back to and read again. And they argued over which one should risk the Dodo's displeasure by asking for so grand a favor. It was a competition, of course, and not like the Caucus Race at all. Here there would be a winner and a loser. Here they would all know how things stood.

The whispering by the riverbank. She could not recall the words but she could bring back the feeling, the fear that he would overhear their whispering, conspiratorial and competitive at the same time, for each of them was daring the other to ask the favor, defying the other to try, each convinced that her own claim on the affections and attentions of Dodgson had to be superior. Alice was complacent because Dodgson had given the heroine her name. Edith had her own reasons, but her belief was every bit as strongly held.

"All right," Alice said at last. "I'll do it." And that became a challenge Edith instantly took up. "I'll do it," she answered.

"No, I said I'd do it and I will," Alice insisted.

The quarrel continued, although the positions had quite reversed themselves, for each of them was now claiming the right to ask the favor, jealous that the other's request might be granted—or really jealous of the other's claim.

Alice asked. And, as if in some fairy tale, she put into movement a process that brought her down a torrent of time and across an ocean, to lie and remember it still. It is like a burr one picks up on a country walk that clings to the hem of one's skirt and will not let go. Years later it persists, still hanging on by its little hooks and spines, as if nature itself wished to turn the closet into a wilderness of weeds.

Nature is correct, as usual. The house is as likely to fall down as not. The burr may yet strike earth and sprout. Wilder coincidences manifest themselves all the time. Alice's fencing with Edith, possessive, vainglorious, spiteful as it was, differed in only trivial ways from that interview, so many years later, with Isa Bowman, just after Regi died. The same surface of good manners just barely observed—and beneath it the same desire to wound. Only, on that July day, with Edith, it was a confrontation of children. She'd been a ten-year-old girl, one of those models of virtue in whom it was impossible to suspect anything so gross as sexual feelings, let alone sexual jealousy and the cattiness of a demimondaine quarreling with a rival over their quarry.

Is it better now or worse, she wonders. Back then, the presumption of innocence was a burden on each child—who knew herself to be a monster, depraved beyond the imagination of any adult. Now, young people may not be quite so isolated in their thoughts, may not feel so absolutely cut off from the general experience of their kind, but are they not encouraged in these ways to grow up too quickly, to indulge their fantasies and develop their baser natures?

Understanding, when it comes, is too late to be useful. How can she change anything now, how can she revise a word, a look, a gesture of seventy years ago? She cannot even escape the scene by closing her eyes, for it only presses upon her with an even greater force, the voices babbling in her ear as if it were all happening in the next room. Those voices, the amplified blaring voices that came bouncing back this morning as they echoed off the buildings, could have been a foretaste of the booming decrees of angels, endlessly reading out the list of her misdeeds. She can see the little girls on the riverbank—but in a ghastly light now, for she knows what will happen to them. She understands how this trivial falling-out will result in an enmity only the most severe Victorian, Oxonian, and Christian constraints will be able to gloss over, suppressing it if not hiding it altogether.

She had been an ungracious winner, gloating over the fact that Dodo had taken her name for the heroine of his story. But it had not been a pure triumph, which was why she needed to gloat. The others had all been transmogrified, so that Edith was the Eaglet, Lorina was the Lory, and Dodgson the Dodo, and even Duckworth was the Duck, but she was still just plain old Alice, not turned into anything remarkable, tiresomely the same, and—as she thought then and still thinks—not very nice in the story but petulant and pouty. She didn't let on to Edith, of course, but put on it the best face she could, pretending to be confident and happy . . .

As one learns to do, is obliged to go on trying to do for most of one's life, pretending to be confident and happy because the contraries are tiresome and an imposition upon others—who have all they can do to pretend, in turn, to be confident and happy too. Or that was how it used to be. These days, there is a wallowing in misery and pain, a public declaration by physicians and analysts as well as by novelists and playwrights of the torment of human life. It is not much different, Alice believes, from what it always was, except that there is a decay in civility, a deterioration of good manners.

In the end, she asserted her rights not merely as heroine but as the elder. Lorina of course was older than Alice, and of the three of them, if that was to be the deciding factor, it would have been Lorina who ought to have asked Dodo. But both Edith and Alice knew Dodo wasn't interested in Ina. Ina was along for the ride, a kind of chaperone almost, a necessary encumbrance, there being no way to avoid including her in the invitation. So Dodgson had invited all three girls, and had brought Duckworth along to help with the rowing and to entertain Ina while he paid his particular attention to the younger two. They both knew that, and that was another reason for their whispering, so that Ina wouldn't hear them. Surely, had she been aware of the subject of their dispute, she'd have settled the question by forbidding either of them to be so forward as to ask . . . It wasn't done. It was like asking for a present, or asking for food. One waited until it was offered or went without. In the heat, one might request a drink of water, but nothing more. That was a rule. Both Edith and Alice knew it. But they also knew how rules could be suspended, could be bent all out of shape, could be made ridiculous in Dodgson's company, because he was always doing it himself. He was obliged to find ways of getting around the rules, for otherwise his life would have been insupportable. He'd have had to present himself at the doors of a hospital or a prison.

So small, so pretty . . . They really were beautiful children! And yet so knowing, too, able to size up a situation of that intricacy and degree of risk and blithely negotiate for advantage, fighting one another for the opportunity of going to Dodo for the proof of his special favor. Alice won and she approached him, feeling about her the breathlessness of mid-afternoon when the birds are hushed and only an occasional butterfly punctuates the stillness by its flutter of color. A warm day, and she can remember the dank smells of the riverbank and the sweeter, lighter smells of flowers about her. But most of all she remembers that stillness, the warmth of the afternoon, the remarkable slowness with which the little puffs of high wispy clouds crossed the pale blue of the sky. It was a moment that had been distilled from nature and suspended in a crystal, and she had no fear in her at all as she approached him, confident in him, in herself, and in the disposition of the world. Of course he'd grant her request! In such a mood, she might have prayed to any god in the pantheon and whatever she asked would have been granted.

She did not even have to speak. She stood there, looking at him, knowing that he would look at her, would delight in her, and would virtually offer, before she had the occasion to make a formal request, anything she might want—the world, immortality, love and happiness forever.

"Yes, my dear? What is it that you want?"

"Could you write it down for me? The story you've been making up for us, could you write it down on paper so that I could have it forever and ever?"

"Whatever for?" he asked.

"I shouldn't like to forget a single word," she said.

Lorina glared. Edith stared at the Dodo, not sure whether she would prefer a yes or a no, trying to read his expression. And Alice? She was as certain of his answer as she was sure of her own name.

"Why not?" Dodgson said.

AND IF EDITH HAD ASKED? Almost certainly Dodgson would still have assented. The manuscript would have been prepared, would have been presented to one or another of the Liddell children, and would have eventually passed to Alice. Surely, when Edith died, Alice would have been the one to whom it would have been passed along. Or even if, in some strict accounting, the three sisters had been given equal shares in the manuscript, Alice would have been the beneficiary, when Lorina died in 1930, of the book that was intended for her from the beginning. And how much pain might have been avoided!

Edith was wrong to have resented Alice's triumph. They had agreed, more or less, that Alice was to ask him. He agreed to write it out, and then did, and presented the manuscript to Alice. Even then, had she managed to suppress her satisfaction with herself, had she not gloated to her younger sister, had she not affronted the tender sensibilities of an eight-year-old girl, then there might have been less reason for Edith to seek revenge.

Nothing less. A grand word for a little girl, but the emotions were large and blunt, undiminished by subtleties, undimmed by the wear of living. Experience and wisdom are all very well, but they do nothing to intensify feelings or the clarity of perceptions or emotions. We know how this, too, will pass and by that knowledge diminish pleasure as well as pain, love as well as anger. Children are less qualified in their feelings and Edith hated Alice with a purity no sane adult could have mustered, for Alice was a sister, a friend, and had nevertheless betrayed her. Alice was the ally who had turned against her and robbed her of a wicked pleasure, which is of course the sweetest kind.

There were few opportunities, however, for an eight-year-old to do anything to an elder sister that would be satisfyingly drastic. Physical violence, even if Edith had entertained such an idea, was out of the question; properly raised young ladies did not go about striking one another. Alice was two years older and larger, and the general limitation applied: it was no good trying to hurt Alice in a way that would bring on Edith's own head a punishment from their parents more unpleasant than anything Edith could do to her sister. She was a cunning one. All younger sisters are cunning, having to work in indirect ways, having to bide their time and wait for their opportunities. They seem to be dreamy and self-absorbed, but are like snakes sunning themselves. If there is a dream, it is of striking.

(No, that's not true, she realizes. Think of Rhoda. But Rhoda was different, the last child, an afterthought. By the time Rhoda came along, she didn't have all those brothers and sisters to contend with. She was like an only child with a great many young uncles and aunts. And she refused to play the kinds of games Lorina, Alice, Edith, and Harry habitually played. She rejected fantasy—except the fantasy that one could live that way, without dreams or illusions, without flinching from the actual world. Alice admires her sister but cannot altogether believe in how she lives.)

Edith waited, then. To be charitable—as Alice can afford to do, now that so many years have passed, and as she'd like to do because it is more comfortable for her—she can suppose that Edith forgot, from time to time, that her intention was retribution and that her object was to inflict some kind of hurt, either on Alice or on the special friendship Dodgson had conferred upon her by naming the heroine after her and giving her the manuscript copy of the book. Edith wanted to destroy what she could not have, herself. Sup-

pose her not altogether a monster, or, while allowing that
she was monstrous—we all are—remember her as an ordinary mortal, frail even in her monstrosity. Let her have had
hours and days that went by without any thought of Alice or
Dodo, or her vendetta. It would have to have been that way,
if only to get through the summer days of the long vac, the
breakfasts and tea times, the ordinary society of the family
and its demands. But buried, waiting to be roused back to
life like a sleeping dragon in a children's story, there was
that affront and Edith's resolve to extract from both of
them some payment. It was an intermittent but persistent
annoyance, like the rough place on a tooth, Alice supposes.
It would have been something to which Edith returned,
perhaps at the same time every day after supper, in the late
summer twilight, watching the real objects in her room fade
away into the gloom and letting the dragons back into the
kingdom of her soul. Perhaps, then, it was in exactly this
kind of gloom, as she played idly at the end of the day, that
the thought came to her of what she might do, what it
would feel like, how she would exult when the great reversal was finally accomplished, how Alice would never forget
her . . .

That part, anyway, turned out to be true. Edith remained
alive for Alice in a more vivid way than anyone. Fifty-six
years now? Yes, Edith died in '76 when she was twenty-two.
So, fifty-six years ago. And here she is, practically nudging
Alice off the bed, filling the room's gloom as surely as those
dragons of jealousy had filled her own head in the same
kind of half-light. Because she was right! Because, had their
positions been reversed, Alice would have done exactly as
Edith did, or would have tried to. Alice is not confident that
she'd have had the same success. Or the same luck, which
was what it amounted to.

No, no. Give Edith credit, she tells herself, trying to be
fair to the younger sister. It wasn't just a matter of seizing

an opportunity, but of improving on it, embellishing the actual event and presenting it in such a way as to make it serve her purpose. And to claim for herself that particular primacy in the Dodo's affections she'd felt was hers and had been cheated of, that day on the river when Alice had asked for the story to be written out.

The nakedness was only the beginning of it. The nakedness was for the photographs and drawings. The costumes were there to be changed into and, more important, out of. The thing the Dodo wanted more than breath itself, the thing he was willing to trade his breath for, gasping in excitement and delight, was the romping of two kittens, two puppies, two otters, quite nude, on the cushions of his sofa, the carpet of his floor, the chairs at his round table, or upon his lap. Isa Bowman had been quite right about that. It was their shared secret, the bond that united them to Dodo and to each other. *All women are sisters that the same man loves.* Who said that? She remembers hearing it and thinking, at first, of nuns. Only later did it come back to her, abruptly applying to Edith and herself. Accusingly? Mockingly. For sisters can feel jealousy and spite as easily as any two females anywhere on earth.

When was it, then, that Edith realized she had the weapon at hand and could at any moment terminate the relationship, shattering the secret circle within which they all played? Did it just cross her mind one day? And did she, on the very same day, speak—or did she enjoy herself, continuing as if nothing had changed, feeling her power, letting it lie there in the nest of her lower jaw—her own tongue, a familiar part of herself and yet a stranger, almost a foreign creature with its own life and will?

Even though Alice knows she was to be the victim of Edith's tongue, she prefers to imagine, on her dead sister's part, the greatest possible enjoyment of the imminence of action, the sense of power, all the richer for its rarity in the life of a small child. Children do what they're told, eat what is put before them, go to sleep when someone bids them sleep, and wake when they're roused. They are told to mind their manners, watch their step, scrub their hands and faces clean, and keep their lips sealed. They hardly exercise control over their own bodies. To have any real influence on the lives of other people, to impinge that way, inflicting their own wills on the external world, is all but unimaginable. Without for a moment taking away any of her sister's intention, Alice thinks it is quite possible that Edith did it but couldn't believe she was doing it. Alice has read convincing accounts in newspapers of women who have shot their husbands or lovers, squeezing the trigger over and over, discharging all the bullets in the gun, and yet not quite able to connect the movement of the finger, the loud sound, and the odd smell with the wounds in the person across the room. Edith must have brooded for some time, daring to do it and daring to believe that her doing it would make any difference. There could have been a considerable degree of pluck involved in her decision. Alice much prefers to allow to her sister as much thoughtfulness as pure spite, as much self-awareness as the moment would seem to have required. It was the one great act of Edith's life. After that, as if she had spent her entire capital of character and originality in one supreme effort, she was the perfectly ordinary Victorian girl—up until her death.

Alice has no doubt about Edith's embellishment, or until now she has never seriously doubted it. Had there been any real attempt on Dodgson's part to do anything immoral with either of the girls, surely Alice would have known of it at the time. She would have some recollection of it if he'd pressed her further, more intimately than was his custom. And had the object of this moment of self-forgetfulness been Edith, then she'd have boasted directly to Alice, wouldn't she? Because that would have been the more satisfying way to deal with it, the best use to which Edith could have put so delicious a piece of information. And it wouldn't in any way have affected its usefulness later on if she decided, that day or the next, or whenever she felt so disposed, to turn around and tell her mother. Their mother. In the absence of any such memory, Alice has to assume that Edith made it up, willfully extending whatever truth there may have been into an uglier, more substantial charge against the man who had made her unhappy—not by being importunate but by his restraint, not by his faults (and there were faults) but by his good manners. She had served up the most sensational charge she could devise . . .

But there is no need to exculpate the Dodo absolutely. He must have known that there were dangers, that he was playing a risky game. Little girls are more mercurial in their moods and deeper in their feelings than was then supposed, but he knew them better than most adults, was able to talk to them, think like them, and become their equal. It was a rare gift then, and there have been few rivals since, even though we are now all supposed to be so much better informed about the human psyche and its development. Carroll had done enough to plant the idea in Edith's head, running the risk from the first kiss, or touch, or even look. On the other hand, it could have been that Edith overheard some Christ Church undergraduate, or spied one of them walking with a young lady with whom he'd been smitten and had made the connection from that to her own feelings for the Dodo. Something else might have intervened. In any event, it wasn't until the following summer that the break came, the definite rupture between Mr. Dodgson and the Liddells. That was when Mama burned the letters. That was when Mr. Dodgson was forbidden the deanery.

Alice can still remember the interrogation, not the particular questions but the mood of it: her mother asking whether he had touched her, and where, and how, and how often, and whether he had touched Edith, and—if so—whether she had been dressed or undressed.

Her answers were grudging, evasive, as if she were the guilty party—as, indeed, she felt herself to be. As Edith had necessarily implied she was, for if Edith had complained and not Alice, wasn't Alice the willing partner in these unspeakable practices, the shameless one, the outcast? The prohibitions were so strong, and the sense of wrong so sharp, that ordinarily reasonable causes and effects were irrelevant. Instead, it was one of those charged situations, like a dry day in winter when the most innocent movement of the hand toward a doorknob may cause a spark of static electricity to fly. And how has the static built up, in the body, the rugs, the walls, the very air? Nobody knows, but it's there. As the feelings of shame were there, waiting to be discharged. Of course, she felt as guilty as if she had made the advances toward the Dodo, as if parading about his rooms naked had been her own idea, or as if she and he together had thought up a way of corrupting Edith—which only Edith's good moral sense and strong character had been able to resist.

Any child, no doubt, could have dreamed up some wild accusation; but only an artful and subtle one could have picked out a charge that was in part true, and of a kind that could not be easily denied. Even the accused—as Alice felt herself rather than Dodgson to be—conspired in the incrimination, a part of the mind chiming in, offended and deploring, so that her protestations of innocence were half-hearted. There was, in Alice's look and demeanor, something evasive and cringing that seemed, to a parent, to be an admission of guilt.

Not that she ever directly admitted anything in words—nor did her mother press her to. There was a reluctance on both sides to dwell upon such matters, but there was a more particular constraint that affected them, for earlier that summer little Albert Liddell had died. Had been born and died. His godfather, the Prince of Wales, had chosen the names—Albert Edward Arthur Liddell. Albert Edward for himself. And Arthur for the other Arthur Liddell, the baby who'd come after Lorina and before Alice and had died when he was three.

Those two deaths were in large measure what had turned Dean Liddell away from the world and into the refuge of his study and the lexicon. Their mother had no such refuge but had somehow to carry on, running the household, looking after the obligatory social life and the rearing of the children as well as attending to her husband's moods. The death of her infant son must have had some effect upon her —the taking back of a lovely, innocent baby after the teasing glimpse fate had given her of the new life. In order to survive, one needs faith or a kind of hardness, an inner toughness. Perhaps faith and toughness are closer together than most people suppose. Life isn't easy, and if faith obliges us to accept life and give thanks for it, it must also require us to acknowledge what it is, to see it in its harshness and bloodiness. Farmers know what the slaughter is like, and they raise their chickens and ducks and lambs and piglets, knowing how it is, giving thanks at table . . .

It would have been in such a mood of—at best—grim acceptance, brave forbearance, something just a little spunkier than abject resignation, that her mother held these interviews, first with Edith and then with Alice. Perhaps with Lorina as well. And Pricks, Miss Prickett, their governess? But Lorina would not have known anything, nor would Miss Prickett. The ordinary secretiveness of children would have been enough to keep from either of them any knowledge of diversions considerably more innocent than those with which Alice, Edith, and the Dodo were occupied. Lorina was not a grown-up yet, but the Dodo must have been put off, intimidated probably by the first suggestion of breasts and hips. And Lorina was, in any event, less apt to enjoy the Dodo's childish wordplay and nonsense.

Pricks was always easy to fool. So neither of them would have had anything to report to Mama, who would have had all the more reason to question Alice as closely as possible. A man's reputation and career were at stake—as well as the safety and well-being of her daughters. She would have been aware of responsibilities that came with the power she shared with their father, the Dean of Christ Church. Somehow, she would have managed to convey that responsibility, to communicate the gravity of the moment and the importance of Alice's replies. She could not lie.

Edith, there, had the advantage again. Edith didn't have to lie. She could color the facts, as one might tint a photograph, bringing out certain details, emphasizing this or that particular feature. But she didn't have to lie. At the bottom of her charge, there was a truth. He did, yes, fondle them. He did kiss them. He did stroke their hair. He ran the balls of his fingertips down the middle of their backs, featherylight, stroking the almost invisible golden down that glinted in the direct sunlight, or touching the protuberant vertebrae of their spines, imagining strange beasts that lurked just beneath their skins (and, of course, the beasts were there, purring in delight). It was a sensual adoring, a thing any fleshly creature enjoys, kitten or puppy or child, a kind of preening, a lovely kind of love that was so sharp—so heightened in its delicate balance between yearning and gratification—as to produce in the girls almost the same sweet trembling as it produced in him. Anything so sweet and sharp, anything with such heights of feeling had to be bad, a secret and therefore shameful experience, not the kind of thing one could report to one's mother as one tried to obey her demands: "No, you look me in the eye, young lady. Look at me when you're speaking."

She tried. She made her back rigid, drew in her chin like a guardsman, looked straight at her mother, and answered the questions her mother put to her: what he did, where he'd touched her, how he'd touched her. But what her mother never asked was the one question Alice most dreaded—whether and where Alice had touched him. It was for fear that such a question would come sooner or later, or perhaps to prevent the question being put, that she let the tears well up, willing them to spill over and pour down in rivulets, all the while keeping that stiff guardsman's pose.

So her mother knew there was something to what Edith had said, that the charges were more or less true. It hardly mattered about the details. The important issue wasn't what kind of monster Dodgson was but that he was a monster, a paedophile, a molester of young girls. In Christ Church, the most prestigious college in the university and a chapter of the cathedral! Unthinkable! Unpardonable!

"You may go to your room," her mother said. And she kissed Alice's cheek to comfort her, and to let her know that it was all right. That it would be all right.

"WHY? WHY DID YOU TELL?"

No answer except the smug smile, tight as if to demonstrate that her lips were sealed. The stable door locked, now that the horse was gone? She would not condescend to an explanation. Alice asked her, that day and the next, and Edith said nothing. Figure it out for yourself, she might have meant. Or perhaps, your question isn't even worth a reply.

Defiance invited defiance. It became a game, not merely a contest of will between the two sisters but a re-enactment of a hundred other such contests, the difference between them important in itself but also functioning as a cue to which the response of each of them was automatic. They were both bright children, clever little girls, and they were joined in ways other than battle. Alice, for her part, had to win because Edith's triumph needed to be redressed. All the strategies of bullying, badgering, cajoling, and intimidating had to be brought to bear, because Edith was perfectly well aware that the stakes were higher now.

But it didn't matter, finally, what the stakes were. Once they both understood it as yet another game in the long series of games, there were rules to appeal to, even if they were not written down anywhere. Like the British constitution. But Alice remembers that her advantage was a willingness to break the rules, to do anything necessary to force her sister to talk—because, in Alice's view, Edith had already broken the rules.

It must have gone on for a week or even more—time is difficult to gauge for a child, almost as difficult as it is, now, for an old woman. A day was an eternity then, and a week a dizzying vista. But the question was there, to be posed again and again, with mounting threats, exclusions, bribes, and, toward the end, actual physical violence. Horse-bites on the muscle of the upper arm. Sharp kicks to the shins. Defying Edith to tell again, to be saddled with the title of tattletale that she'd earned anyway, having peached on the Dodo. Alice dared her sister to report her to Pricks or even their mother. Father was off in his study, writing citations of Greek words on small slips of paper, on the trail of his own wily beast, the *hapax legomenon.* He was not to be disturbed by anything less than a death. Or by anything other?

Finally, she did talk, confessing that she told, "because I wanted to. Because he was hateful. And you were hateful too."

"You were jealous," Alice accused.

"*You* were jealous."

"I wasn't."

"You were. You are," Edith insisted.

There was nothing more Alice could get out of her. As if
that weren't enough. As if it weren't true. They were both
of them jealous, which was Edith's way of saying that the
Dodo had come between them.

That, of course, was the one thing Edith couldn't admit—
that the Dodo had loosened their bonds as friends and
sisters, that she was frightened, not just by Alice's behavior
but by her own feelings. That telling their mother was a way
of restoring the *status quo ante.*

The shame of it could make her blush, not just then but
for years afterwards. When Edith died, that was what Alice
remembered. Twenty years after Edith's death, Alice could
still go back to that failure of hers to appreciate Edith's
motives—not just understand them but endorse them—
and cause her skin and the blood vessels to do whatever it is
that they do. If she is inured now, it is only because she has
a different and lower idea of what life is about, expecting
less of herself and everyone else. But Edith was able to give
the Dodo up because of her love for Lorina and Alice. And
Alice didn't love Edith back—or not enough to forgive her.
That's the shame of it. Always has been. That's the terrible
truth to be faced over and over. There weren't three girls in
England closer to one another, more united in their tastes,
jokes, enthusiasms, and dislikes, and more in tune aestheti-
cally and spiritually. And at the first man to come along,
two of them were at each other's throats, ready to betray
each other for any advantage, however slight, in the affections of a poor sad pervert.

"Oh, Edith," she says aloud into the gloom of the artificial twilight, knowing there is no point to it whatsoever.
Edith has been dead more than fifty years. Either she knows
without the words being pronounced or she doesn't. Saying it won't help. It won't even make Alice feel any better.

She knows this, for she has tried before. Many times.

ALICE'S REALIZATION of Edith's probable motive had come later, too late to be useful. By then, she and Edith had dropped away from each other, the relationship between them having altered and set. They were still sisters but no longer best friends. Nothing was different and yet everything was different. Alice understood it as what happened to Adam and Eve when they were expelled from the Garden of Eden. The same plants, the same animals, the same weather, the same sun shining down, but everything different. Apparently, it happens to everyone sooner or later, which is what keeps that story charged with meaning.

Her concerns, at the beginning, were less with Edith than with her parents. And with the Dodo. What would happen to him? Would Edith's mischievous blabbing ruin the man? Would their father come bursting forth from his study, leaving his slips of paper behind to bring judgment and punishment to the poor Student? Would there be a scandal?

Would Alice have to run away? How could she bear to be held up as the poor victim of the depraved don, the object of juicy gossip and prurient pity? Would her parents send her away? Forever?

Those were the questions she worried about, but as the days passed and then weeks, and nothing happened at all, she began to relax and then to wonder. Were there no consequences to what Edith had done? Were there no consequences to what they had all done together, the three of them, Alice and Eaglet and the Dodo? There were, indeed, but not those the young girl had first feared. Her parents had explored the same possibilities but had come to different conclusions. Or, putting it another way, it took Alice a lot longer to figure out what was immediately obvious to her mother and father—that the reputation of Christ Church ought not be sullied, that the reputation of the Liddell family must be preserved, and the daughters kept free of the taint of scandal. No harm that the Dean could do to Dodgson was worth doing, whether for the sake of revenge or of more abstract justice, if it hurt the reputation of his house and of the House.

An interview, very likely, took place in which the Dean let Dodgson know that he knew and disapproved. That Dodgson remained only on sufferance. That any misstep would bring immediate dismissal and disgrace. That the Dean was actually of a mind to thrash the deacon, as if the former were back at Westminster and the latter reduced to the status of unruly boy. It hardly had to be said that the deanery was off limits thenceforward to Dodgson. He was no longer welcome. There would be no further intercourse between the Liddells and Mr. Dodgson, except for those official encounters that were a part of college life.

Which went on, all the time, for the rest of their lives! In public, they had not only to tolerate each other but to behave toward one another with scrupulous correctness. A cool correctness, perhaps, but with no show of enmity or resentment. It was like those extravagant novels by the Brontës in which some terrible secret—embodied in a madwoman—is locked away in a tower, making noises at night and threatening the rest of the household with a calamity that ultimately comes, satisfying the reader who can stand only so much suspense, so much dread. In real life, people put up with what they have to for as long as is necessary. And if the catastrophe never arrives, they are grateful. The difference between the novels and real life is that the novels take a week or two to read, but a life stretches out over decades, and people find ways to bear these burdens, developing the right muscles, building the right calluses.

That added burden came at a time when her parents already had more than enough to carry. Little Albert's death was not merely sad but an occasion for reconsidering the question they had managed to put aside when Arthur, the three-year-old, had died. In . . . '53, that would have been. And they must have asked themselves how such a thing could happen, how God could permit it to happen, or how—if God did permit such things—it helped in any way to have such a God. One might as well live like an atheist, like a pagan.

Which was, perhaps, what her father was trying to do. The study of Greek was perfectly respectable, inasmuch as Greek was the language of the New Testament. But it was also a door to all of pagan thought. And his task was of such scale as to fill up the days of a lifetime and not threaten to desert the laborer. How to endure? How to accept such a thing? An innocent human life, given and then snatched back. It was, quite literally, beastly. What you'd do to a lamb for the chops. Or a pullet for broiling. And next to that beastliness, this from Dodgson?

To which there was no recourse. Had her father been a duke or an earl, he could simply have horsewhipped the man and very probably would have done. But having more power over the Students and the Chapter than any duke, he had no such option, was limited to a private discussion, expressions of contempt and disgust, and then . . . for-bearance. Patience. A long, slow hardening of the soul.

That was what came over the household, a darkening, as if, immediately beside it and to the south, a tall building had been erected that turned the sunniest rooms dim. Alice blamed Edith. Edith refused to take that blame. She blamed Alice for blaming her. The love that had previously obtained between the two young girls soured, curdled as love can. And they were cast out of Eden.

Out of Wonderland? That too.

2

"ALICE? ARE YOU AWAKE?" Rhoda asks, not quite whispering.

"Yes. I've just been lying here, resting."

"They say that that's almost as good as sleep. They're wrong," Rhoda says. "Whoever *they* are."

"Yes."

"Are you upset?" Rhoda asks. "By this morning?"

"Not really."

Rhoda waits, not challenging what Alice said, but not immediately accepting it, either.

"Not by this morning," Alice says, at last.

"Then by what?"

"Oh, this entire business. The way it's become so . . . public."

"You can always plead illness or fatigue. A woman of your age has an excuse that is likely to be believed."

"People are very kind," Alice says.

"People are vultures, you might better say."

"I might think so . . ."

"What is upsetting you?" Rhoda asks.

"I've no idea what to tell Caryl. For the newspaper. I must tell him something."

"For the newspaper, you tell him what they want to hear. For yourself—or himself—that's another question. Perhaps another time?"

"No, I've always said that. But if there's to be a time, then this is the time. I've avoided it all these years . . ."

"Why not?" Rhoda asks.

"Why not tell him?"

"Why not continue to avoid it? Who's going to challenge you? Not Caryl, surely."

"I simply can't decide which is likely to do him more hurt," Alice says.

"Him? Or yourself? They're not quite the same. Both are legitimate concerns, I should think."

"Yes."

"There are no deadlines," Rhoda reminds her. "And there will be the crossing back to England. Plenty of time, really."

"That's true," Alice agrees.

Rhoda stands at the window and adjusts the blind so that she can look out at Park Avenue below, with beds of flowers set out in the islands between the streams of traffic.

"The worst of it's over," Rhoda says.

"Yes, I suppose so," Alice agrees.

"Would you like some tea? Or bouillon?"

"Bouillon, please."

"I'll call down for it," Rhoda says. "You'll come out?"

"Yes, very shortly," Alice promises.

Rhoda goes out into the parlor of their suite, closing the door behind her. She is a brick, Alice thinks, a tower of strength. But the decision still has to be made about what she should tell Caryl. In spite of Rhoda's reassuring words, Alice knows that if she does not speak now, she never will.

Rhoda knows most of it. Very possibly, she has been able to guess at the rest. But Rhoda wasn't involved in it. Indeed, Alice often thinks the organizing principle in Rhoda's life has been the avoidance of involvements, the refusal to descend to the messiness of living. Which was why Rhoda had never married?

It isn't up to Rhoda, however. It is Alice's decision, whether to speak or not speak, whether to suppose that Caryl will be strengthened or broken by hearing how other people bore up after having done . . . grievous wrong.

SHE REMEMBERS the last time she saw the Dodo. It was forty
years ago and she'd gone up to Oxford for her father's
retirement from the deanship. Parties, dinners, ceremonies, and in amongst them all there was the note from
Dodgson inviting Alice to tea. Not alone. *You would probably
prefer to bring a companion; but I must leave the choice to you, only
remarking that if your husband is here he would be most very
welcome (I crossed out most because it's ambiguous; most words are, I
fear). I met him in our Common Room not long ago. It was hard to
realize that he was the husband of one I can scarcely picture to myself,
even now, as more than 7 years old!*

The invitation to bring a companion was a declaration
that he would not be a danger to her—which was obvious.
The misstatement, that he could scarcely picture her as
more than seven years old, was tantamount to an undoing
of their entire relationship. She'd been ten when he'd made
up the Wonderland story, and eleven when the break came.
He had photographs he'd taken—presumably, he'd held on
to them—of her at ten and eleven. "No more than 7 years
old" was to suggest that he'd set the clock back to the very
beginning, when they'd first met, before anything had happened between them except a mutual interest and approval
that enabled the rest.

She showed the letter to her mother, not for permission
now, but as a curiosity. A thirty-nine-year-old married
woman doesn't need permission from her mother to take
tea with anyone. Her mother showed her an extraordinary
letter she'd received from Dodgson a fortnight or so earlier. He said, among other things, "The Latin Grammar
tells us that the more money we get, the more the love of it
grows upon us: and I think it is the same with *honour.* Having had so much, I now thirst for more: and the honour I
now covet is that a certain pair of young ladies should come
some day and take tea with me. I have a store of ancient
memories of visits from your elder daughters but I do not

think that Miss Rhoda and Miss Violet Liddell have ever
been inside my rooms: and I should like to add to my store
one fresh memory at least, of having had a visit from them
. . . If I were 20 years younger, I should not, I think, be
bold enough to give such invitations: but, but, I am close on
60 years old now: and all romantic sentiment has quite died
out of my life: so I have become quite hardened as to having
lady-visitors of *any* age!"

"Extraordinary!" Alice said.

"Isn't it?" her mother agreed.

"It's as close to an apology as he could come," she said.

"He can afford it," her mother said. "In his way, he's
won. He's outlasted Henry. Henry retires. Mr. Dodgson
stays on."

Alice was excluded? Omitted, at any rate. "I do not ever
ask more than 2 ladies, at a time, for tea: for that is the
outside number who can see the same photographs, in
comfort: and to be showing more than one at a time is
simply distracting." But then, the invitation came to Alice
herself. The first letter, perhaps, had been a kind of scout
sent ahead to find out whether the terrain was passable. A
tentative foray? As he sat there in his rooms, was he waiting
daily for some sign from the deanery whether this renewal
of an old association was now to be tolerated? Or was he
daring a refusal, now that the Dean was stepping down and
most unlikely to bring proceedings against the old Student?

It hardly mattered. What mattered, Alice decided, was
that he still cared. And that he was sorry. He admitted a
boldness. To both mother and daughter, he had as much as
confessed to at least some share in the blame. Alice had
never objected to his attentions. And she was fairly certain
Edith had been eager for more of them.

But tea? With his waving about of the teapot as in the old
days. Tea, as with the Mad Hatter and the Dormouse? No, it

was too much. She offered to call, but not for tea, and she brought Rhoda rather than Regi, knowing how frightened Carroll was by imposing men, by husbands. The following day, in the afternoon, they crossed the quad and spent half an hour with him. So that Rhoda could see him—she hardly remembered him, having been too young, back then, for him to pay much attention to. Too young for any impression she might have formed of him to hold itself fixed in her mind.

And so Alice, herself, could see him again, not only for the sake of seeing him but as a way of visiting Edith's grave. The grave of their good times together. Or the scene of the demise of that relationship.

It was a formal, rather stiff visit. He was altogether cordial, said he was happy to see her, delighted to see them both, but he was nervous. The old stutter that was there for outsiders, when he was self-conscious, betrayed the fact that his feelings were, at the very least, mixed. There may have been pleasure but there was also apprehension. He must have looked at her with a complicatedly refracted vision, considering—as Alice did not at the time—how many little girls had come to sit in her place, admiring his jokes and conferring upon him what tokens of affection he might want or be able to accept for his performance. She mentioned the names of her children—Alan, Rex, and Caryl—and he nodded but did not inquire about the coincidence of the sound of the last with that of his own nom de plume. Caryl then was . . . four? They spoke of her father's retirement plans, which were to move to a sizeable property nearby from which he could maintain his connection with the college, see some of the Christ Church men who came back to the House from time to time, use the Bodleian . . .

"Yes, yes. All very wise, very sensible. He has done quite well by the college, I think."

"He's tried," she said.

Dodgson showed Rhoda one or two of the photographs from the old days. And he had a little postage-stamp case he'd designed, which he gave Alice, inscribing it "To Mrs. Hargreaves, from the Inventor." It was a funny little thing that held different denominations of stamps and slipped into a cover on which there were pictures of the Cheshire Cat and of Alice holding the Duchess' baby. When one pulled the interior case out of the holder, the baby in Alice's arms turned into the pig, and the Cheshire Cat on the back disappeared, all but the smile.

An odd gift, but it was what he had. And formally inscribed, but then he was afraid to call her "Alice."

All the while, she kept thinking that it wasn't worth it, that she should never have fought with Edith over this. They'd made a terrible mistake, throwing away their childhoods in a dispute for this little man's affections. When she could bear it no more, she announced that they had to get back to the deanery. Rhoda loyally rose. Dodgson bade them good-bye.

She never saw him again. But that evening, at the deanery, she talked with Rhoda. She didn't actually have to say much. Rhoda had been well aware of the coolness between Edith and Alice which had gone on for years. All Alice had to say was, "He was what we'd fought over."

"Oh?" Not prying, but inviting her to say more if she was so disposed. Rhoda was very good at that kind of thing, almost too good. Professional.

"It was a terrible mistake," Alice said. "On both our parts."

"Oh?"

"Edith told mother that he'd been behaving improperly. Indecently. But it was really because she was jealous."

"But that wasn't your fault, was it?" Rhoda asked.

"Oh, yes. I knew she was jealous. I could have made her

feel better about it, could have coped with it. I ought to
have done so. As one ought to take care of a younger
sister.''

Rhoda, a younger sister, said nothing. She couldn't agree
or disagree without wounding. Or ask if Mr. Dodgson really
had been indecent—to either of them.

"It seemed so important at the time.''

"And all these years, Papa did nothing?'' Rhoda asked.

"What could he do? Without hurting the college and us,
what could he have done?''

"Yes, I see,'' she said. And a minute later, having thought
about it, she said, again, "Yes, I see.''

Alice looked at her, inquiringly.

"In fact,'' Rhoda said, "I don't see how anyone could
have done differently.''

"No,'' Alice agreed. "That ought to make it easier, but it
doesn't.''

"No, it never does,'' Rhoda agreed.

RHODA OF COURSE FANCIES herself as the expert on suffering. She even has an OBE for her work with all those poor
broken people at Netley Hospital. It is inevitable, Alice
supposes, for sufferers to resent—to some extent—experts
in suffering. Rhoda is likely to expect that, too.

"The bouillon is here, dear,'' Rhoda announces.

"Yes, yes. I'm coming,'' Alice says. She slips on her
quilted robe, puts her feet into the slippers she has placed
carefully beside the bed, and goes out into the parlor.

"Caryl is out?'' she asks.

"I'm afraid so,'' Rhoda says. Neither of them alludes to
the overwhelming likelihood that Caryl is out in some
speakeasy, drinking himself toward numbness and beyond.

There is too much show about the bouillon. Service
ought not call attention to itself this way. But the Waldorf-
Astoria has its reputation to maintain with people who do

not have the habit of good servants and feel the need to be impressed. After all, they've paid for it. So there is more flourish than the pouring of bouillon from the heated metal container into the heated double-eared cup requires. The laying out of the napkins and spoons has been a ritualized performance. Or a way of intimidating guests into tipping more than they otherwise might?

"Thank you," Alice says, exactly as she would say it at home.

The room waiter retires, recognizing a quality performance when he sees one.

The bouillon is good, very hot and not too salty. Alice approves. "A good idea," she says. "Thank you."

"Whatever for?" Rhoda asks.

"For suggesting this. It's just what I needed."

"This is all very taxing," Rhoda says. "Any way you can baby yourself, you ought to do it. You deserve it."

"But I haven't done anything. I felt like an impostor this morning. A doctorate, for goodness' sake! They must be mad!"

"They couldn't give it to the book. They couldn't give it to Rosenbach. And Dodgson's dead, so they couldn't give it to him. You were the only one left."

"Yes, I know. Still, I felt ridiculous. And I kept thinking about Edith. If only she could see me now. It would be her . . . Not quite revenge. Satisfaction, perhaps. Something like that. She'd have been amused."

"You think she was that spiteful?" Rhoda asks gently.

"Aren't we all, just a little?"

Rhoda decides that Alice is at least partly teasing. She likes to do that, to be mordant. Rhoda is surprised, then, when Alice continues, not teasing at all but quite in earnest. "I remember thinking, when she died, that she'd had the last word. That she'd left me with an apology I never really had the chance to make to her. And that she'd been true to our childhood romance after all, dying that way, just as she'd announced her engagement . . ."

"Fiddlesticks!"

"Perhaps. But so much of what we deeply and truly think may be fiddlesticks. Bargains we make with God. Bring home my sons, and I'll do thus and such . . . It's all nonsense. Nobody's listening. Nobody's there. There aren't any bargains, except in our own minds. But Edith was going to marry Aubrey Harcourt and I'd been looking forward to that as if it would put things right between us. She'd have had Aubrey Harcourt and that wonderful old house. She'd have been able to forgive me. She'd have sensible things like a husband and children, and I wouldn't. I'd more or less resigned myself to being an old maid. It would make it all right between Edith and me. But then she had appendicitis and peritonitis and . . ."

"Yes."

". . . and it was as if she'd decided to remain true to Carroll, or to Wonderland, or to our long silent battle, after all."

"That's nonsense," Rhoda says. "She had a ruptured appendix. She didn't decide anything or remain true to anything. That's all in your mind."

"I know. But knowing doesn't make it go away. It remains in my mind."

"Did you feel you betrayed her or Dodgson or anything or anyone when you married Regi?"

"No one cared. It didn't matter," Alice says.

"Of course people cared!"

"No, what I mean is that no one cared the way Edith would have cared. And she didn't care because she was dead. Because she had won."

"Because she was dead. That's all," Rhoda says rather sharply.

"As you like," Alice says, not really conceding anything.

She picks up her bouillon cup and drinks the last drop. She remembers the shock of it, the way she had been hoping Aubrey Harcourt might make it official, promoting Edith into such success, happiness, and assurance that the two of them—she and Edith—might manage at last to repair the old rift, bridge it or simply fly across it in the soaring of the moment.

But Edith came down with measles, a perfectly silly thing to do, a child's illness that she ought not to have had. Amazing that she hadn't been exposed to it before! But there she was, covered with ridiculous spots and kept to a darkened room. All the festivities of the commencement exercises going on, the balls, the dinner parties, and Edith was kept to her bed like a naughty girl with that almost laughable ailment. She was in no danger. All the physicians had agreed it was simply a minor nuisance for Edith to wait out, a trial of her patience. And on top of that trivial ailment, there came the trouble with the appendix. And the measles perhaps masked some of the appendicitis symptoms. By the time any of them knew anything, it was too late, the appendix having already ruptured, the peritonitis having set in.

The infection. The grave looks of specialists called up from London. And, abruptly, unreasonably, peremptorily, the death.

With the quarrel between them as yet unsettled. There is no way to answer the accusations of the dead. They may be unreasonable, but they are final. One contrives, somehow, to live with them.

And one feels guilty even about that.

CARYL APPEARS. He has been drinking but he is not drunk. Or not beyond a slow and ponderous demonstration of his competence to walk, speak, sit, and comport himself as if he were sober. It is the result of long practice, this ability to absorb alcohol up to the very point of insensibility and not yet cross the line. An art, really. It is his art. Some men have a talent for business. Others have a knack for painting or drawing or writing. Some have a gift with animals and can ride well or manage dogs. His forte is drinking. He is suited to it physically, temperamentally, and spiritually.

He takes it, therefore, as more of an inconvenience, almost as a personal affront, that the Americans should have decided to prohibit the sale of beer, wine, and spirits, taking a bizarre leap backwards in time to some quasi-religious puritanism. He feels as though he were visiting in Arabia Deserta, where the bedouin have similar views about booze. But they make an exception for visiting Europeans, turning a blind eye to the ways in which the French or English provision themselves for tours of duty there. The Americans, believing themselves to be civilized, make no such allowance for the requirements of their betters. When he arrived in New York, the customs inspector took a quick look at Caryl's face, judged him accurately and immediately to be an imbiber, and went minutely through all the luggage, not only Caryl's but his mother's and his aunt's, too, looking for hidden flasks. Caryl took it as a challenge more than an affront, and he was almost disappointed to find how easy it was to get a drink in New York. Still, remembering the face of the customs man, and in consideration of the precautions the speakeasies have to take with their payoffs to the police, their expensive smugglers, their gangster connections, there is a particular pleasure in drinking here, as if he'd discovered a new cocktail that, after a few days, still is appealing.

He has been out having a drink, of course. For the drink, partly, but also to get away from all that unbearable uplift of the morning's exercises. The way they treated his mother was silly. The way they oozed dedication to the good, the true, and the beautiful was utterly loathsome.

They were all fools. And in the speakeasy, there was a wonderful clublike atmosphere of conspiracy against fools and foolishness. Neat whiskey in a teacup is the only possible answer to pious nonsense and a humorless passion for self-improvement. The children of darkness may have their difficulties, but they tend to be more modest and therefore more companionable than the children of light. In America, anyway. In a speakeasy, there is the quick fraternity of outlaws—for they are all of them violating the law just by being there. The fact that it is a stupid and barbarous law doesn't change anything, or not in the saloon. What it does is underscore all of the daytime activities of the city, giving an ironic twist to perfectly reasonable pieces of discourse. Mealtimes are a joke—without wine? Academic gatherings are hilarious, with all these people pretending to be civilized and humane, living in the middle of an intellectual, artistic, and moral Sahara. The strenuousness and famous pace of New York are a joke, because the pursuit of happiness to which the nation is supposed to be dedicated is as much of a sham as the life and liberty that are supposed to go along with it. The decent people are inside, sitting at a polished wooden bar, feet curled around a barstool, watching the bartender pour drinks with the melancholy seriousness of priests in an atheist country where religion is outlawed. Or sitting at a table in what is trying to look like a restaurant, drinking whiskey from a teacup . . .

Caryl enjoys this because it suits his temperament. What was left of him after the war was a fondness for the absurd, a permanent non-salute to authority, a devout suspicion that the more impressive and sober a man or an institution sounds, the more full of shit he or it is likely to be. He doesn't expect his mother or Aunt Rhoda to agree with him in any of these views. But he needs to get away every now and then in order to keep up the silent assent on his part to their pathetic gratitude—to America the bountiful and to

Rosenbach the swindler; to Nicholas Murray Butler, the stooge; to Columbia University, the institutional toady. And to Eldridge Johnson, the Victor Talking Machine Company president, who is the greatest ninny of them all. Rosenbach bought the manuscript at Sotheby's for $75,000, only to turn around and resell it to Johnson for $150,000. A profit of 100 percent then, and a sum that was princely. Regal! The trip to America was the least he could offer. And the reason for it is painfully obvious—to boost the price further, to make Johnson think he got a bargain. To have Columbia, and Butler, and the New York *Times* endorse the value of the object he's laid out all that hard cash for.

This is altogether clear to Caryl, but his mother dislikes alluding to it in any way. Caryl has no objection, understanding perfectly well that there are some things one just doesn't talk about. He is forty-four years old and has held the King's commission. He isn't a child, but neither is he a perfect fool. It seems excessive—and foolish—to him at least, to carry on in private as if the academic pomp and circumstance and the trip itself were all the natural outpouring of the generosity of the Rosenbach brothers, or Mr. Johnson, or America as a whole. They've done well for themselves, as far as Caryl is able to see. Certainly, the Rosenbachs have come out of it with a lot of cash and at the same time a reputation for great public benefaction. Astounding!

It is a piece of hypocrisy that seems to go along with the other, larger hypocrisy about drink. If you can speak English—or presumably Chinese or Hindustani or any other language intelligible to God—and are tall enough to see over the bar, you can get a drink in New York. Not necessarily a good drink, and certainly not a cheap one, but it will have alcohol in it. You can get sozzled. And all the time, there are these insane pretensions about purity and health and whatever damfoolishness it was that they had in mind when they passed this dotty law. Or amendment to their Constitution, actually!

Inasmuch as he isn't a citizen of this curious republic, Caryl sees no particular reason for having to participate in the egregious flummery that seems to be the national pastime. His mother's collaboration is regrettable, as is his Aunt Rhoda's. But he owes them a filial deference that keeps him from arguing about it. He can raise the question —and has done so. But he cannot press his views beyond a certain point. They have long since reached that point. So, from time to time, he finds it necessary to excuse himself, dart round the corner, repair to some amiable watering hole, and brace himself with a stiff double whiskey. He's been advised that the whiskey is safer than the gin.

Now that he is back, he is prepared for a couple of hours of foolishness. With luck, he'll be able to get all the way through dinner. And then? Well, his mother is eighty, goes to bed early, and will leave him free for whatever remedies the wear and tear of the dinner hour have demanded.

"Is that you?" his mother asks.

"I've never quite known how to answer that question," he says cheerfully. "Certainly, it's me. As any burglar could honestly claim."

"You know perfectly well what I meant," she says.

My God, he thinks. We're back in the book. Drowning in the damned treacle-well.

SHE REFRAINS FROM ASKING. Indeed, the question is so restrained that it seems to lunge, like an unruly dog on a short lead, all but snapping at him. He disarms it by announcing, "I thought I'd go out for a quick drink before we set to work."

No reply. Except that it might now wait until after dinner.

Is it an accusation? Has she been sitting here, waiting to work, all this time?

"I had a nap," she announces, which may be a way of letting him know that his absence has not been an inconvenience. She is careful not to add to his burdens, but her care is a burden. To be taken care of thus by a woman of that age is a burden of great weight.

They eat rather early, return to the suite, and he is at the ready, a writing tablet on the little fruitwood desk and his fountain pen neatly placed beside it, ready to uncoil its wreath of words. But now she is the one who seems unwilling. She claims fatigue—which is always possible at her age, also always possible to claim. She did have a nap in the afternoon, or said she did. Rhoda confirms that, but Rhoda would, whether it were the truth or not. Are they perhaps daring him to go out for another drink? Are they testing him, trying to determine how irresponsible he can be, how selfish?

Next to the tablet, there is the letter from the New York *Times Magazine* editor with its list of questions, "the answers to which—as much as possible in Mrs. Hargreaves' own words—will make a piece in which our readers are likely to be interested." So the editor thought and so Caryl is inclined to believe, himself. He is interested in what his mother is going to tell him, not really expecting any long-suppressed revelations but rather curious as to how she plans, this time, to keep him at arm's length.

He has been dragged along as a further exhibit, but also to support and protect his mother and his aunt. He agreed to come because it was impossible to refuse, would have been unthinkable to allow his mother to undertake such a journey without him. It was also, coincidentally, a good time to be away from London and from Madeleine, who can sometimes be a trial.

In fact, he has already learned more than he thought he

would on this absurd expedition. He understands, for example, that it wasn't just Carroll's deplorable behavior that his father always resented, but the strange way in which his mother turned the event—or allowed the world to turn it—into some special badge of honor. She had used it to keep the rest of the world at bay. Caryl has the clear impression that she manipulated her secret the way a little girl might do, who wanted to drive her playmates wild with jealousy. His mother was subtle about it and more adept than a little girl, but the operation was much the same. She enjoyed this morning's exercises, he is quite convinced, because they were the world's acknowledgment that, yes indeed, she has a secret.

"Whatever you say," he replies. "But the man is coming tomorrow afternoon."

"We can do it in the morning," his mother tells him.

"It won't leave me much time to make a fair copy. Or even to put it into any sort of order."

"They'll do all that," she says. "They're paid to do that."

He hardly thinks it worth while to point out that he, too, is being paid. This pose of hers, of the unconcerned gentlewoman, is wearisome, but she indulges in it all the time. It is her way of reproaching him for not having taken any of the money from the sale of the manuscript. Or for having married Madeleine. The worst of it is that, about the marriage, he sometimes wonders whether she mightn't have been right.

"Whatever you say, mother," he says again.

She thanks him for his reasonableness and goes to bed. It is quite early. He can go out, find another saloon, or go to a film. Or he can stay in, read the new *Collier's* and a recent *Punch* he picked up at a news stand. She may emerge in an hour or so, ready to go to work. It wouldn't be at all surprising—no more than it would be for him to discover that this was a test of his loyalty and attentiveness. She is forever devising such tests, and he is forever failing them.

But it is also possible that she is reluctant to talk about Dodgson, reluctant to admit that there isn't any secret. Or that the secret is a terrible one. But what could bother her after all this time? Except for the fact that he is still alive, that the war spared him, there isn't much that embarrasses Caryl any more. He assumes his mother must be even more inured, or resigned, or whatever it is. Different routes to the same end.

She sleeps. He sits and reads magazines. He decides to write a brief note to Madeleine, for form's sake. It is a relatively easy way to maintain the pretense that he has no idea what she's doing in his absence. There are men in his position who can say in all truth that they simply don't understand what their wives may be doing. He, on the other hand, understands all too well. Madeleine has worked out a desperate way to punish herself for her infidelity to Felix, which is what she considers her marriage to Caryl to be. The remedy, of course, is further infidelity, a series of infidelities to Caryl that are so absurd as to be depressing. He has learned that the worst thing he can do is pretend not to notice, to maintain a willful blindness for as long as possible. And then, when that fails, to forgive her. She finds that quite infuriating.

Of course, the worst thing is what he always does, partly because it is the kind thing to do, but also partly because it is mean and hurtful.

Other than that, the marriage is a great success, thank you. He has money to live on. They get on well and enjoy each other's company. They have even surprised themselves, the world, and Caryl's mother, having produced a daughter, nearly a year old now, Mary Jean Rosemary Alice Hargreaves. They are not likely to have any more children.

The note is a minimal gesture. But the hotel paper is

there, inviting and of good quality. The fountain pen is out anyway, accusingly ready for action. It may as well be used. He scrawls a cheerful greeting, writes the address on the envelope, and tucks it into his pocket to hand in at the front desk for posting. In the morning? Or now? He considers going down to post the letter, himself. He could take a short stroll.

No, that would be the moment his mother would choose to appear, looking for him, ready to work, or saying she was, and feeling abandoned.

He puts the letter on the desk beside the yellow tablet and goes into his bedroom to prepare for bed. Along with the magazines, he has a new Dorothy Sayers and can get by with that. There are worse hardships than comfortable hotel suites and dull evenings of what is by now almost pure sobriety.

In the morning, he is ready to work again. He wakes early, knowing his mother's habit is to rise with the sun. He breakfasts with his mother and aunt, and then, together, they face the editor's questions.

"What was your first meeting with Mr. Dodgson?" he asks, reading from the editor's letter.

"I don't remember," his mother answers.

"Oh, they'll love that," he says, and he commences writing: "My mother does not remember her first meeting with Mr. Dodgson."

"It's the truth," she says.

"And very gripping, too." Caryl teases.

"Well, I was four when your grandfather became dean and the family moved to Oxford . . ."

"Wait," he enjoins. And he writes: "She was four years old when my grandfather became dean of Christ Church and the family moved to Oxford . . ."

There is nothing new that she has to confide to the *Times*. Or to Caryl? He waits, writing in a large clear hand, filling up the sheets of the tablet, putting down the familiar details of the excursion up the river to Godstow. Some details that he knows, she censors—such as the nickname for Miss Prickett, "Pricks" being undignified. Caryl doesn't argue. His mother says things that are clearly untrue—implying that her friendship with Dodgson continued on until his death. Caryl knows this to be—at the very least—an exaggeration. He says nothing. His fountain pen rolls on.

The one surprise she has for him is Dodgson's last letter to her, which is remarkable only in that she has carried it with her—keeping it as a talisman, or using the *Times* to advertise the fact that she possesses yet more treasures? It is Dodgson's invitation to tea back in '91, when his mother was up at Oxford for her father's retirement. She opens it, unfolds it, and places it on the desk before Caryl for him to copy. He does so, but as his hand forms the words he cannot help wondering what the letter proves—that Dodgson still cared about his mother? That his mother still cared enough about Dodgson to have carried the letter about after all that time? Or that something was fundamentally peculiar about the connection? Why should Dodgson have said, "You would probably prefer to bring a companion," unless there were some impropriety in her visit or the risk or memory of one?

"Who was your companion?" he asks. "Did Father go?"

"I went," Aunt Rhoda tells him.

Speaking at the same moment, however, Alice says, "Certainly not."

It takes Caryl only a moment's consideration to realize that Aunt Rhoda was protecting Alice, then and now. She is still, by her attempt to answer Caryl's question, shielding her sister. "Why do you say, 'Certainly not,' that way?"

She looks at him, looks at Rhoda, and looks back at him. He waits. He is convinced she will avoid the question somehow, that she will keep him away.

"They disliked each other," she says, "your father and
Dodgson. My father and Dodgson disliked each other as
well."

"Why would Dodgson dislike Grandfather?" Caryl asks.
He ostentatiously screws the cap onto the pen as if to let her
know that he is asking only for himself and not for the New
York *Times* or its readers.

"Because your grandfather disliked *him*," his mother replies evenly. "It was a misunderstanding that had gone
back for many years."

"Of what sort?"

"It hardly matters any more," Alice says.

Should he insist that it matters to him? Is that too obvious to need saying? Would it be too overbearing?

"Tell him," Rhoda prompts. "I think you should tell
him."

Alice looks at Rhoda blankly. Caryl, at any rate, cannot
tell whether she is angry or resigned.

"You don't like to speak ill of the dead, I know, but it was
none of your doing. It was Edith, after all," Rhoda
prompts. "Tell him."

Alice blinks. Is it a secret they have shared together? Or
is he right in supposing his mother is surprised that even
Rhoda has guessed it?

"Your Aunt Edith—your late Aunt Edith, I should say—
made some accusations about Mr. Dodgson's behavior, accusations I believe to have been untrue and to have been
prompted by jealousy . . ."

"Of your mother," Aunt Rhoda explains.

"Yes, of me. And I am afraid that while they may not have
been believed they were not altogether disbelieved. There
was, from that time onward, a coolness between Mr. Dodgson and your grandparents that lasted all their lives. I find it
most distressing. Very sad, actually. You will not make any
reference to it . . ."

"Of course not," he assures her.

". . . either in the newspaper piece or anywhere else."

"Never," he promises.

"Thank you," she says.

"I think it's better out in the open this way," Aunt Rhoda says.

"Out, and then put away," Alice says. "At any rate, that visit with your Aunt Rhoda was the last time I ever saw him."

He opens the pen once again, and writes at the bottom of the page, "As far as my mother remembers, that tea was the last occasion on which she saw Mr. Dodgson."

"Will that do?" Alice asks.

"I think so," Caryl says. He has no idea whether the question is about her having satisfied the editor or her having satisfied him. In either case, the only decent, the only possible answer is the one he has given.

And probably, they are—he and the editor—likely to be satisfied to about the same extent, less than they might have wanted but more than they really expected.

At last, he lays down his pen.

3

THE MAN from the *Times* seems pleased. He sits in the parlor, having read Caryl's manuscript and having asked a few questions of his own, the replies to which he has written down in a small spiral note pad. It will be up to him to rewrite, emend, and perhaps entirely to recast Caryl's pages. Caryl understands that the fiction of his authorship is a way the *Times* has found around its own rules. If he is the author, then the newspaper can allow him and his mother a look at the galleys. Apparently, it is not a custom of the paper to let the subjects of its curiosity retain control, but for Alice Hargreaves they have waived their rules.

Rhoda offers coffee. The *Times* man refuses. He is eager to depart, as uncomfortable with these unorthodox arrangements as anyone else. His own professional standards prompt him to be gone. "We'll be able to reach you here?" he asks.

"Until tomorrow at least," his mother says. "Perhaps until Friday. Then we'll be in Philadelphia. Dr. Rosenbach will know where we are."

They can find Dr. Rosenbach easily enough. Caryl assumes that Rosenbach was the one who got the *Times* interested in the first place. One needs only some prestige and a little nerve to approach them, and Rosenbach seems to be lacking in neither.

"Yes, of course," the *Times* man says, not quite admitting that Rosenbach's name and phone number are already known to him. He rises, thanks Caryl on behalf of the paper, and extends his hand in admirable insincerity.

"Think nothing of it," Caryl says, sure the man will think as little of it as possible.

"Miss Liddell, Mrs. Hargreaves, it was a pleasure."

"Thank you for coming," his mother says.

When the *Times* man is gone, Caryl watches his mother retire to her bedroom, fatigued or simply wishing to be alone for a while.

"We mustn't push her any further," Rhoda says quietly.

The "we" is intended in a friendly spirit, Caryl supposes. Still, something perverse in him wants at least to press his aunt a bit further. "About what?" he asks. "Do you mean physically? Or about Dodgson?"

"About Dodgson. She dislikes speaking of those things."

Caryl sits down on one of the sofas, gets up, walks to the window, looks out, looks back at Rhoda. She says nothing. There are questions, of course. And if he is not to press his mother on the subject, it would be reasonable for his aunt to volunteer her own opinions, but nothing is forthcoming.

Can it be as simple, then, as what his mother at last confessed? Wouldn't his grandfather, the Dean, a man of some experience and judgment, have seen through Aunt Edith's charges if they had been utterly false? Wouldn't his father have been satisfied by such an explanation? Had it ever been offered and rejected?

Rhoda's silence is huge, fills the room, weighs on the furniture like heavy brocade. Can she find no word to add, no syllable of authentication and reinforcement? But she says nothing. Indeed, she is looking at him, waiting for him to decide whether to believe or disbelieve his mother's latest revelation. Whether to stop there or go on, to the next set of questions. He has a giddy moment of perception in which he comes to the understanding that Aunt Rhoda is waiting to see what kind of person he is, how obtuse or acute, how rigid or flexible. He will settle on whatever truth he can stand, whatever story he can devise that will be at the same time tolerable and satisfying. And the result, with which she dare not tamper, will be a function of the balance between head and heart.

He looks down at the traffic on Park Avenue. "I think I may go out for a while," he says at last.

"Shall we expect you for dinner?" she inquires.

"I'm not sure," he tells her. "Don't wait for me, if I haven't turned up."

"Very well," she says, looking at her shoes. She knows perfectly well where he is going.

HE WINDS UP, several hours later, in a whorehouse in the East Forties, having been steered there by a bartender in one of the speakeasies on his serendipitous tour. It is an impressive place, almost comical in its staginess, with a large crystal chandelier in the entrance hall and flocked wallpaper in crimson and black. Blackamoor sconces holding electric candles. Bowls and vases of flowers on impressively heavy sideboards and ornately carved and gilded tables. There is a bar-room and a parlor, and upstairs there are the private rooms. It is all very decorous, with the girls in long robes that, nevertheless, flash open from time to time to reveal a glimpse of milky—or swarthy—thigh.

Caryl is in no hurry. What he wants, more than sex, is the company of strangers, the honesty of strangers who are brought together in a situation where there is no nonsensical pretension about how splendid any of them are and who can relax and enjoy themselves. This is the human condition. This is what it is all about, something to drink, something to eat, and someone to hold on to for a little while. The rest is foolishness. The pomposity of Columbia University or of Christ Church leads directly to rats' alley and the stinking bodies caught between the trenches. It is a dreadful association, but that is the way the world works—so that there is something a little disgraceful in the very idea of survival. To avoid the trenches, to celebrate the kick of booze, or the taste of food, or the warmth of another human body is—in the world's terms—a bit louche, a childish self-indulgence. The high-minded fellows do their Latin and Greek, sit for their exams, and then go over the top to be mown down by cannonades.

"You're new here, aren't you?"

It is the madam, addressing her first-time customer. She is a handsome woman, a former working-girl, perhaps, who has made it to management. "That's right," Caryl says. He tells her which bartender recommended him. He admits what is obvious, that he is an Englishman, visiting the States "on business."

"Welcome," she says, meaning either to the United States or to her establishment, or both.

"May I buy you a drink?" he offers.

She is a little surprised but she accepts, signals the black servant—a kind of butler-cum-bodyguard—and asks for a

bottle of champagne and a couple of glasses. While they are
waiting for the champagne, she asks Caryl, "You have
something special in mind?"

"No, no. Just to sit here, really, and have a pleasant
evening. I like the atmosphere. It's like . . . like a good
club."

The servant brings the champagne. Caryl pays him and
lets him open the bottle and pour. The madam offers a
toast, "Mud in your eye," and takes a healthy sip. Caryl
drinks to that.

"Of course, it isn't just as a good club that we manage to
make a living here," she reminds him.

"I appreciate that. And I'll be going upstairs, eventually.
But it's a nice place. I thought I'd enjoy myself a bit."

"Name of the game," she says. "Still, when people buy
me a drink in my own place, it generally means that they've
got something a little bit special in mind."

"Oh, no, nothing like that, I assure you," he tells her, but
he wonders what it is that she thinks he wants. It had been
just a friendly impulse, the offer of the drink. Could it be
such an unusual thing?

"Sure, sure," she says, with a big stage wink that demon-
strates her conviction that, sooner or later, he is going to
ask for . . . dwarfs? Fire hoses? Hot mud?

What strikes him as funny isn't simply her misunderstanding, but his own realization that there is a mirror
image to the pretentiousness of the morning. One can pretend to vice as well as virtue, to the supine as well as to the
upright. There is a kind of glamor to coming in as the
depraved foreigner with bizarre compulsions. Ought he to
admit, out of patriotic pride, to a fondness for *le vice Anglais?*
Does he, in fact, want to take advantage of her offer? Would
he disappoint her if he contented himself with an ordinary
girl's entertainment in the ordinary way?

"Really, the enjoyable part is the anticipation. The confident expectation of pleasure," he explains, "is as much a source of gratification as the physical encounter."

"Whatever you say," she counters. "Still, when you've decided what your pleasure's going to be, don't be shy, you hear? You just let me know what you like. Within reason, we can provide whatever it is that you like. Isn't that so, Harry?"

Harry, a rather nattily turned-out fellow in a dark blue lounge suit, has come up to greet the madam. He is, Caryl assumes, an old customer. A friend, perhaps.

"Harry's my bootlegger. This champagne we're drinking, Harry brought it. Down from Canada. Harry and his boys. In trucks with fellows riding shotgun, like in the old days out west."

"No, back then, there were only the Indians to worry about. We got the cops to dodge. Or pay off. Did I catch your name?"

"Caryl," Caryl says.

"No, no. Your first name. We use first names around here. It's friendlier. Also safer, you know?"

Caryl is about to spell his name, but he changes his mind. "Lou," he says, straight-faced. He even invites the bootlegger to sit down with them.

"He's coming on shy," the madam says. "I don't think he trusts me."

"You could whisper in her ear, Lou," Harry suggests, flashing a conspiratorial grin. He turns to the madam and says, "Or maybe he wants you to guess. Like twenty questions."

"As long as the champagne keeps flowing, why not?" the madam asks. "At least one of us will be making a buck."

"You do all right on the refreshments," Harry says. And to Caryl, "Don't take it personally. She gives everybody a hard time." He signals with a broad grin that that's a joke.

Caryl smiles. "Have a drink?" he offers.

"Sure, thanks. But the next bottle's on me."

"Thank you," Caryl says carefully. He has drunk rather a lot at the speakeasies. The wine is mixing with his earlier indulgences somewhat heavily.

"Whips and leather?" the madam inquires.

"What?" Caryl asks.

"Is that what you want? Whips and leather?"

"No, no."

"Boys?"

"No."

"Two girls?" Harry asks.

"Hardly."

"A fatty?" Harry asks.

"I beg your pardon?"

"A real fat woman. Nellie's got one, you know. She must weigh three hundred pounds."

"No, no. Really, I'm not looking for anything exotic."

"Little girls?" Nellie asks. "Children?"

He looks at her, not quite knowing what to say. It is not such a shocking notion, no more peculiar than fatties or whips. And Caryl knows that there are paedophiles in the world, that such men exist . . . It is the neatness, the absurd reversal of the morning's academic rites that leaves him unable to know just how to reply.

"That's it! Look at him!" Harry says.

"It's all right," Nellie assures him.

"No, no," Caryl says, and he is about to explain what is on his mind, his distaste for the molestation of children, his curious position as the heir to the celebrity—or notoriety—of his mother's connection with Lewis Carroll, but he realizes that that simply isn't appropriate. It isn't right to be discussing his mother in a whorehouse, or her connection with Carroll, no matter how suspicious that connection may have been. "It . . . just never occurred to me," he says, knowing that it sounds feeble and that, in their places, he wouldn't believe it either.

"But now that it has been suggested, you find it suddenly fascinating, eh? A wonderful thing to try once?"

"Once upon a time, eh?" Harry suggests. "Or is that only for fairy stories?"

Caryl wonders whether Harry is drunk too. He knows he is a little drunk himself.

"We can arrange that," Nellie says, her voice low and rather flat, perfectly matter-of-fact. It is business she is talking, and business carries a solemnity about it, even here.

"I've no doubt," he says. It is supposed to be a concessive introductory remark. He is supposed to come up with the *but* and a graceful way out of it. But he can't think clearly enough. He can't tell her he is shocked. That would be bad manners in a place like this, would reflect unkindly on her and her business. He can't tell her—not any more—that it just doesn't happen to interest him. It is interesting. He isn't at all sure he wants to do this, wants actually to fuck a little girl, but he is struck by the idea of it, and the light it might shed on the question he has been carrying around for years like some genetic tendency toward a disease. He wonders what it would be like—just to talk a bit with the girl, to find out what she's like. Does she, he wonders, play with her toys and dolls between sexual workouts? Does she get any pleasure from the sex? Does she do it for sweets?

"It'll cost you fifty, Lou," the madam tells him.

It is a lot of money, even if it is dollars rather than pounds. He notices that her look has changed ever so subtly to one of appraisal. Is he good for it? Will he turn out to be a piker about his pleasures? It is, in a purely financial way, as much a challenge as a barrier, a price like that. Caryl's attitude toward money is, in any event, mixed. He has had moments of depression as he has looked about him and seen the way some people in the world just have the knack of finding it, stumbling into it, attracting it. On the other hand, he knows all sorts of men less deserving than he who seem to piss it away with a careless abandon he envies as much as he has ever envied anyone for the power to earn or attract it.

If Madeleine can atone for her marriage to him by being unfaithful, then he can expiate the shame of having married into comfort by pissing it away. Some of it, anyway.

Besides, he has made money, has accepted the *Times*'s payment for a non-job, simply to maintain the polite fiction by which they could let themselves treat his mother so delicately. It is a joke that makes the money unwelcome, almost as unwelcome as the money his mother got from the manuscript itself. Here is a suitably undignified way of getting rid of the *Times*'s check. "Will you take a check?" he asks. "The New York *Times*'s check?"

"You're kidding," she says.

"Not entirely," he says, to himself as much as to her. "But I can manage the cash."

"That'd be better," Harry says with a sage nod. "Nellie's used to dealing with cash."

It seems to have been settled. It doesn't much matter that Caryl has no intention of actually consummating any sort of sexual act with this child—or near-child, or mock child—that Nellie is about to produce for him. He is interested in talking with the creature and in wasting the money. Both these requirements will be harmoniously and pleasingly met. And there is no occasion for fear of the whore's impatient contempt, which he might have had to risk with one of the more mature professionals. That is an interesting, and perhaps vital, part of the attraction of children: that one needn't be concerned about one's performance or dignity. Children aren't threatening that way. They are like lapdogs. Like pets.

It isn't altogether true, but Caryl can see how it is true enough. With a man like Dodgson, that must have been a good part of the attraction of children, of small girls particularly—that they were small and strange and not threatening. That he could talk to them, as one can't to a spaniel or a terrier, and see in them a certain animal attractiveness, an otter-like grace. Not all children have that, of course . . .

"What does she look like," he asks, taking a sip of the champagne.

"A beautiful little girl. Slender. With big, wonderful, soulful eyes. We've been paid many compliments."

"And that's not all you've been paid, either," Harry says, cheerfully.

"How old is she?" Caryl asks.

"How old did you have in mind?" Nellie asks, her candid expression an admirable mask. Within very wide limits of plausibility, Caryl knows that any age he specifies will be the one the girl just happens to be.

"I trust you," he says. And it is true. Whatever age is most popular or the best compromise between what is possible and what the customers want, the likeliest way to meet the exigencies not of the actual patrons but of their fantasies, their imperious whims, that is what this shrewd woman will have. He trusts, then, not in her honesty but her knowingness, her calculation. "You have her here?" he asks.

"Oh, yes. She's very popular."

"I see."

"It's quite unfair, really. I've always maintained that all the arts of pleasing require practice, experience, the investment of time and energy. But in this house, there is always a place for raw youth."

"The rawer the better," Harry chimes in.

"So many of you seem to prefer it. Like *naïf* paintings, I expect."

"It's not that," Caryl tells her.

"What is it, then?" she asks. As if he were really a paedophile and had given thought to reasons for his predilections. Pretending, he considers what it might be. "They aren't threatening," he says. "And they are a way back."

"Back to what?"

"To when we were young, ourselves. To when everything was new, clear, sharp, fresh." He has surprised himself. He has surprised Harry, too.

"He's right, you know. That's it. That has to be it. I've always told you that what you're selling isn't flesh at all but dreams. We're in the same business after all," Harry says.

"Oh, shut up," Nellie says, but it is affectionate.

"More champagne?" Caryl offers.

"My treat, remember!" Harry reminds him.

Nellie signals for another bottle.

HE NOTICES THE ROOM FIRST. One can't help noticing the room, the way it has been done up like a nursery. There is wallpaper with a pattern of dolls, toy soldiers, stuffed animals, and balloons repeating endlessly from panel to panel. The colors of the chintz curtains and of the oversized chairs are pale pink and white. Of course, oversized! To jog one's memory, to make one think of the scale of furniture back then, when one was small. One could sit in a chair and have one's feet barely touch the ground. Caryl feels the size of the furniture and responds to it.

He realizes the light is dim. It is a night-light with a parchment shade on which the same procession of dolls and toy soldiers parade. That light is helpful for the girl to pretend to be whatever age is demanded. It allows the customer to regress a little too, if he is so disposed. And that is the point. That is what he stumbled on, downstairs, talking with Nellie and Harry, and up here he is convinced of its truth. To be . . . fourteen, say, and back at Cuffnells, and fooling around with the stableman's daughter in back of the carriage house. And she'd have been thirteen then? Twelve, for God's sake? He'd hardly touched her, simply put his hand on her just barely discernible breast, on her chest rather, for the breast was as much in his mind as it was there under her rough linen singlet. He remembers how he'd been seized by a trembling, a breathlessness, an ecstasy he was not to know, not with that intensity surely, at any time in his life thereafter. He is not back there in the gloom of the carriage house, but the dim night-light has put him in mind of it, has suggested it somehow. That is enough.

"Good evening," the girl says. A nice little girl. A well-behaved, proper little girl. Which is also quite right. One doesn't want a whorey little creature, a dwarfish version of the sluts and drabs downstairs.

"Good evening," he says. "And what's your name?"

"Juliet," she tells him. She is wearing a large hair-bow, black patent-leather shoes, white socks, and a filmy robe, full but short, so that it comes down to her fingertips.

"Juliet," he repeats. Of course. To remind people that Shakespeare's heroine was very young. To suggest, therefore, that this is not so unusual a taste. "Is that your real name?"

"No, but it's nice. I like it," she says. "It's from the play. Would you prefer to call me something else?"

"What's your real name?"

"Alice," she says.

He laughs. He can't help himself.

"It's not such a funny name, is it?" she asks, not defensive but rueful.

"It's a fine name," Caryl says. "It's every bit as good as Juliet. I was laughing at them for changing it."

"They thought Alice was too plain."

"Hardly," Caryl says.

She smiles. She is glad that he likes her name.

He is relieved that he has managed to avoid hurting her feelings. But "Alice"! He drains the champagne that was in the glass he brought up with him. He sets the empty glass down on the nightstand beside the dim night-light.

"Would you like to play?" she asks, her voice low and conspiratorial. Oh, they've trained her well! They know what they are doing.

He realizes that he is fooling himself, that he has discovered what he has come to find out, that there is no exculpatory intellectual excuse for him to remain longer. If he stays, it will be because of the girl herself, her blandishments, her sad hair-bow, her Mary Jane shoes.

"Would you like to lie down for a little while? Just to rest? I know how to relax you, just with my fingertips on your forehead. It's lots of fun. Very floaty. You'll like it."

"I'm sure I'd like it," he tells her.

"Just for a little bit?" As if he would be pleasing her, as if it were what she wanted. The poor thing!

But it is also true that the customer's position is difficult, a disturbed struggle between temptation and guilt, fear and desire. Grown men have come here, men much like himself, and needed to be invited to lie down, to be reassured that all the little girl was going to do was massage their furrowed brows into some momentary relief, a promise of ease and repose. Certainly, she seems less troubled than he feels himself to be. She has the advantage of experience, of course. And of being on home ground, as it were. But she is a young girl. No more than fourteen or fifteen? Perhaps even less.

He realizes his jaws are clenched tight, that he can hear the pounding of his heart in that artery in the ear, a deep boom of some dreadful processional.

"Just for a little bit," she repeats, reassuring him.

The bed has a white counterpane on it. Like a good little boy, Caryl takes off his shoes so as not to dirty it. He lies down on the bed, exhausted, barely able to breathe, still hearing his heart pounding. He closes his eyes. He feels her bounce onto the bed beside him. He feels her fingertips making light semicircles above his eyebrows. He opens his eyes and looks up. He can see the silhouette of her slender torso through the robe, back-lit as she is by the lamp. He can make out the little buds where her breasts are just developing. He closes his eyes, unable to bear it.

He is happy. It is an awful thing to admit, but he is delighted, the little gamine's innocence taking away the curse of the situation, the bawdyhouse setting, the sense of wrongdoing that the heartiness downstairs of these men of the world cannot conceal. It is all wiped away, as though by a stroke of her small smooth hands, her little girl's delight in his evident enjoyment of what she is doing and going to do. He is smiling. He hears her say, "That's better, isn't it?" and he can hardly find the strength or focus of intellect to say "Yes," but only make an affirmative "Mmmhmnn," that is quite sufficient. She knows perfectly well that it is better, better and better. And to be more comfortable, to be able to touch him more easily, she climbs astride his chest so that she can touch his temples, run the balls of her fingertips down his cheeks, feathery-light, and go back to the corners of his jaws only to sneak under the jawbone and stroke the delicate skin of his chin, just under where the tongue lies in his mouth, so that his salivary glands spill forth from sheer pleasure. He swallows.

He can feel the bones of her buttocks on his chest. It is excellent, exquisite. It is something that he cannot imagine doing in England, but here, in America, where they are all mad and pious, and hypocritical, and far away, where nothing is real, not even the money, he can learn about himself that he is not so different from Dodgson, that many men, perhaps most men, maybe even all men long for the restoration of their youth and innocence, and that what they suffer is as difficult to bear as what the girls suffer.

Not that Alice seems to be suffering much. She looks healthy enough, is radiantly beautiful in that perfect, Dresden-doll way that young girls have, and seems intelligent. Skilled, surely. And dexterous. She seems, moreover, to be enjoying herself, to be in touch with that free, delighted, primal prompting that was born in an Eden the gates to which have long ago clanged shut. A little monkey brought back alive from that prelapsarian jungle, she sits upon him, unselfconscious, doing her little grooming tricks and spontaneously delighting in his delight.

He hates to end it. But he knows that it cannot long continue. He has an erection, a turgid, painful erection, so hard and tight that he can imagine his penis breaking off. Or vibrating like a tuning fork if it were touched, sounding a note of metallic clarity. And if she moves down just a little, she'll know about it. Probably she knows about it already. It is her job to know about such things. It is the reward of her attentions up until now.

But he doesn't think he'd be comfortable with himself, later on, if he allowed any further or more direct intimacies.

Along with his moral distaste, there is another, more purely aesthetic reluctance, a recollection as much as an actual judgment now, that his appendage, engorged as it now stands, is a bit ridiculous. He provoked with it an altogether unexpected burst of laughter from that stableman's daughter, who was familiar with the members of horses—having seen them mate—and who thought his miniature human version was, in her word that he carried with him for the rest of his days, "darling." A diminutive, of course. And diminished even more by the amusement in her voice. Martha, her name was. She had a bridge of freckles across the upper part of her cheeks and over her nose. They looked like a saddle, he'd thought. He remembered her amusement that—later on—he told himself had been mixed with relief. The members of those horses had been formidable. His own had been reassuring, unfrightening.

But that relief had weighed less than the whole legacy of Victorian *pudeur* that was as much a part of his birthright as shooting birds and playing cricket and going to Christ Church. One's prick was a shameful thing. And women were supposed to think of it as they might think of a krait or cobra, a nasty, snake-like thing with deadly venom. The younger the woman, the greater, presumably, would be her loathing and disgust. But it wasn't so! One's own experience spoke to the untruth of the proposition. And one was faced with the choice of believing in the world's wisdom or in the evidence of one's own senses, one's own lived and remembered experience. Cowardly in one's conformity, one chose the world's view instead of that of one's own life. And suffered the shame of the tortured souls in hell at the very thought that a button in one's flies might be undone.

"Little dolly wants to play," Alice croons. "Poor dolly wants to come out and play." She swivels around and scrunches down so that she is sitting on his stomach, her back toward his face, her face toward his prick.

"No," he says. "No, no."

"Can't poor dolly come out and play?" she wheedles. "Poor, poor dolly." She strokes the bulge in his trousers almost as lightly as she stroked his eyelids and his temples.

He tells himself that if he lies very still and does nothing to encourage this naughtiness, then it will not be his responsibility, that it will all be her doing, her own idea, that he is hardly violating the innocence of this girl, that she is, if anything, restoring his own innocence, that he has felt nothing so sweet, so tingling, so marvelous in years, that she is a terrible vixen, that it couldn't possibly get any better than this . . .

Poor dolly throws up and feels better.

He hasn't touched her. Only afterward does he plant a nearly chaste kiss upon her lips. And he gives her an extra ten dollars to hide in her sock.

"Thank you for coming," she says. "I had a lovely time."

"Thank you for having me," he says.

"You'll come to visit me again?"

"If I can," he says. "I'd like to."

"I'd like that, too."

"You're a sweet child," he says.

He does not stop in the parlor to talk further with Nellie and Harry. He takes his coat and walks out into the gentle spring evening, feeling . . . delicate. As if he might at any moment shatter into a thousand shards.

4

IT IS NOT QUITE FOUR in the morning when Caryl returns to the Waldorf. At that slack hour, the lobby is busy with housekeepers running polishing machines along the marble and vacuum cleaners over the endless vistas of patterned broadloom. Caryl asks for his key at the desk, goes to the elevator bank, and ascends to his floor. He opens the door to the suite as quietly as possible, not wanting to disturb his mother or his aunt, both of whom are light sleepers, particularly toward morning. He closes the door behind him in almost absolute silence and is startled to hear his name spoken.

"Caryl?" Aunt Rhoda has been sitting up in the living room, sitting in the dark, waiting for him.

"Aunt Rhoda! What are you doing up?"

"Waiting for you. I wanted to make sure you were all right," she tells him. It isn't quite a whisper, but she speaks in low tones.

"You thought I'd come in drunk," he tells her, teasing.

"That possibility crossed my mind."

"And for mother's sake as much as mine . . ."

"Don't be impertinent, young man. It wouldn't be the first time, would it?"

"No."

"Well, then," she says. "Let us go into your bedroom. Let me have a look at you."

"I'm all right, really."

"Of course you are," Rhoda said.

It is inevitable. The only question is whether to stand there and argue or submit gracefully. She follows him into his bedroom. He turns on the light. She looks at him, searching no doubt for telltale signs of blood, vomit, or whatever else.

"You must be patient with her," Rhoda says. "She'll tell you, perhaps. When she can bring herself to do it."

"It doesn't matter," Caryl assures her.

"But it does. You were troubled. I could see that. And she could, too. She cares about you, but it is a painful subject . . ."

"Believe me, it doesn't matter. Not any more."

"Promise me you won't say anything."

"There's nothing to say. Really. The subject is closed," Caryl says. He appreciates his aunt's effort, but he is tired. And it really doesn't make much difference any more. He can live with it, whatever it is. He can live with it, not even knowing exactly what it is.

"Promise me," Aunt Rhoda insists.

"I promise," he says. He lies down on the bed, not bothering now about his shoes. He isn't the good boy any more.

"It wasn't Dodgson himself, so much. That isn't what has troubled her all these years. Or I don't believe so. It was our sister, Edith. Edith and your mother were jealous of one another. It was one of those silly jealousies that sets, somehow, and goes on for years. That one did. And when

Edith died, there was no longer the possibility of making it
up between them. So it has remained, all these years, a sore
spot in your mother's memory. Worse than that, it remains
a difficulty in how she thinks of herself, how she judges
herself. A moral lumbago. Changes in the weather can
bring on a pain about which there is nothing to do and for
which one's patience has been exhausted. Or it's a phantom
pain. Some of the wounded veterans have that, you know. A
pain in a leg that has been amputated. Or an itch. One
wants to scratch it, but the leg isn't there. It's like that with
your mother."

He lies there, thinking not so much about his mother and
her sister Edith—Aunt Edith, she would have been, if she
had lived—as about his Aunt Rhoda, the sweet, sharp little
lady who has sat up most of the night in order to speak
these words. She cares about him. She cares about as-
suaging pain. She believes in doing what she can to make
better whatever is about her and in want of improvement.
"It was really very kind of you to do this," he says.

"Nonsense," she tells him, as he could have predicted.
She puts this kind of thing down to duty and then writes it
off as not worthy of mention or even notice, except in the
breach.

He is more than tired. He is new-fledged, or even freshly
hatched. He is vulnerable as one of those primitive creatures between two skins or two shells, like a lobster or a
crab. He is all but overwhelmed by a feeling of tenderness
toward his aunt, about whom he has hardly ever stopped to
think, putting himself in her place and imagining how she
must feel. She has always been there, solicitous, admirable,
dependable. And he has taken her for granted as plants
take the sunlight for granted, a benevolent force, a condition of life. But her life has been difficult and giving, and
she has worked hard to be the good aunt, the good admin-
istrator, the good nurse, the good Samaritan, as if by her

efforts she hoped to earn herself a place in heaven. Or, no, not heaven, but something more immediately at hand. Her own unsentimental and rigorous esteem. Her own self-respect. As generous as she has been to others, she has been rigorous with herself. There is a kind of saintliness Caryl sees in her, a generosity that, at this moment, is enough to bring him to the brink of tears.

Tired though he is, he forces himself up, first to a sitting position and then, with effort, to his feet. He takes his aunt in his arms and holds her.

"I tell you, you're being ridiculous," she chides. He doesn't care. He kisses her on her brow which is cool and dry and makes him think of parchment. "It hasn't been easy for you either, has it, this trip?"

"She needed me. And for all I knew, you might have needed me, too."

"That's not the point," he insists. "All this nonsense, this fuss about mother and Lewis Carroll . . . What has it to do with anything important?"

"I don't know what you mean," she says.

It's possible. He isn't being clear. He doesn't want to be too clear because he doesn't want to risk hurting her feelings. But it seems to him enormously clear that there is something hideously unfair in the way life has worked out for these two sisters, his mother and aunt. The one is a virtual saint, a servant in the vineyards of the Lord, and the other, for no particular reason, has been touched by a physical grace that happened to catch the notice of old Dodgson a lifetime ago, fascinating him, transfixing him, as the Juliet-Alice fascinated and transfixed Caryl earlier in the evening . . . And from that his mother has been promoted to a kind of immortality, a place in the firmament, the New York *Times*'s and Columbia's view of heaven.

All of which is another burden for Aunt Rhoda to bear. For while Caryl loves his mother and respects her as a son ought to do, he is by no means blind to her defects. He is able to see that selfless Rhoda is the more remarkable of the two, the more generous and giving. And Rhoda must have been ten or eleven or twelve once, must have been possessed for a little while of that gazelle-like grace and of the hope we read into it, the physical delight that seems to suggest a spiritual clarity.

Sometimes it happens and sometimes it doesn't, and there is no accounting for the fairness or unfairness of it—the way the one trudges up a hill that the other has ascended on the wings of grace.

"Are you sure you're all right?" she asks.

"I'm fine," he says. "Really, I'm fine. I appreciate what you've told me. And I shan't say anything to mother."

"She may yet bring herself to tell you . . ."

"It's not necessary. She oughtn't do anything that causes her distress."

"I'm glad you understand."

"I do."

"Yes, perhaps you do," she says. "I'll go to bed now. We go to Philadelphia this afternoon. I must get some rest."

"Me, too," Caryl says.

She kisses him on his brow, as if he were a little boy and she were putting him to bed.

Well, he is. And she is.

The light has started to show. Dawn is not far off. It is almost like going to bed as a child when it's still daylight out there, as in the Robert Louis Stevenson poem. He undresses quickly, crawls into bed, and falls asleep almost immediately.

ALICE, RHODA, AND CARYL go to Philadelphia later that week to stay with Dr. Rosenbach in his big house on Delancey Street. This little side-trip is as much the object of their visit to America as the Columbia University commemora-

tive exhibition and the awarding of the degree. Eldridge
Johnson, the president of the Victor Talking Machine Company of Camden, New Jersey, and the purchaser from Dr.
Rosenbach of the manuscript, comes to lunch the next day
to meet Alice, to show her his manuscript (her manuscript!)
and to boast to her about it and how it is going to be kept in
a watertight, fireproof, steel safe—aboard his yacht, so he
can take it with him when he sails to the Caribbean.

And Rosenbach, in his quieter way, is boasting too, how
with his academic standing he can arrange such things as
the degree and Alice's appearance. Or, more to the point
and to Alice, how he can play any game she proposes and
win it, easily and gracefully. He took the challenge of her
postponement, from January to May, from Carroll's birthday to her own, and, having taken it as a challenge, showed
her how he could use that, too. He arranged for that cake
from Oscar of the Waldorf, and had the photographers
from the newspapers come to take pictures of her cutting
the enormous cake with eighty candles and figures that
looked like the Tenniel drawings all over it. It was a pleasant enough gesture, except that Alice suspects there may
have been some arrangement behind it, some understanding between Rosenbach and the hotel that the bill would be
reduced somewhat, in consideration of the publicity that
her visit had generated. The closing ceremonies at Columbia, in the university gymnasium, with those same charac-
ters hanging on the wall behind them, huge as nightmare
figures, was another declaration, Alice believed, that Rosenbach could wrest even her own birthday from her, make
it public, turn it to his own uses.

But Alice has had long experience in this kind of squab-
ble, having begun long ago, with Edith. The best strategy is
to pretend to be ignorant, to smile serenely as if it never
crossed her mind that Rosenbach might be showing off or
that his living depends largely on his ability to impress such

captains of industry as Mr. Johnson. Rosenbach has to impress them and amuse them in order to keep their interest and respect. There must always be something beyond what their money can buy, something elusive and valuable, something tantalizing and delicious for them to crave. Johnson has bought the manuscript, but Alice is a live person whom he can meet and will have to remember—like any other mere mortal, without the help of his millions. And her memories of Dodgson, whatever they are, aren't for sale.

He's bought a package—the manuscript and two copies of the first edition of *Alice in Wonderland*, the edition that Dodgson had withdrawn because he hadn't liked the quality of reproduction of the drawings. The quality had nothing to do with the rarity that resulted from this decision, and the consequent prestige of the few stragglers that survived the recall. As if the "first" edition were something special, representing some literary virginity these people craved!

But whatever Alice thinks about the matter, she smiles, says little, is the gracious old lady—a role she knows how to play for tiresome people. She has come out well. She has provided for Caryl. And for Caryl's daughter, too, if they are sensible.

Caryl behaves himself in Philadelphia. She was afraid that, in a private house, he might fret and chafe, might sneak out and look for speakeasies. Might resent the way they were all being treated as . . . as objects. Something between wild beasts from the Asian steppes and amusing pets. But he is quiet, polite, attentive. He puts up with a lot and smiles through it like the good soldier he was and is. She is grateful

She owes him an explanation of what he calls "the truth" about Dodgson. Some of it, anyway. Something more than he wrote down for the New York *Times*. Rhoda has said so.

And Alice has more or less resolved upon the return voyage as the most auspicious moment. There will be plenty of time and few distractions. It will be a nice way of ending this journey, putting it all at last behind her.

There is no need, she thinks, to let Caryl know of this resolution. It would be better if the subject could be raised naturally and in the course of things. And failing that, she hopes to pick a moment when she is comfortable, when his mood seems receptive and cheerful, when circumstances generally appear propitious. She is surprised then, when they return to New York, by Caryl's decision not to accompany Rhoda and her on the *Aquitania*. He has decided to remain in New York a while longer and follow in a week or ten days on the next suitable ship. There are some business matters he wants to look into.

Alice presses him as far as she can, but he is not forthcoming about details. She is concerned about him but is also uncomfortable about her own relief. Can she avoid the discussion altogether? Or is she now obliged to bring it all out into the open on their last night together in New York, back at the Waldorf?

Curiously, Rhoda is no help at all. She has no opinion, which is most uncharacteristic. She says it is entirely up to Alice, that she can't imagine which would be better—to have it over and done with or postpone it to a calmer time, knowing that there is always the risk that no such time might ever present itself.

In the end, Caryl makes it clear—or Alice thinks that that's what he means—that it doesn't matter. They are in the suite, a different suite from their first stay, before Philadelphia, but just as grand, up in the Towers. They have had an early supper so that Alice can finish her packing and go to sleep. And she decides to plunge in. "About Dodgson . . ." she announces, bravely abrupt.

"It doesn't matter, mother."

"But you had asked me . . ."

"I know. It doesn't make any difference, though. After all this time?"

She doesn't know quite what to say to him.

"What I mean," he says, "is that, at the time, I wanted to be treated differently from the *Times*. I wanted to know more than they did. But that was absurd. What I want now is to treat you differently from the way Rosenbach and Johnson did. To pry, the way they did, seems distasteful now. And . . . unnecessary."

"That's very sweet of you," she says. "It wouldn't be prying . . ."

"Still! You know what I mean. Our lives aren't likely to be changed one way or another, improved or disimproved, by anything you'd tell me."

"No, probably not," she agrees.

The change, after all, happened years ago. With Dodgson, and then with Edith and her parents, and then with Regi. And then with Alan and Rex. Caryl is all she has left. And if he can love her with the unquestioning love we all want and hardly dare expect, then she is content. She even tells herself that it is better this way.

In return, she does not push further her inquiries about the reason for his staying on in New York. There may well be some business deal. In view of his dislike for the States, he is probably not staying for pleasure. There is always the possibility that some woman is involved, but if that is so, then Alice doesn't want to know.

That, she decides, might well be Caryl's motive too. Perhaps he simply doesn't want to know. Perhaps he has come to understand that there are some things about which people don't have quite so much freedom as they'd like to suppose, that they are borne along, unable to change their destinies. She lies in a deck chair on the *Aquitania*, wrapped in a blanket and feeling beneath her the vibration of the ship's propellers and the slow swell of the ocean, the two different motions of human intention and of nature, in harmony now but always liable to contend with one another, and always with an element of risk. To be borne along on the water. It is so restful to the spirit, for one has the clear understanding that the water has its own temperament. One realizes that one has given up a little the illusion of responsibility and freedom and that one is a creature, subject to all the laws of creation.

Alice the child—heartless as most children are—had not wondered at the pool of tears in which one might almost drown. It still strikes her as remarkable that people never refer to that. Is it merely good manners or good taste that prevents them? Musing there in the sun with her eyes closed, Alice decides it is probably simple fear.

She remembers that other day, that day in the sun on the water, with Ina, Edith, the Duck, and the Dodo.

A lifetime ago.